T0245033

AVA

AN INTERNATIONAL SENSORY ASSASSIN NETWORK NOVEL

MARY TING

OTHER BOOKS BY MARY TING

Young Adult

International Sensory Assassin Network Series
ISAN, Book 1
HELIX, Book 2
GENES, Book 3
CODE, Book 4

Tangled Fairy Tales
Jaclyn and the Beanstalk

Adult – Clean Romance

Spirit of Ohana Series
When the Wind Chimes, Book 1
The Seashell of 'Ohana, Book 2

Awards

International Sensory Assassin Network Series

Gold Medal: Science Fiction & Fantasy, Benjamin Franklin Awards
Gold Medal: Science Fiction—Post-Apocalyptic, American Fiction Awards
Gold Medal: Science Fiction, International Book Awards
Gold Medal: Young Adult Thriller, Readers' Favorite Awards
Gold Medal: Young Adult Action, Readers' Favorite Awards
Silver Medal: YA Fantasy / Sci-Fi, Moonbeam Children's Book Awards
Finalist: Action Adventure, Silver Falchion Awards

Jaclyn and the Beanstalk

Bronze Medal: Juvenile / YA Fiction, Illumination Book Awards
Finalist: YA Mythology / Fairy Tale, Readers' Favorite Book Awards
Finalist: Young Adult Fiction, Best Book Awards
Finalist: Unpublished Manuscript, Hollywood Book Festival

Spirit of 'Ohana Series

Grand Prize Winner: Romantic Fiction, Chatelaine Book Awards
Gold Medal: Romance, Kops-Fetherling International Book Awards
Gold Medal: Romance, New York Book Festival
Bronze Medal: Romance, Independent Publisher Book Awards (IPPY)
Finalist: Romance, Next Generation Indie Book Awards

AVA

AN INTERNATIONAL SENSORY ASSASSIN NETWORK NOVEL

MARY TING

AVA

This is a work of fiction. Names, characters, places, and incidents either are the product of the author's imagination or are used fictitiously.
Any resemblance to actual persons, living or dead, events or locales is entirely coincidental.

Copyright © 2023 Mary Ting

Cover design by Michael J. Canales
www.MJCImageworks.com

No part of this book may be reproduced or transmitted in any form or by any means, electronic or mechanical, including photocopying, recording, or by any information storage and retrieval system now known or to be invented, without written permission from the publisher, except where permitted by law.

The publisher is not responsible for websites (or their content) that are not owned by the publisher.

ISBN: 978-1-64548-092-1

VESUVIAN BOOKS

Published by Vesuvian Books
www.vesuvianbooks.com

Printed in the United States of America
10 9 8 7 6 5 4 3 2 1

TABLE OF CONTENTS

CHAPTER ONE – SOUTH KOREA, SOKCHO

HAE JIN

Hae Jin's long ponytail whipped at her back as the small motorboat jumped over rippling water and pushed through the surging tides. She wished they weren't on a basic gasoline-powered boat, but a high-tech hydro glider would draw too much attention.

After being stuck underground when not on a mission, she didn't mind the harsh wind slapping her face. But the bright full moon and the glistening stars didn't quell her pounding pulse.

Behind her, Min Hyuk, Sena, and Jung sat tall in their assigned seats, gazes trained on the red lighthouse at the end of the concrete pier ahead. The Korean ISAN—International Sensory Assassin Network—had captured Japanese renegades hiding at Sokcho beach, but they had escaped during transportation back to their headquarters.

The operation, to capture the Japanese rebels, offered Hae Jin and her team an opportunity to escape. Their desertion had to play out as planned, without a hiccup, or they would be terminated on the spot.

Grayson, their supervisor, braced against the waves from where he stood at the front as the boat swerved away from the placid line of ships that caught octopi during the night. When the engine shut off, the unforgivable breeze didn't slow near the shore. Hae Jin's

1

heart raced the closer they idled toward their destination.

Inhale. Exhale. No amount of oxygen tamed her anxiety, but she couldn't show distress. She had to execute the operation without giving any indication of what was at stake. Too many lives depended on her.

"Get ready." Grayson spoke in English, his voice thick with tension.

The agents used to speak in their native tongue, but once ISAN had moved between facilities in other countries, English had become the universal language. It was a vital part of their training. Most of the new agents didn't have sensory superpowers, but they all had strength, speed, and endurance. With the latest advancements, they only had to sign the contract and agree to an injection of the HelixAVA—Advance Variant Ability serum. The serum then altered their DNA to mimic Ava's.

Grayson's lean and muscular body swayed with the boat's motion. "Put on your mask, and you're good to go. Once you have contained the rebels, meet the guards at the endpoint. They will transport the prisoners to the designated base."

Hae Jin stood and tapped her embedded forearm chip to activate its new gadget. When she pressed the icon, a skin-like fabric rose from the collar at the front of her combat wetsuit and molded to her face.

She brushed a hand behind her back to ensure the Taser was in place. "Ready?" she said to Min Hyuk, her next-in-command.

He teetered from the rocky wave as he offered a curt nod just before the material covered his eyes. The engineered fabric allowed the assassins visibility on land and underwater but appeared a matte black from the outside. Despite the danger, she wanted to laugh. Her teammate looked like a giant fly.

Sena brushed her braided hair back and Jung narrowed his eyes in concentration. They both raised their thumbs, so Hae Jin counted to three with her fingers, and then they dove into the ocean.

The shock of the drop in temperature jolted her stiff. The freezing water wrapped around her muscles, locking them in place. Her lungs burned as she drew a breath, then narrowed her eyes on her team, rocking with the tide.

Fingers gripped her arm. "Are you okay?"

Min Hyuk's worried voice resonated in her slim earpiece, attached inside the mask. She imagined his handsome features twisting. His concern gave her a warm feeling, but it wasn't the time to get all mushy.

"I'm fine." She held up a hand. "Let's go."

Hae Jin pushed through the water with long strokes and quick flapping feet. The single line of teammates behind her matched her speedy swimming pace. They emerged behind the pier and climbed up the boulders.

Streetlights on the pier cast a weak yellowish light over the walkway, and the crashing waves overpowered nearby sounds.

Water dripped from Hae Jin's wetsuit. She tapped on her controller to lower the mask. Her team moved silently, but the damp footprints left a trail signaling their presence.

"I don't see anyone, not even the guards." Min Hyuk's voice came through the earpiece as he sauntered beside her.

"Can you hear anything?" Hae Jin halted and asked Sena, who could hear a pin drop on a carpet.

Sena took a step out of the formation. "Just the waves. It's like radio static. Are you sure of the rebel's location? They might have moved on."

3

Their supervisor had given the order, so why the inquisition?

A cold and sharp stab hit her gut—the kind that meant something had gone askew, well, besides the fact she had planned the escape, and they might not live another day.

Jung placed a hand on Sena's shoulder. "Stick to the plan. We don't have time to waste."

Sena raised an eyebrow. "Speaking of which, why aren't you using your map?"

Hae Jin pinched her lips together, suppressing a scowl. She wished she could shove a cloth inside Sena's mouth to keep her quiet. A delay in pulling up her map gave the Japanese rebels more time to escape, providing protection for her team in case her supervisors could tap into her mind.

Just like the now-infamous Ava, Hae Jin had the ability to detect people's locations and chart blueprints of her surroundings. Though she'd never met the assassin, Ava had inspired her to do what was right, even if it meant betraying the network and the people who had saved her life.

"Follow me." A warm, tingling sensation coursed through her veins as she pulled up her map.

She sprinted and stopped about one hundred feet from the rail in the shadows, away from the lamplight. Her mind showed six guards at the other side of the lighthouse directly above the water splashing about the large boulders below. Before they attempted the escape, they had to knock out the guards first.

Hae Jin nodded at the two male teammates, a cue to let them know it was time. The three had contemplated whether or not to trust Sena, but now had no choice. They had to let her know the details to avoid surprises or complications.

She turned off her earpiece. "Remember when I asked that if

you had the chance to leave ISAN, if you would do it?"

Sena's brown eyes widened.

Being new to the team, Sena was a risk. There wouldn't be a second chance to ask. And if they left her behind, the guilt would eat at her. "It's short notice, but it's happening today." Hae Jin inhaled a deep breath and exhaled a longer one. "Blink if you want to come with us."

Sena's eyebrows pinched in the center, and a moment later she blinked. "Perhaps we shouldn't—"

Hae Jin covered Sena's mouth, fast as a whip. She gave a stern headshake and pointed at Sena's ear, indicating that their leader was listening.

The only person allowed to turn off communication was Hae Jin—and only for a few minutes, to give her quiet time to pull up her map. Her leader understood that she sometimes became overwhelmed by the noises around her.

"Follow our lead. Let's get this done." She turned on her earpiece back on and bolted, her squad keeping her pace.

The details on her hologram chart, beaming in cobalt-blue, indicated the six red dots. The wind howled and shoved her back, but she pushed forward. Whipped higher by the air stream, waves crashed against the rocks with a crack like thunder.

"This isn't the protocol!" the red-haired head guard shouted. "Find the rebels and bring them to us."

She gripped her Taser and pumped her legs harder. As she brought her weapon level, the redhead fired at her. She leaped to the side to dodge the bullet and the other five discharged their weapons.

Bullets dug into the concrete, some ricocheting in pale furrows. The guards couldn't follow Hae Jin's speed, nor see her team jumping over the rail.

Min Hyuk delivered a punch square to a guard's chest, lifting him off the ground. A scream rent the air as he flipped over the edge and crashed into the ocean. Blood painted a boulder from another guard's body, one Jung had knocked in the head with a roundhouse kick.

Fools. They should have run.

Hae Jin got down on her knees with her eyes closed and pulled the trigger. The red dots on her hologram showed her where to point. The three remaining guards collapsed and quivered like they were having a seizure. She rose and scanned the pier. "Everyone, follow me."

Footsteps pounded, as swift and erratic as her heart. She had to get everyone to the secret tunnel inside the lighthouse that Sunjo, the Korean rebel leader, had disclosed to her—the same course the Japanese escapees had taken.

Hae Jin yanked the door open. As expected, a solid wall prevented them from entering.

"Now what?" Jung said, a note of panic in his voice.

She raised her hand and smirked. "Don't worry. It's all good."

"Whatever you're going to do, hurry." Min Hyuk pointed out to the sea. "Grayson is coming."

Hae Jin squeezed her index finger under a panel and found a button on the wood surface. The door slid upward, revealing a dimly lit space. She descended the stairs and reached for her Taser. Four ISAN guards appeared, their machine guns pointed at them.

"Ssi-bal," she murmured. And, "Damn." Min Hyuk said the same word in English.

The Japanese assassins were facedown, their backs riddled with bullet wounds, blood pooling. That was the reason she hadn't seen

6

any red dots underground. The guards' suits had to be made from a material she couldn't detect.

Hae Jin's heart squeezed. *No. How?* She had no time to dwell. She had to get her team out.

"Don't move," a guard said. "You're surrounded."

She scoffed. "You think your old weapons can stop us?" Still, they were still efficient killers.

"No. But she will. We're the distraction."

She? Hae Jin looked over her shoulder as clicking sounds filled her ears. Min Hyuk and Jung dropped like fallen rice sacks as a lightning bolt zapped through her bones. She slammed against the wall, trying to support her body, but she couldn't do anything about her muscles convulsing.

Hae Jin had been Tased before, and she'd been able to break free from it. Sena must have added a stronger charge to her weapon.

The betrayal hurt more than the pain.

"How did you know about the escape route?" Hae Jin clenched her jaw.

Sena couldn't have. She hadn't disclosed their secret to anyone.

"Remember, I have good hearing." Her tone was as cold as her eyes. "Careful what you whisper."

She stumbled forward, refusing to fall to her knees, but the Taser pellets seared like hot coals, scalding every part of her skin. Her eyelids drooped, and the pressure to shut them became too strong. She panted with the effort of staying upright. She had to help her teammates. If they were taken back to the base, they were dead.

"Why?" Hae Jin didn't know if she'd managed that one word when her lips parted. She shook her head to clear the fog and twisted to take another step.

"It's simple." Sena came closer and shoved her chest. "I'm taking your position. It's all I ever wanted."

"No." She groaned. "I ... trust ... ed ... you."

Sena clutched her chin with stiff, greedy fingers. "You shouldn't trust anyone. And this is why I make a better leader than you."

"Save them." She craned her neck to see her teammates, as guilt squeezed her heart. "Don't let them ... be ... executed."

Sena crossed her arms and rolled her eyes. "Once you're dead, you won't even care. Don't bother speaking."

She shoved Hae Jin with one finger. The red door spun and the guards multiplied. Her butt thumped and her back slammed onto the concrete.

Despite the horrendous failure and her impending death, she wept at the beauty of the full moon. Min Hyuk and Hae Jin had recently fallen in love, and couldn't wait to start their new life out of ISAN. That dream now vanished in the blink of an eye.

She had been so close. So close to deserting. But she should have known better. No one escaped. At least, not Korean ISAN. Those who attempted, during missions, had been terminated on the spot with no second chances or memory wipes.

But Ava had broken free, and so had many others.

If Sena hadn't stabbed her in the back, Hae Jin's plan would have worked. As her eyelashes fluttered in one last attempt to stay awake, she gave the traitor the middle finger before her world went dark. At least she'd given it her all, and only had one regret—not being able to take that bitch with her to Hell, the only place waiting for assassins.

CHAPTER TWO – MEDICAL STATION

JOSEPHINE CHANG

Josephine's high heels tapped across the tile floor and stopped at the two hubs. It had been a few days since the ISAN secret base had blown up. Mr. Novak had shot several assassins. She had brought the injured to Mr. San's facility.

She peered down at Lydia's glass pod and stroked the top as if she were caressing her hair. She had grown almost maternally fond of the agent. In fact, people had asked her if she was Lydia's mother. She understood the confusion.

They shared similar features—porcelain skin, a narrow jaw line, and intelligent eyes that said *don't mess with me*. But Lydia had the cutest dimples.

Unfortunately, work had always taken precedence, and Josephine hadn't had time to raise a child on her own. She certainly wasn't going to get married. As Remnant Council of the Former United States, she had to commit to her job, which meant sacrificing romantic relationships.

Lydia reminded Josephine of her younger years, and she recalled how she had recruited the agent. Josephine had exited a meeting, flustered, and bumped into Lydia. Josephine had apologized and extended a hand to introduce herself.

After a brief chat, the agent whispered, "I work for Mr. San. He told me we have a common goal. We should discuss it in private."

Josephine asked her to stop by her office the next day, and their beautiful friendship began.

A beeping noise brought her to the present. The staff she had hired rushed to either side of hub. The doctor injected liquid through the tube and the noise settled to a steady beat.

Mitch, who had been out of the room, came rushing through the sliding door. He scratched the stubble on his chin and brushed a hand through his messy hair, eyes trained on the tubes that ran through Lydia's nose and mouth.

Mitch inhaled a deep breath. "Is she okay? Why was that thing beeping? I thought she was stable."

He sounded as frantic as Josephine felt. Though Mitch stood tall and stiff, he was strung so tightly, a blow would shatter him. The last time the monitor had rung out of control, Lydia's lung had collapsed and they had almost lost her.

Dr. Machine had done its job with Mitch and Zen. Mitch had been released, and Zen was on the road to recovery. But, with Lydia, the infection had spread and her fever would not calm.

Josephine rested a hand on his shoulder. "Let the doctors take care of her."

She guided him to a sofa on the other end of the room. They eased onto the cushion and let out a sigh simultaneously. Mitch braced his elbows on his legs and shoved his palms to his face.

"She's going to be fine." Josephine said it for both of their sakes. She *needed to* believe that Lydia would pull through. Because if she didn't, well, Josephine didn't want to consider the alternative.

Mitch lifted his head, his hands trembling on his thighs. "I should have told her to stay behind. Or I should have jumped in front of her before Novak shot her."

"It's not your fault." She raised her eyebrows. "You can't tell Lydia what to do. And you certainly can't outrun a bullet, so don't think about the what-ifs, or it will drive you insane."

He leaned back. "Novak and Gene are dead, right? Did you get the confirmation?"

Josephine clicked on her chip and read the text Vince had sent her. He had taken over Zen's position since he was out for medical leave.

Novak and son are deceased.

The package safely arrived. I miss you. I can't stop thinking about our kiss.

Though the message only she could see the message, Josephine's cheeks warmed.

Good news. Thank you for the update. I miss you too.

So, Vince was one exception to the no-romance rule.

Mitch cleared his throat.

She ignored him as she read another text that came through.

The DNA test of the subjects matched.

Before her mother passed away, she had revealed that Josephine had a half sister. Josephine had been searching for her, but had come up empty until now.

Her heart stuttered. She shouldn't be surprised, as she had guessed as much already. But, what to do with the result? She had to wait for the right time.

Mitch cleared his throat again. "Everything okay? Did you get the response we wanted? And, are you blushing?"

Was it that obvious? Vince and Josephine hadn't publicly acknowledged their relationship, or whatever they had, but if Mitch had picked up on something, others might have, too. She'd like to keep her personal and professional lives separate. He didn't need to know her business, so she skipped over the last question.

Josephine shut off her chip and crossed her legs. "Yes. ISAN has confirmed that Novak and Gene are dead."

"Good." Mitch nodded and raised an eyebrow, smirking. "Who's the lucky guy?"

She snorted. "Now I see what Lydia sees in you."

He sat up straighter and tilted his head. "*Now?*"

Mitch was a known ladies' man outside of the network. Who knew if the rumors were true?

"You have a reputation. But, perhaps—"

"They're wrong," he said. "Maybe I played around before, but it's different with Lydia." His features softened when he said her name. "I love her." His gaze shifted to the hub. "I would trade places with her. I didn't understand what Rhett meant when he'd say *love is everything*, but now I do."

Josephine smiled. "Thank you for being there for Lydia. Because of you, she didn't feel so alone spying on Novak. She thinks the world of you. She told me that people don't give you enough credit."

Mitch swallowed and scrubbed a hand down his face. He didn't seem surprised, but rather, appreciative.

He released a long breath. "She thinks the world of you too, Councilor Chang. And so do I. As do the rebels." His grin faded and his expression turned serious. "Please, do everything you can to bring Lydia back to us."

Josephine gripped Mitch's shoulder. She was about to say

something when her chip binged and Rhett popped up on her screen.

She typed: *Call you back soon.*

"Your brother has called every day to check up on everyone," Josephine said. "I didn't tell him that you woke up this morning. I figured you would want to give him the good news. And Ava and a team will be heading to South Korea soon."

"Thank you. I planned to call him after our conversation." He clasped his hands and tapped a foot. "I hope you don't need me." He glanced at Lydia's hub. "My head is not in the right state of mind to help anyone."

"That's what I thought. I need you here, anyway. I have a plan in motion to bring down Korean ISAN, but I need more information. Sorry to make this short, but I'm expecting an important call."

Josephine rose and fixed the sleeve of her silk blouse. She sauntered toward the sliding door, then pivoted.

"Oh, Mitch. I almost forgot. Rhett has something special to tell you."

Josephine had been shocked when Ava and Rhett had told her about Avary. A miracle, indeed. She couldn't be happier for them, and she had a feeling they would retire soon.

"What is it?" Mitch, heading toward the medical pods, halted. She smirked. "A sweet bundle of joy."

Her name is Avary, named after her maternal grandmother.

Confusion set on Mitch's furrowed brow as he continued his stride. Perhaps he had heard wrong. He had been through so much, he might be too occupied with Lydia's condition to process her hint.

A beep came from Josephine's chip. Her smile faded when she

read the message from a squad Rhett had sent out to Korea to bring the escaped rebels to the Remnant Councils of the former US.

"What's wrong?" Mitch asked. He must have seen the worried expression on her face.

Josephine closed her eyes and opened them, sighing. "There's trouble in Korea."

CHAPTER THREE – AVARY

AVA

I opened my eyes to the ceiling, my back sinking into the too-soft mattress. Rhett planted on a chair, his knees touching our bed. His hands curved around Avary, bundled in her pink blanket beside me.

Disoriented from waking up from a dream, I sat up and twisted at the waist. The cold stone chilled my bare feet and tears wet my cheeks.

The computers on the table, pushed back against the wall, hummed, and the faint smell of soil tickled my nose. I was in Rhett's room at the rebel base in the mountain.

Not dreaming.

Avary and I were safe. Oh, thank God. I released a long exhale and my shoulders slumped.

"Babe. What's wrong?" His eyes grew wide with concern. "Why are you crying?"

"I dreamed about my mom again." I wiped my eyes.

"At the secret compound? The same nightmare?"

ISAN's base, the one Mr. Novak had demolished. My father. He had bombed his own facility when he had been found.

"Yes." I let out a sigh and stared at Avary's peaceful face. I could look at her all day.

The dream always began with my mom and I separated,

15

divided by a splitting ground big enough to keep us apart and prevent me from saving her. And Novak would try to take Avary from me.

He gently grazed across my cheekbone with his knuckles. "I'm so sorry, babe. Do you want to talk about it?"

I shook my head and adjusted the necklace he had gifted me. The small pendant had a pressed dandelion encased in a flat, see-through locket. Novak had taken it from me, but my mother had tucked it inside Avary's blanket. She'd known it was mine.

The ache of missing my mom pierced my heart. I could still feel her presence, but it only served to remind me how much I missed her.

"If you change your mind, I'm here." Rhett caressed Avary's dark mop of hair. "I wanted to take her, but you held on as if someone would steal her."

I snorted and drew my nose closer to her face. She smelled like honey, and she made the cutest coo as she slept.

"I think our daughter is dreaming." I snickered.

Our *daughter*. A phrase I never thought I would say. We were told that female assassins couldn't conceive, but ISAN had lied to us. The Helix serum that suppressed our abilities was also a form of birth control.

Rhett leaned and kissed my forehead, then Avary's. His smile radiated warmth and love for us.

We had talked about adopting later in life, when we escaped from the network, but Avary had been the most amazing surprise. At the same time, taking care of a child was a huge responsibility. It was one I wasn't ready for, especially as a war brewed between ISAN and the various resistance groups. And … I knew nothing about being a parent.

"Babe, do you want to sleep more?" He placed a hand on my shoulder, pulling me back from my wandering thoughts.

I scooted over and brought Avary with me, careful not to disturb her. Rhett stretched his long body on the bed and fixed his eyes on her face. The three of us were a tight fit on the twin side-by-side mattresses.

"She's beautiful, like her mommy." He traced Avary's feathery eyebrow.

Avary's lips puckered and she wiggled her cute button nose.

"It might be feeding time," I said.

A soft knock came from the door. "Ava? Rhett?" called a muffled voice.

"We should answer," I said.

"Hold on." He sighed, sounding annoyed. "I just got in bed."

Avary's eyes opened and she stared at the white ceiling, alert and curious. She craned her neck toward me and her lips parted and closed repeatedly. It had been a few days since we'd brought Avary home, and we were still trying to figure out what she needed when she cried. And boy, did she have a great set of lungs.

Wiggling and fussing meant she wanted to be fed, have her diaper changed, or be burped. Rhett and I were on pins and needles. Babies communicated by crying, but it made me want to sob along with her.

Another knock.

Rhett jolted to his feet and raked a hand through his hair. As he spoke, he moved backward. "She's starving. I'll warm up a bottle. Or, does she need a diaper change? Probably both. Papa will be back."

The pounding on the door got louder.

"I'm coming." He clenched his teeth.

He turned and nearly collided with the medicine cabinet. He braced a hand against the wall, then headed toward the door. When the door slid open, Ozzie and Brooke entered.

"We thought Avary would be hungry," Brooke said.

Ozzie gave an exaggerated grin, his blue eyes gleaming as he held up the glass bottle.

I pushed up and smiled. "You're the best auntie and uncle."

"Thank God." Rhett grabbed the bottle as Avary wailed.

Ozzie leaned against the cabinet and covered his ears. "Holy mother of all mothers. Well, her lungs work."

"Hurry, she's famished." Brooke sat at the edge of the bed.

Rhett passed the bottle to me and I stuck the nipple into her mouth. Her crying stopped as quickly as a light switch. All was quiet and she was happy. My tight shoulders eased as I scooped her up, then scooted back on the bed until I hit the wall and settled in to watch her drink.

"Any updates?" I asked, keeping my eyes on the gradually lessening milk.

Ozzie meandered across the room and sat in front of the back table. As his fingers brushed over the hologram keyboard, he said, "We should shop for formula. And add diapers to a list."

Rhett loomed over his friend. "I already have a list. And we shouldn't wait too long."

I'd thought Ozzie was looking up something for Councilor Chang, but to find out he had been taking his time to focus on Avary made my heart warm.

Every day I sent silent thanks to the nameless person who had stored baby necessities at the mountain base. Wipes, diapers, and even clothes. I was especially grateful for the canisters of baby food.

Brooke crawled across the mattress and planted himself beside me. "Any news about Korea?"

"A message came through from Councilor Chang." Rhett swiped across the hologram screen. "The squad that was supposed to pick up the Japanese and Korean rebels aborted."

"What?" I lifted a finger. I was still wearing a mother hat. "Hold that thought. Let me do this first. She's a fast drinker."

I put down the empty bottle on the cot, gathered Avary in my arms in an upright position, and patted her back. She gave the cutest burp. I thumped the small of her back once more and handed her over to Brooke.

"What happened?" As I scooted off the mattress, my foot nudged Avary's emergency backpack under the cot.

The bag held my father's journal and phone, and a backup supply of everything she would need if we had to leave the mountain base. I hoped that day would never come.

I squeezed between Ozzie and Rhett in front of the screen, which flashed a grainy, still image of a pier at night. The camera had been mounted on a lighthouse at Sokcho. We had access to the feed because Rhett had directed a crew to plant the recorder.

Ozzie pushed a button and a video played.

I had planned to take a trip to Sokcho with a small team after I settled Avary. But, the day after ISAN's secret compound had been demolished, an agent named Sunjo had sent a message to Councilor Chang asking for help.

Korean ISAN had captured the Japanese rebels, and the timing couldn't have been better to execute the escape of a group of sympathizers.

Sunjo had planned to coordinate the mission and send a squad led by her second-in-command, Hae Jin. Once they got to the end of the tunnel, they needed assistace to escape their country.

Rhett clicked the button on the panel that controlled the aerial shot. "It's not playing. Are you sure the recorder was on?"

Oz hiked up his eyebrows and scoffed. "Do you even know me?"

I pinched Ozzie's cheek. "You're fine, Einstein. Never mind Sniper."

Ozzie shrugged and rubbed his face. "Let me try something." His fingers danced about the hologram letters and numbers. "Holy mother of all mothers. Look. There."

The three of us leaned in closer to the screen. It was difficult to make out the low-resolution figures, and glitchy static made the image jump, at times. Something had blocked the reception, but there was no doubt that the four people in wetsuits were assassins moving stealthily across the pier. After they took out the guards, they entered the lighthouse and the video died.

I tapped my knuckles on the table as I stared at the display, my heart breaking. "Someone ratted them out. There's no other explanation. Either the rebels are in prison, or they've been executed."

Rhett pushed back against the wall behind us and peered at the ceiling. When he spaced out, he was usually sifting through countless thoughts and possibilities. He blew out a long breath. "You're planning to go there, aren't you?"

I swallowed and stepped in front of him. "I promised my mom I would. Besides, Councilor Chang asked me to lead a team. You remember, don't you?"

He pulled me into his chest, the dandelion pendant pressed between us. "I would never try to stop you, but damn it, Korea is too far."

Rhett was a good fighter and an excellent marksman, but one

20

of us had to stay behind with our daughter. I also didn't want him near the super-soldiers, who had been lobotomized and shot up with the latest serum, HelixAVA.

He furrowed his brow. "But what if—"

"Novak and Gene are dead," I said with finality. If my mother was, they'd better be.

His concern made sense, since we hadn't seen the proof. But it would have been impossible for them to have live through the destruction. I clung to that thought.

Rhett's warm breath brushed the shell of my ear as he let out a sigh. Then he kissed my forehead. I pulled back to meet his gaze those bright golden eyes entranced me, especially the tenderness they held. I felt and saw the depth of his love for me.

We'd been through so much, and we still had more danger ahead, but we would pull through. We *had* to.

He kissed my lips, tender and soft, and it nearly brought me to my knees.

"You two need to get a room," Ozzie murmured as he headed toward Brooke.

"This *is* my room." Rhett snorted, his eyes still boring into mine with want.

A beeping sound from the monitor broke us apart.

"Councilor Chang." I reached over to tap the audio speaker on the panel, but Rhett grabbed my wrist.

"Let's get some breakfast first." He squeezed my hand as he said, "I'll talk to her on the way to the cafeteria."

Next to Brooke, Ozzie tickled Avary's chin. They smiled and babbled sweet nonsense at her. She was lucky to be loved by many. We at least deserved a little reprieve before we had to separate again.

CHAPTER FOUR– SOUTH REGION

MOMO

Momo stared out the window as the glider passed over the ocean. She focused on the blue sky and the white fluffy clouds, to calm her nerves.

Going back to where Debra and the other half of the rebel squad had died had her pulse jumping all over the place. Momo's stomach coiled and her throat knotted. She needed air. No, she had to be on the ground, searching for survivors. Every passing second meant the possibility of ISAN finding them first.

Ever since Vince had told Jo that his men had spotted a group of young ones in the south territory wearing caps with *Renegade* printed on them, Momo had been racked with guilt. They should have stayed instead of fleeing with Rhett, even if they had been under attack and the building had collapsed around them.

Debra, the rebel leader in her division, would understand. She would tell Momo she had made the right decision. Safety for her team came first. No turning back—only move forward, because that was war.

Easier said than done.

So what about the guilt? In ISAN, weak emotions weren't allowed or talked about. Her superiors hadn't taught her how to process those feelings, only to ignore them.

"You okay?" Coco placed a hand on her arm.

"Just thinking," Momo said. "I hope we find them."

"We're here." In the front passenger's seat Marissa adjusted her Renegade cap, the same kind all four of them wore. The hats would either make them targets or would help Debra spot them easier. Momo hoped for the latter.

"Get ready to land," Jo, second-in-command to Debra, said, and turned their transporter on autopilot.

The glider began its descent. Clusters of high-rise buildings came into view. Commercial towers displayed ads on exterior walls constructed with built-in screens. People meandered over bridges and streets covered with steel-reinforced domes to protect them from the occasional tsunami, and transporters flew in orderly streams.

They reached their destination when they neared the town, which was peppered with abandoned office structures and shopping plazas. The glider landed in an empty church parking lot that was as quiet as the ruined city neighborhood.

Jo handed out weapons and pushed the release button for the door. "Stay behind me."

Momo and Coco bolted down the ramp and Marissa scurried beside them, their Tasers aimed outward. Her jeans and T-shirt stuck to her skin as a wave of humid, hot air hit her, and she wanted to turn back.

Momo stepped over used paper mugs, ripped cardboard, and plastic water bottles swept into dirty piles by the wind. The heat from the scorching sun did not lighten her mood. She wished a draft would come from somewhere.

Scattered sandwich wrappers blew past them on a gust of hot breeze that sprang up suddenly, as if her prayer had been answered. She lifted her arms, glad, at first, for a bit of a gust, but her gut told her that something didn't seem right.

"*Run.*" Jo's voice came sharp and urgent. "Follow me."

Jo's warning confirmed her intuition, and her stomach dove into her shoes.

Four sets of footsteps pounded across the asphalt in the silence of the abandoned city as Jo guided them past a bank with smashed windows. Then they entered a liquor store, its door hanging by the hinges. Jo thrust out a hand to tell them to halt, her chest rising and falling from running fast.

"Why are we here?" Marissa pivoted and peeked out the window.

"We have unwanted company," Jo said after finding her voice. Her eyebrows arched in concern as she divided her attention between the three young people beside her and the deserted street.

Coco's fingers twitched, a thin line of electricity crackling between them.

"How do you know?" Momo glanced over her shoulder, lifting her arm to wipe away the sweat dripping down her temples.

Most of the shelves were empty, but she spotted a toothbrush and laundry detergent. The items in the cooler were all gone, but a handful of chocolate bars were scattered in the third aisle.

Momo licked her lips. She should be alert for danger, but she couldn't stop wanting to take the goodies on the dusty tile floor.

"That wind didn't come from nowhere." Jo shoved her fingers through her hair and sighed. "Their invisible transporter landed nearby. It also means they might have seen us."

"What do we do?" Marissa whispered, holding her trembling hands to her chest.

"We stay until I—" Jo took a step back to the counter and her elbow hit the flipped-over cash register. She caught it just as it fell, but something dropped in front of Momo with a tiny metallic *ching.*

Momo grabbed a brown circle of metal with Abraham Lincoln's face on it, the sixteenth president of the United States. It was a copper coin that had been used before the meteor devastation.

She recalled an adage she had read online. *Find a penny, pick it up. All day long, you'll have good luck.* Despite the danger around them, Momo felt excited, and she shoved the coin inside her pocket. They certainly could use all the blessings.

The thumping of boots in steady sync made her pause. No other rebel team knew of their mission. Jo was right: their enemy had arrived.

Momo leaned closer to the door and counted heads. About eight girls. Not many. The four of them could take them down, right? And, with her speed, she would likely knock out half of the squad on her own. But, for the first time, her confidence faded.

The assassins moved like ghosts, wearing sleek, form-fitted combat suits. No Tasers or guns. So, what superpower did each possess?

She couldn't put it into words, but something was different about the terminators. Their features remained fixed and robotic, as if they felt no fear or *any* emotion. Even in the heat, none of them fanned their faces or wiped sweat off their foreheads.

Momo held her breath, praying the ISAN team would pass. She'd rather skip the introduction, rescue Debra's crew, and go home.

"Do you hear anything?" the assassin with dark braids said.

The redheaded girl next to her whipped her head in Momo's direction. Momo's pulse raced, despite her long breaths to calm her nerves. She wondered if those assassins could hear her heart beating.

"No, Davina. But something is out there." She pointed straight ahead to the cluster of abandoned shops where Momo's squad had planned to venture.

Great. Just great. Why couldn't they go in the opposite direction?

The leader, Davina, signaled with her fist raised. The girls marched forward.

Coco lowered her electrifying fingertips and pressed her back to the wall, releasing a sigh. Marissa relaxed her white knuckles. She had been holding Jo's shirt like a lifeline.

Jo held up a hand, indicating they would be on the move. "I have a plan. They know where our missing team is located, or have a good guess. So—"

"We follow them." Momo pushed her hair back and readjusted the cap. "But, first, does anyone want chocolate?"

"Momo." Jo frowned, but then the tight lines across her forehead softened. "You have five sec—"

She dashed off before their leader could finish and shoved the items she gathered inside her pockets. Coco and Marissa did the same.

"Let's go." Jo stepped out onto the pavement with a Taser readied in front of her chest.

Momo looked from left to right, ensuring that no soldier had lingered. A favorite ISAN tactic was to lure their victims by letting them think they were safe while the assassins strolled onward, leaving behind a few for a surprise attack.

The terminators passed several parked trucks. They were far enough ahead that they wouldn't detect the rebel squad. Silent as a thief, Momo sprinted beside Marissa to the next hiding place behind the closest abandoned stores.

Momo wiped the sweat from her forehead and pressed her back against a bookstore wall. A large sign hung sideways and creaked, shifting in the breeze. When Jo gave the signal, Momo tiptoed in beside Coco.

She could almost envision what had once been a beautiful store before the meteor and the looting. She picked up a paperback from a tilted small table, and her heart skipped a beat. Momo knew what a book looked like, but she'd never held one until now.

Momo ran a hand down the torn flap of the cover and flipped through its stiff pages, rippled with water damage. She read a paragraph and stopped. She could get lost in a good story, and this wasn't the time.

"Look at all these books." Marissa weaved around a fallen shelf and peered up the immobile escalator.

"I don't think anyone …" Momo's heart lurched as something black dropped from the third floor. It happened so fast that if she'd blinked, she would have missed it. "It's a—"

She didn't have the chance to finish the word *trap*. She spun and fired her Taser at the tall shelves in the back of the store.

"Get out!" Jo shouted, running toward the exit.

A thudding boom cut through the air, and a strong wind came from where the surprise attacker hid. Clusters of hardbacks and ripped pages soared as Momo flew, her back arching like someone had socked her in the stomach.

She collided with the wall. A few inches to the side, and she would have gone through the broken window. Strange: no pain coursed through her body, but blue and purple filaments of zapping lights engulfed her in midair. Coco had saved her.

Momo landed in a crouch and ran to the back. The redheaded soldier, standing with her feet apart with her arms extended outward, had a gadget looped through her fingers, the band strapped to her wrist.

Zeke had shown her the same glove contraption, capable of a powerful air blast that hit like an invisible punch.

The redheaded assassin's eyes grew in surprise. She must not have expected Momo to recover. When the soldier closed her fingers into a fist, Momo heaved a chocolate bar at her. Momo moved faster than the assassin could detect and Tased her from behind.

"Mine." Momo picked up the chocolate and shoved it back inside her pocket, then her jaw dropped. She had made a mistake by turning her back.

Coco had jumped in front of Momo and thrown out her hands. Blue electricity crackled, engulfing the redheaded assassin. She should have been on the ground, convulsing, but instead she remained standing, as if she had been untouched. Not possible, but Momo didn't have time to process it.

"Watch out!" Marissa bellowed by the door as Jo grabbed her beside the cash register counter.

Another assassin had jumped from the second level, but Coco detained her in midair, with her abilities. The soldier's dark eyes held no fear and she pointed at Coco, as if to say, *I'm coming for you.* Then she smirked.

Momo knew that expression. It was the kind she would make if … yup … she should have looked behind her.

A punch of air hit her like a ton of bricks. Her cap flew off her head. Pain seared her back as she soared forward and smacked against the menu posted above a counter. A coffeemaker joined her

28

on her way to the floor, and shattered. She twisted to the side to avoid the shards flying every which way.

Momo groaned, but she gathered into a ball. With one hand planted on the cabinet, she crawled up to a standing position as the earth tilted beneath her feet and flashes of white dotted her vision.

There was no time to rest. Davina, the girl with dark braids who had attacked her, gave a mocking grin. Only the counter divided them.

"Your kind is pathetic," Davina spat.

"My kind? Then, what are you?" she asked, to buy some time. The walls continued to spin, and Davina split into three.

"What am I?" Davina hiked her fists on her waist, her chin raised. "I'm a variant with advanced ability."

"You're freakin' crazy." Momo groped for something, closed her fingers around an object, and flung what turned out to be a bottle of syrup. She tucked and rolled under the counter, swiped her leg out, and knocked the assassin onto her back.

The variant leaped to her feet as if she hadn't just fallen and reached beneath the counter to grab Momo by the hair. Momo screamed as her scalp lit up with searing pain as the soldier dragged her out.

"I'm also known for breaking bones, girl."

"And I'm good at taking things." Momo adjusted her grip on the long-handled spoon she'd grabbed from the counter and jabbed it into Davina's waist. Then she slammed her head back as the assassin bent forward. That crunch sounded like her nose.

Blood spread on the variant's hip. She should be crying out or trying to stop the flow, but she just stood there and threw a daggered gaze at Momo.

"You bitch!" Davina pointed at her. "You ruined my uniform.

No more games, little mouse. I'm going to—"

"You talk too much." Momo seized her fallen hat and sprinted. She would surely outrun the soldier. Her speed surpassed all her friends, even Ava. But a hand yanked at the back of her shirt and she hurled over the broken tables as if she were a doll.

Momo smacked into a bookshelf near the door and dropped to a sitting position with her legs spread. Books toppled to the floor, one falling on her head, the corner of the hardcover jabbing into her tender skull. Stuffed animals from a display tumbled over Momo. Her cap was lost in the mix.

Davina approached, her purposeful eyes on the target. She needed to get up, but she couldn't move. For the first time, she wasn't sure if she could outrun her opponent.

The variant stopped a few feet from Momo and raised an eyebrow. "As I said before, you're no match for me. I'll let my *weakest* teammate teach you a lesson." She put her thumb and forefinger into her mouth and blew a shrill note.

The rest of the ISAN super-soldiers leaped over the rail from the second and third level and landed without a sound. They must have been told to stay in position until further notice.

Coco's blue electrical light zapped across space and wrapped around Davina in a blink of an eye. She didn't convulse from the shock, like the redheaded assassin. Momo fished her cap from under the mess and sprinted to stand beside her teammate.

Jo grabbed Marissa and hid behind a shelf near the escalators. Coco released Davina and tossed another assassin through the broken window, then she and Momo slid between the tall bookshelves toward the back.

"You can't hide from us," Davina said, her voice laced with confidence. Her boots crunched on shattered glasses in the center of the bookstore. "This place isn't big enough. Why don't you come out and save me the trouble?"

The terminators scattered outward, and one of the assassins stuck a small gadget on the wall by the exit. A bomb?

Davina picked up two mugs and read them out loud. "'I've got no shelf control.'" She scoffed. "'Books are like coffee. They warm the heart. Lame."

"If you were a reader, you would understand." Momo shouldn't have spoken, but she wanted to say something—*anything*—to deflate that giant ego of hers.

Davina knew where she was hiding, anyway. She was taunting them, keeping them occupied and in place. That's what predators did before they killed.

"I'm going to count to three," Davina said. "Either you come out and turn yourself in, or I burn you to ashes. One …"

Momo went to the other side of the bookshelf and sneaked a peek to catch Jo's attention. Momo was not the leader. She needed instructions. She could easily escape out the door before the blast, but she couldn't carry everyone in her squad with her.

Jo raised a hand, telling her to wait.

Momo's heart pounded even harder when something whizzed through the air in their proximity.

"I can—" Coco didn't finish, and her face paled. Her eyes grew, and she stood frozen in place. Scarlet liquid came from the tender spot between her neck and shoulder.

Momo aimed over Coco and fired her weapon at the soldier who had snuck in close enough to fling the dagger. Just like before, this assassin remained standing, with no reaction. It seemed her suit was Taser-proof and she felt no pain.

She grabbed her friend before she fell and held Coco in her

arms. Her heartbeat thundered in her ears. "Jo! Jo, Coco is bleeding. I need Mar—"

Momo's world had flipped over and she was losing control. She shouldn't have disclosed the names or the status of her squad member. Almost all her training had vanished.

Coco couldn't die. She had already lost Bobo. Momo had sworn she would do anything to keep her "found family" safe. The dagger in place kept the blood from gushing out, but she didn't know what else to do.

"You're going to be okay," was the only solace she could give. "Just hold on."

Coco blinked as tears slid down her face. Momo tried to keep her comfortable, placing her friend's head on her thigh, but that left them both vulnerable. If death came for her, she would be fine dying with her friend.

Footsteps thudded. Jo and Marissa crouched beside them.

"I'm so sorry I failed you." Jo took Coco's hand in hers. "Davina knew you could save us from the blast, which was the reason why they took you down."

"I can heal her," Marissa said.

"Not enough time." Jo stroked Coco's face.

"Two and three." Davina let out a halfhearted laugh near the exit. "No time to play. My order was to kill you, so we're leaving. You and this bookstore …" She waved a hand, snarling, as if disgusted. "… will be nothing but ashes. And don't worry about Debra's unit. We've got their location, and the same thing will happen to them. Say your goodbyes and count to five."

"I love you, Coco." Momo gripped her hand as tears streamed down her cheeks. "You're my soul sister."

"Mo … mo." Coco coughed and shivered. "Get out. You can

do it."

Perhaps Momo had seconds to escape, but how could she? They were her family. She wouldn't be able to bear the guilt. Besides, renegades never left anyone behind. *Ever.*

"Take … the dagger out." The words gritted through Coco's teeth as she bit back the pain. "I can shield us … I can do it."

Momo wiped her tears, ignoring her friend's request. Her breath shuddered as she tried to remain composed. She would die with dignity, and with those she loved.

Momo thought of Rhett and Ava and all the people she had met at the rebel base. Escaping ISAN had been the best decision their squad had made, and to be able to live in freedom for this long was a gift. She only wished she had more time.

Jo and Marissa wrapped their arms around Momo and Coco, forming a huddle. Just as the bills of their caps touched, the roar of the bomb exploded in Momo's ears, and blazing heat engulfed them.

CHAPTER FIVE– CATCHING UP

MOMO

Momo *should* be dead, but the ground stopped moving and the scorching heat vanished. She thought Coco had somehow found the strength to protect them, but her hands rested on her stomach, her gaze focused over Marissa and Jo.

Momo craned her neck and gawked at the incredible sight.

Some kind of invisible bubble shielded them. Red and orange flames danced over the sheltering sphere and blue and purple electricity crackled and fissured, as if they were in a lightning storm.

Debra and Jessa held their palms upward while Hector extended his arms outward with fierce concentration. The missing squad stood in the bubble with them, concrete and wood flying all directions. The explosion had destroyed every inch of the bookstore, including the ceiling and the four walls that once held the foundation.

Ashes fell like a soft first snow as the wind carried the settling debris and burning pages. The sound of paper flapping amid lingering cinders filled Momo's ears. Despite the destruction, she squinted at a slanting ray of sun that peeked through the clouds and sighed, thankful the team had survived.

When Debra's team dropped their arms, the invisible barrier and toxic smoke had disappeared. Momo snapped out of her daze when Jo and Debra exchanged hugs.

Marissa wasted no time. While she carefully slid the dagger free from Coco and placed her hands on the wound, Momo squeezed Hector and then Jessa. Both wore their Renegade caps.

"It's good to see you." Debra patted Momo's shoulder.

Momo beamed a smile, blinking back the tears. Surely, more of their teammates had survived.

Debra kicked away a bit of ash-covered wood. "We've encountered ISAN super-soldiers too often to count. We weren't prepared for their skills or their special weapons. Daniel and Pete are out there somewhere. I need to find them. We've lost so many."

Debra had always been all business, refusing to let her emotions into her voice, but her fingers trembled as she pointed west.

Momo's stomach filled with acid, and the urge to vomit became strong. Most of her friends were dead. She didn't want to believe it.

Jo shoved broken pieces of a mug to the side with her feet. "These assassins are different."

"They were created to be robots." Debra shook her head.

Momo continued to stare at Debra in awe. What were the odds of them being at the bookstore at the right time? Unless …

"Were you following us?" Momo took off her cap and slapped it on her thigh. Ashes flew upward, and she flapped her hand in front of her face.

"Momo?" Jo's voice rose a pitch, a warning.

She hadn't meant to sound accusatory or use a sharp tone. Momo dipped her head and shrugged.

"You're the perceptive one," Debra said.

Momo flashed all her teeth and raised her chin.

"Yes, you're right." Debra scuffed one boot at the ash-covered ground. "Every time ISAN soldiers came to our territory, we followed them. And never did I imagine seeing you."

Jo smiled at Hector and Jessa, still huddled around Coco and Marissa, and wiped a tear at the corner of her eyes.

"We hoped to find you, but the rest of our ..." Jo turned her back and sobbed quietly.

Tears streamed down Momo's cheeks. The moment held both joy and sadness. Forty young assassins and two leads, Debra and Jo, had escaped ISAN from the south territory, but not many had survived. She didn't want to count their losses anymore.

Debra met Coco's gaze, then Momo's. "Where's Bo? The three of you are always together."

When Coco closed her eyes and Momo shook her head, Debra released a long sigh. No words were needed. The silence said it all.

"Hector and Jess, help Coco up and let's go." Debra snapped everyone back to reality as her voice carried the authority she'd assumed in the ISAN compound.

A small smile played across Jo's lips. "We have much to catch up on. So much has happened since we got separated."

Momo couldn't contain her excitement. "You're never going to guess who we ran into."

Debra angled her eyebrows. "I want to say Rhett, since you couldn't stop talking about him, but other than that, I have no clue."

Momo grinned like she held a secret and hiked one leg over the pile of ashes. "I can't wait for you to meet him and the rest of the rebels." She batted her eyelashes. "Rhett is so dreamy—well, you'll understand when you see him. As Jo said, we have much catching up to do."

CHAPTER SIX–BETRAYAL

HꞆE JIN

Hae Jin opened her eyes, only to close them again when the ceiling spun. Her head throbbed and her muscles ached as if she had been body-slammed against a glider. She sat up and supported her back on the wall to settle the acid bubbling in her stomach.

"Ssi-bal," she murmured.

Was she in hell? She had to have been executed. But the gray walls with no door indicated otherwise. At least Min Hyuk and Jung were with her, though knocked out and sprawled on the tile floor.

She tried to pull up her map. A warm, tingling sensation crackled through her chest, but fizzed out. Definitely back at the base. All their facilities had some type of sonic vibration, preventing their assassins from using their power.

Oh, God. She couldn't hold it in. She jerked away from her teammates and retched. Nothing came out of her mouth, but she felt like her insides had turned out. She pressed her hot cheek onto the cold tile and sighed, the burning sensation easing.

"Are you okay?" Min Hyuk asked, his voice groggy. He pushed himself up, crawled a few feet to her, and collapsed.

"I've been better." She moaned.

Hae Jin sat up and focused on her teammate. He must have

been drugged, too.

Four things were certain. They were back in ISAN. Sena had betrayed them. The Japanese rebels had been assassinated. And the three of them were in a whole lot of trouble.

She patted her body, checking for injuries, and realized she wore an ISAN gray training outfit and not the sleek combat suit she had worn on the failed mission. It was unsettling to imagine some goon stripping her and her teammates while they were unconscious.

"Wake up." Hae Jin shook Jung. "Wake up."

She tapped his face and waited for a response. When none came, she slapped him harder.

Jung flashed his eyelids open and rolled to his feet. He stumbled a few steps and planted his hands on his face.

"Whoa. We're back in ISAN. What happened?" He sank next to Min Hyuk, lowering his head between his raised knees.

Min Hyuk pressed his back to the wall and crossed his legs. "I'm going to kill Sena. How did she know the details when she shouldn't have known about the escape plan?"

Remember, I have good hearing. Careful what you whisper.

"Her ability. She spied on us," Hae Jin said. "And I'm going to help you kill her. The Japanese rebels are dead from her doing, and we won't be able to join the western team."

"Maybe Ava will rescue us," Jung said.

She inhaled a deep breath, despair rising in her chest. She shouldn't have trusted Sena. That was what she got for caring.

"Why would she?" Hae Jin said, her tone rising, and then it softened. "Why would someone we don't know risk her life for us?"

Min Hyuk shifted to face her, the tips of his lightweight canvas shoes touching hers. "It's not only the three of us she would be saving. Once we escaped, we help the CODE children. Don't you remember that plan?"

"If we live." Jung glanced about the walls, likely searching for the door. "Grayson is going to kill us."

Hae Jin rubbed her temples, head throbbing. "Speaking of leaders, Sunjo might have been found. I think she ..."

Was executed. She couldn't say it out loud. She didn't want to think anymore. Hae Jin had to find a way to keep her squad alive. Bargain?

Min Hyuk scowled. "Maybe we can beg for forgiveness."

She scoffed. "We did nothing wrong. I'd rather die than be in this hellhole. It's so—"

Part of the wall slid open. Mr. Park Ji Woo and Sena ambled in and staked their positions in the center of the room. She almost didn't recognized Park, clad in a training outfit instead of his usual suit. His attire made him appear younger than his mid-thirties age.

The three of them jolted up and bowed at the waist. Damn the Korean culture. She didn't want to give them any respect, even to the elder. As for Sena, it took every ounce of Hae Jin's will to tame the urge to pounce on her.

Nothing was welcoming about Park. He was cold. Stark. And no matter how many times she had seen the pale scar running from his left eyebrow down to his chin, she couldn't stop staring.

Park's shadowed eyes narrowed on her. "You despise this hellhole so much, you'd rather die?"

Ssi-bal. He had heard!

As Park paced in front of them, Hae Jin felt small and inferior. He towered over her, his shoulders thick with muscle. Still, if it weren't for the gun in his holster, she could bring him and Sena down to their knees. She had to be careful ... play her cards right and get on his good side again.

Hae Jin bowed. "Mr. Park. I didn't mean—"

"Silence," he snarled. "Tell me who organized this ridiculous plan."

Sena pointed at Hae Jin. "She did."

Hae Jin clenched her jaw, quivering with rage. One did not betray a team member. But then again, Sena had already stabbed her in the back.

Park sauntered behind Hae Jin. His warm breath brushed the shell of her ear when he spoke. "Did you do this?"

Hae Jin's heart pounded and she said nothing. *Steady.* Park did not tolerate fear.

"I did," Min Hyuk said, his gaze rooted at the part of the wall that had opened earlier.

Park stepped in front of him. "How noble of you, but we all know you don't have the guts or the brains."

He grabbed Min Hyuk's arms, twisting and locking them behind his back. Min Hyuk's face contorted in pain, but he made no sound.

"Stop!" Hae Jin put up a hand. "I did it. I'm the one you want. Let him go."

Park let go. "That wasn't so bad, was it?" He took the pistol out of his holster and pointed it at Hae Jin's forehead.

"No! Please." Min Hyuk dropped to his knees, desperation in his tone. "Don't kill her. I'll do anything."

Jung lowered beside him and pressed his head to the floor in a gesture of respect and a request for forgiveness.

Park rolled his eyes. "How touching." He turned to Sena. "I wonder if they would do the same for you?"

Sena lowered her head and kept quiet.

"So, what to do?" Park said. "Here." He handed the weapon to Sena. "Prove your loyalty. How far would you go for ISAN? Hae Jin was your leader, but she has betrayed us. What are you going to do about it?"

Sena's lips curled wickedly as she pointed the gun at Hae Jin's head. "Your position is finally mine."

Jung jolted up. Then Min Hyuk rose, sweat beading on his temples.

"Why?" Min Hyuk asked. "Hae Jin was nothing but kind to you. When you were bullied by other teammates, she protected you."

"Shut up. Shut up. Shut *up*." Sena scowled, but her hand trembled.

"Prove yourself." Park patted her shoulder. "Show me you have the guts to be the leader."

"Shoot her now?" Sena asked, sounding uncertain. "Right here?"

"I gave you a weapon, didn't I? Do I need to demonstrate how to use one? Because, if I do, you're the target."

Hae Jin snarled. "Do it. What are you waiting for?"

"Are you crazy?" Min Hyuk's pitch rose, his fists trembling by his side.

Hae Jin ignored him and said, "Let me tell you this, Sena. When I die, I swear I'll come back as a ghost and haunt you for the rest of your life. Hell, I'll even do it during the daytime. You'll be so scared you won't be able to function."

"You …" Lines creased on Sena's forehead. Her body trembled from rage. "Just die."

Sena tightened her finger on the trigger. Jung reached for Min Hyuk, but Min Hyuk dove in front of Hae Jin as the gunshot rang out in the room. Hae Jin fell, Min Hyuk on top of her.

Hae Jin screamed and tapped his back. No blood. Strange. Had it been one of Park's mind games? But the acrid smell of hot metal stung her nose. When Min Hyuk helped her up, she stepped on a pool of blood that came from Jung's chest.

"Jung!" Hae Jin dropped beside him. Crimson liquid soaked through his shirt and seeped out of his mouth.

Park held the pistol instead of Sena, who stumbled backward to the wall with wide eyes. What in the world had happened?

Hae Jin stood with her fists rounded. "Tell me why!"

"You don't know your teammates well, do you?" Park grabbed Sena's arm and shoved her.

Hae Jin backed away in time to avoid the collision.

Park scoffed and rubbed at his scarred eyebrow. "Sena, did you really think you could fool me?"

"What are you talking about?" Min Hyuk's eyebrows pinched to the center.

"She didn't double-cross you." Park raised a gun at Sena.

"Enough!" Hae Jin jumped in front of her ex-teammate, her pulse racing.

She used a disrespectful tone, but she didn't care. And she couldn't believe she was protecting a traitor who'd tried to assassinate her twice.

Park glanced at the blood on the floor. "Jung told me about the lighthouse and your escape plan. You should be thanking me for killing him."

"What?" Hae Jin shook her head, confused. "Sena Tased us, not Jung. And you gave her the pistol to kill me."

The muscle on Park's face twitched. "Sena wasn't going terminate you. She was planning to shoot me. Isn't that right,

Sena?" His narrowed eyes became colder. "So I killed Jung. I had planned to execute him anyway. Now, you three catch up and prepare for the next assignment."

Unbelievable. Park lied through his teeth, and Sena had no acting skills. Jung would never betray them. Did he think she would buy his story? What was his motive in killing Jung? So they could trust his spy again?

Hae Jin had no choice. To stay alive, she had to pretend to accept his justification.

Park strolled toward the exit, then halted. He looked over his shoulder as the door slid open, "Just so you know, you're not dead only because I still have use for you. My gut tells me Ava and her team will be headed our way. And you make the perfect bait—and her terminator."

Hae Jin imagined another life, swimming in the ocean with her friends and eating raw fish and spicy ramen with kimchi at the famous beachside restaurant instead of being a prisoner in Korean Isan compound.

CHAPTER SEVEN—SHOPPING

AVA

R hett held a bundled Avary in one arm while I sauntered beside him to the cafeteria. Ozzie and Brooke strolled behind us, holding hands.

Councilor Chang ordered us to go shopping first. She hoped to hear from Sunjo soon, then she would decide on the course of action. My gut told me she had been found out and terminated.

The cracking of boiled eggs and laughter filled the room, the smell of fresh bread warming my stomach. Tamara, Naomi, and Reyna ate across from Payton and Justine. Mia, Ella, Cora, and Nina sat at another table.

I had placed Payton and Justine with Tamara's group to ensure their safety. The rebels wanted her even less than Payton at the mountain base. I had announced they had left ISAN, and I also surprised everyone with the news that Mr. Novak was my father, and Justine my half-sister. I understood the confusion, especially since she had blond hair and blue eyes.

"Good morning." I gave a curt nod as I passed our friends, and then stopped in front of Tamara, Rhett, Ozzie, and Brooke beside me.

Justine and Payton smiled, and then focused on the boiled eggs on their plates.

"How's Avary?" Tamara leaned back and peeked around me to

Rhett. "She's so adorable."

"The cutest baby in the world." Rhett kissed our daughter's forehead.

Reyna took a big bite of bread and set it on her tray as she chewed. "I still can't believe Avary is yours." She waved a finger from Rhett to me, still chewing. "Do you think she'll have a special ability?"

I shrugged. For her sake, I hoped not, but the chances were high. Novak had made her unique. We had to wait until her power manifested.

Justine cracked her egg against the plate and began to peel the shell. "Ava, I heard you're going to South Korea on a mission. I would like to go with you."

"I'm not sure if—"

"Nobody in ISAN is aware I've deserted," Justine said, sounding desperate. "But they know who I am, and I can get you into the Korean ISAN compound."

"I can go with you too." Payton tore off a piece of bread. "Nobody knows about my status, either."

"They have a point," Naomi said, and bit into an apple.

"You're going to trust them?" a guy from a table at the back of the room asked.

Apparently, people were eavesdropping.

"Don't go. It's a trap," a female next to that guy said.

I raised a hand and said in a calm tone, "That's enough. If you have questions, come see me, but not in front of everyone."

Rhett strode to the guy who had spoken earlier and stared down at him. "Tom, you should know better. If I hear another word, your duties will quadruple and you won't have time to sleep. Do you understand?"

"Yeah." Tom scoffed and chomped on an apple.

"I like Justine's idea." Brooke went around the table and stood behind her. "*We* can't just show up. All of the ISAN regions know who we are, and would kill us on sight."

"Talk about this later," Ozzie said. "We need to eat and go diaper shopping. The clock is ticking."

Brooke and I sat across from Tamara while Rhett and Ozzie went to grab our breakfast.

Justine's features contorted into a frown. "When will you be back?"

I wondered if she worried for her safety among the rebels.

"I'll be back soon. We can discuss about Korea after. Sound good?"

Justine's lips curved just enough to hint at a smile, and she nodded. I met Tamara's gaze and jerked my chin toward Payton and my half-sister in a reminder to keep them safe.

Tamara winked at me, a confirmation.

Naomi had seen the interaction between us and hiked a thumbs-up. *Good.* Two more people who would watch over them. I would have asked Reyna, but no way in hell would she ever protect anyone outside her circle of friends.

Deserting ISAN took guts. My sister's choice was genuine. She had left Novak *before* he died. I sympathized over what she must have been through. Our father had manipulated her for her whole life, leaving her arrogant but desperate for his attention.

After breakfast, the four of us left the cafeteria and headed to the glider. Rhett took the driver's seat while I held Avary in the back with Brooke.

When the transporter rose higher, the sun peeked through the clouds. Avary closed her eyes against the brightness. One day she would be big enough to see the mountains surrounding our base, the stream snaking around them, the skyscrapers in the cities, and the giant bubble protecting the citizens from tsunamis.

I angled my daughter to face the window. "Look at all those gliders. You're in one now."

Brooke leaned closer, her shoulder touching mine. "Can you see all those beautiful buildings? They're colorful during the night."

Rhett landed the transporter on the twentieth floor. The seatbelts automatically unbuckled and I handed Avary to him, as he already had the baby carrier strapped to his body. He positioned our daughter, her stomach to his chest, and lifted the flap of material to cover her head.

We strolled out and entered the department store. Some people shopped online and had the purchased items delivered to their homes, but we had to do it the old-fashioned way, for obvious reasons.

Baby products flashed on the wall screens and mothers pushed their strollers. A toddler screamed, hugging a robot while as his mom tried to pry it out of his hands. Another child wailed, frightened of the mobile dog toy spinning in her path.

Not looking forward to that stage.

Ozzie placed his palm on a tall hologram post at the front of an aisle. A list of infant products appeared. He scrolled and swiped at words and images. The last time I'd been at a store was with my mom, ages ago.

"We can go here for diapers." Ozzie pointed at the star inside a circle.

"Why are we looking at the map when Ava can use hers?" Brooke raised an eyebrow.

Ozzie slapped his forehead with his palm. "That's right. Go ahead."

I gave them an *are you kidding me* look. "I can find *people*, not baby formula."

"We don't need directions. This way." Rhett grabbed my hand and led me down the aisle, passing bassinets and cute stuffed animals.

Floor-to-ceiling aisles—I had never seen so many different brands of children products in my life.

Rhett peeked at Avary, who was fast asleep, and picked up a pink bottle of shampoo. "How about this one?"

"Unicorn sprinkles?" I took it and read the label. "Says it's organic."

Ozzie narrowed his eyes. "Her hair isn't going to turn pink, is it?"

Brooke snorted and slapped his arm. "Stop being silly."

A young mother with a toddler inside a stroller stopped beside Ozzie. "You know, I thought that, too. But don't worry. You'll love the sweet scent."

Ozzie shrugged sheepishly and offered a shy grin.

I scanned the bar code with the laser projecting from my chip. It took my 4Qs from the bank. Rhett had transferred money to my account before we left. Good thing he had plenty. Children were costly.

I had registered under a fake name and address that Councilor Chang had set up for me. I couldn't go around telling everyone my true identity. ISAN would find me in a heartbeat. I was wanted for the murders of Novak, Gene, and all those who'd died in the blast.

Mr. Novak was gone, but someone else had taken his place. As important as he had been to the network, the organization was much larger than him, and had influence throughout the countries. "On to the next thing on the list." Rhett rounded the corner to another aisle.

"How cute are those?" Brooke hugged a stuffed white dog and looked at me with puppy eyes. "Can we buy one for Avary? I don't have 4Qs, so I'll need to borrow some. I want to gift one to her."

"Of course." I smiled. "Thank you for thinking of her."

Gratitude filled my heart. Avary had such great aunts and uncles. Though I wished my mom was alive to help raise her, I was lucky to have friends I considered as family. Rhett and I couldn't raise a child alone, especially in the middle of a war.

After we were done shopping, we headed to our glider. Two gentlemen came out of the service door and handed us fifteen large bags containing the items we had purchased: diapers, canisters of formula, baby bottles, clothes, toys, and much more that weren't on the list.

Rhett passed me a fussy Avary, who smacked her lips nonstop. I went inside the transporter and fed her with a bottle we had brought from the mountain base.

"Need help?" Rhett took the seat beside me and watched Avary drink.

Brooke and Ozzie remained outside. Something was up.

"You got the call from Councilor Chang, didn't you?" I asked.

He inhaled and exhaled, chest rising and falling. "Yeah. She wants you to get your team ready."

I swallowed and choked up as I looked at our daughter. I had fallen in love with her so fast and hard, I couldn't stand the thought of being away from her.

"I don't have a choice, right?" My voice dipped low. I didn't know if he heard me.

Rhett lifted my chin. "Babe, no one is going to judge you if you decide not to go. You're a mother. And for my selfish reasons, I don't want you to go, and I don't want to be apart from you."

"We already talked about this," I said softly. "I go. You stay with our daughter. Just in case, she needs at least one of us."

The thought of us being separated gutted me. We had enjoyed peace, though short, but our lives were on the line again. When would the war end? I already knew the answer. When we brought down ISAN.

Rhett caressed my cheek, and I savored his warmth and love. His nose twitched and his lips became a thin line. I wondered what he was thinking.

"She needs her mother, so you better come back. And I need you, too. More than you'll ever know."

I pressed my face into his palm. He kissed my forehead, then Avary's. There was so much I wanted to say, but I didn't want to tear up, and we needed to get home.

"Have you made up your mind on who you'll take with you?" Rhett asked.

I placed the bottle on the seat, positioned Avary over my shoulder, and tapped her back. "I'm taking Brooke, Justine, and Tamara. A large group will be too hectic. A small group is easier to manage, and having people I've worked with before will make things go smoother."

"Brooke. Justine. Tamara." Rhett snorted. "How we've come full circle. Your second team is now fighting against the people they fought for."

That was life. So unpredictable. Never would I have imagined this scenario. Never had I predicted Justine would go up against the father she had worshipped.

"I almost forgot to tell you." Rhett stood and held out his arms toward me. "Councilor Chang would like to see you before you go to Korea."

I had planned to stop by Mr. San's secret medical facility, regardless of Josephine's request, anyway. After I passed Avary to Rhett, I took off my necklace and shoved it inside his front pocket.

"What are you doing?" He frowned.

If I don't make it back, I want you to give it to our daughter.

"I don't want to lose it." I swallowed, biting back tears and suppressing the words I wanted to tell him. I kissed our daughter's forehead, then kissed Rhett's lips. "I love you both with all my heart. You are everything to me."

Rhett gathered us in his arms, and we stayed like that for many heartbeats.

CHAPTER EIGHT—PIERRE VERLOT

JOSEPHINE CHANG

Josephine blinked, adjusting to the brightness after the blindfold was removed. When her vision had cleared, an attractive man seated across from her smiled, a metal table dividing them.

"My apologies again for the hood, Councilor Chang." Mr. San placed his folded hands on his lap.

Someone had escorted her, blindfolded, to San's office, like the last time she'd gone to the ANS—Advocacy Network for Superhumans—facility.

"As I said before, I understand." She ran her fingers through her hair as she admired the oil painting of the ocean behind him.

He dipped his head and grinned.

"Thank you for your help," she said. "The package arrived safely."

He rubbed his chin with a finger, looking pensive. "I hope it was in your favor."

Josephine crossed her legs and leaned forward. "The DNA match confirmed."

The gratitude she felt toward him made her want to hug the man.

San cleared his throat. "Can I offer you a drink?" He flicked a thumb at the table with water and sodas.

"I'm fine, but I'm in a hurry, so if you—"

"Why do you want to see the prisoner?"

For crying out loud: she was a member of the Remnant

Councils of the former United States, and didn't need his permission.

Josephine shifted on the black vinyl chair and rose. "Please take me to Verlot. You are welcome to join me. I'm not excluding you." San paused a moment and nodded. He stood and said, "I got my hands on some ISAN battle suits for your rebels. Remind me to give them to you before you leave. ANS is designing one based on their tech."

Josephine followed him out the door and halted by the glass wall. His people were monitoring streets and highways in different regions.

"Vince told me Jo and some of the younger rebels went searching for Debra," she said. "Have you seen them?"

He pointed at the largest screen in the back wall. "My team picked up an ISAN glider and a group of their assassins. A bookstore blew up. If anyone was near the building, they wouldn't have survived."

Her heart pounded and a wave of dizziness washed over her. Hopefully, Jo's squad hadn't been in that region.

San led her past the grand chamber where a group of teen girls practiced self-defense with boxing gloves on. One had a metal band over her forehead, and the others didn't. Perhaps that one had a special ability, but Josephine didn't ask.

They rounded another hallway and went down the stairs. Cool air and dim lighting gave her goose bumps, as it had the last time she'd visited this facility. They passed through the first door into the prisoner's cell.

Verlot's eyes widened and a slow, wicked grin grew on his face. He took a bite of a burger and wiped his mouth.

A burger? She flashed an incredulous glance at San.

"Hello there, Councilor Chang," Verlot said around a mouthful. "You should try this. It's so good. San does special favors for me. I think we will be best friends. What brings you to my humble home, Beautiful?"

Don't call me that. She wanted to tell him off, but the panel next to the cell door blinked a red light, indicating while she could hear him, he couldn't hear her.

Josephine's lips twitched. How she loathed him with every inch of her fiber. She wanted to take that burger and smear it all over his face. And maybe San's, too. Josephine clenched her jaw, eyes burning with rage.

"Before you say anything, hear me out. I promised him a treat if he gave me information."

She scoffed, anger scorching her veins. "What did he tell you?"

He held up his chin. "The location of where the CODE assassins are being bred."

What Josephine had to say would make San look like a fool.

With a straight face and a calm voice, she said, "In South Korea."

He gave her a sidelong glance and shoved his hands inside his pockets. "You already knew, which explains your long face. Who gave you that information?"

She angled an eyebrow and turned to face the glass barrier, then spotted a movement from the corner of her eyes. Verlot got up and threw his trash inside the small sink. He passed the toilet and sat back on the cot—the picture of good health and contentedness, not like someone who had been locked up.

When she didn't answer, he said, "You have the right country, but you don't have the location of the Korean ISAN base where the CODE soldiers are bred. That's my next question for him."

54

Josephine took a step closer and jabbed his chest. "Get me the facts, and stop feeding him what he wants."

She turned and yelped, startled by Verlot's face pressed to the glass. Her hand went to her chest.

San pressed a button on the panel next to the cell door. A beep echoed, and the red light turned to green.

"So nice of you to visit me, Councilor Chang." Verlot smirked. "How can I help you?"

He spoke in a honeyed voice, but his eyes held no warmth. His words sliced through the air like knives and she clenched her fists, longing to strike his face.

"Cut the crap." Her nostrils flared. "Tell me where the Korean ISAN base is located."

Verlot's eyes flashed with rage as he slammed his palms on the barrier, making the glass shudder. His fingers curled and his knuckles turned white against the transparent surface.

"Listen, Chang." His voice was low and strained. "Your pathetic rebel unit is no match for my super-soldiers. Save their lives and stand down. If you do, I'll give you the same treatment you have given me. I think that's fair. So, how about you let me out?"

She took a step back and snarled. "You will never get out," she said with conviction. "Even if I have to give up my own life, you will never leave this hell I created for you."

"Chang!" Verlot's chest rose and fell, his hot breath fogging up the glass. He scrubbed a hand down his face and said, in a calmer tone, "Fine. See if you can find them without my help." Verlot narrowed his eyes at San. "We had a deal, but I've changed my mind. You can thank Chang."

Verlot sauntered away and grabbed a book off his cot, flipping through the pages without a care. Anger seared through Josephine's veins, but she stood her ground, keeping her face passive. But her fists clenched so tight that her fingernails dug into her palms. She pressed the panel in the wall, and the red light flickered on.

"Don't worry." San gave a curt nod. "I'll get an answer for you."

"We need the location today. I told Ava to get her team ready. I hate to admit it, but we're no match for their super-soldiers. And I want something from Verlot."

"Yes, of course. Anything."

"I need an official memo from him to Mr. Ji Woo Park. He runs Korean ISAN. I've already drafted one and sent it to you. It's imperative you send it to me as soon as possible."

CHAPTER NINE-HIDE OUT

MOMO

Momo, Coco, Marissa, and Jo flanked Debra on the left, while Hector and Jessa guarded the right. They followed their leader stealthily down the street, passing abandoned cars and ruined shops to reach their shelter.

Thick gray clouds tumbled across the sky, and a cool gust scattered the paper trash. Momo slammed a hand on her cap to keep it from blowing away. So far, no sign of Davina's team.

Debra extended her fist and made a sharp turn into a vacant office building. To Momo's surprise, the first level wasn't in ruins, like most structures.

Footsteps pounded up the stairs. Momo and Coco fell behind and covered the rear, their Tasers aimed outward. She was relieved to climb stairs that weren't broken or missing. When they reached the tenth floor, they settled where the chairs lined the wall and blankets were piled on a desk.

Canned foods, bags of chips, and cereal boxes occupied the table beside the rusty file cabinets. Had Debra's unit been hiding here all this time?

Jessa grabbed a small trash can beside the desk. Hector rubbed his hands over the wood inside and, from his power, a fire was kindled.

Debra sat on the ground and the rest followed suit, in a circle.

"How do we find Daniel and Pete?" Jo placed her palms out to take warmth from the flame.

Jessa raised her hand and spoke before being given permission. "If we get separated, we meet at the grocery store not too far from here. The sign is destroyed, so we don't know the name, but we have the location."

Debra rested a hand on Jessa's shoulder. "We'll wait until it's dark. ISAN searches for us during the day, so hopefully they'll retreat before the sun sets." She clutched a leather bag from under the table behind her and revealed white, pearl-sized medicine. "I found these water pills in the office kitchen. It should last you for a day."

After Hector swallowed the capsule, he reached over to the rusty cabinet. "We have emergency supplies. Flashlights, a first-aid kit, dried food, and ..." He took out something from the bottom drawer and beamed with excitement. "And ... chocolate."

Momo's eyes widened, even though she had some in her pockets.

"Here." Hector tore off the wrapper and tossed broken pieces to them.

Momo exchanged glances with Coco and Marissa. Their faces lit up with smiles despite the horrendous day. They had to enjoy the little things, for even the next hour wasn't guaranteed.

"Yummy." Momo savored the sweet, creamy confection melting on her tongue.

Her stomach rumbled with hunger, but she wasn't going to complain. She'd had a good meal that morning—boiled eggs and bread. And it was more than what Debra, Hector, and Jessa had.

She reached inside her pockets and pulled out the chocolate bars she had found at the liquor store. And also a penny. She had forgotten about it.

Perhaps the coin had brought her luck. They had survived the blast at the bookstore, and they had found Debra's team.

Momo wanted to keep the sweets for herself, but since her friend had shared, she offered hers, and Coco and Marissa did the same.

"How did your squad get separated?" Jo asked.

Debra rubbed her hands by the flame, her eyes gleaming against the firelight. "Daniel and Pete were on the other side of the building when Davina found us at the grocery store. I didn't want them to get captured, so I made some noise and ran. But Hector and Jessa tailed me, and I had no choice but to hide to keep them safe."

Jessa licked a smudge of melted chocolate on her finger. "We followed the assassins to the bookstore, but we didn't know you were inside until I spotted the four of you huddled by the back wall. Davina's team was on their way out."

Hector crumbled the bar wrapper and tossed it into the flame. "Debra and Jessa shielded us from the blast. And I pushed back the fire and the debris."

"Lucky for us, you showed up." Coco tugged at the dried blood stain on her shirt.

"How are you feeling?" Marissa asked.

She pressed her fingers on the wound. "I'm sore, but I'm fine."

Marissa's blue eyes twinkled. "It's a good thing I came. I may be small, and people might think me useless, but I'm powerful."

Jo ruffled her hair. "And don't ever let anyone make you think otherwise."

Debra opened a file cabinet drawer and handed Coco a dark sweat shirt. "This might be big for you, but it's better than what you're wearing."

"Thank you," Coco said, then took off her cap and turned around to change.

"What's our plan after we get Daniel and Pete?" Debra asked.

"Depending on the situation, we might have to go to South Korea." Jo leaned back against the wall and crossed her arms.

Debra glanced behind her between the rusty cabinets. "Sorry, I thought I heard something. Anyway, why?"

"They're creating CODE soldiers. The acronym stands for Constructed Ovum Designed Engineering. These assassins are injected with a serum called HelixAVA, which can make a super-soldier out of anyone, whether they have a unique power or not."

Debra shoved a piece of chocolate in her mouth. "How do you know?"

Jo tapped her forearm where the chip had been embedded in her. "I'm in contact with a man named Vince. He's working with Councilor Chang."

Debra blinked and furrowed her brow. "What? Councilor Chang?"

Jo inhaled a deep breath. "I have much to tell you. And, Momo and Coco, please feel free to jump in. You've had your own journey, as well."

Momo couldn't believe all that had happened within a short amount of time. So many losses—but she had to hold on to the hope that it all meant something. And she would never forget Bobo or the friends who had sacrificed their lives. Momo swore she would avenge their deaths.

Renegades forever.

CHAPTER TEN-MEDICAL FACILITY

AVA

Brooke, Justine, and Tamara followed me into the glider and we departed for Mr. San's secret medical facility. I punched in the coordinates Josephine Chang had sent me and the transporter flew us to our destination.

Clusters of skyscrapers loomed over department stores and cute boutique shops. The people below looked like ants going about their daily business. I wondered if those of us who had escaped ISAN could ever have a normal life.

The glider passed the city to uninhabited territory—nothing but destroyed houses and restaurants. We rounded the tallest office buildings and entered a underground parking lot. As soon as our transporter neared the wall, the structure opened to a wide, polished space.

Tamara slapped the button on the control panel and the door slid open.

"Go ahead," I said. "I'll be down soon. I need to send a message to Rhett."

> Landed safely. Miss you and Avary already.
> I'll keep you informed.

I rose out of my seat and jerked back. Justine stood in front of me.

"Sorry." She retreated a few steps. "I didn't mean to scare you."

61

I understood her reservation and the reason she lagged behind. "I already told Councilor Chang you're part of my crew. Rhett, Mitch, and Russ are also aware. You'll be fine, I promise. Now, put your head up and come with me."

Justine pressed her lips together and curled them with a hint of a smile. When I descended the ramp, my team waited for me in a resting stance and my sister joined them. Déjà vu. Reminded me of our mission days.

Russ and Mitch stood side by side, blocking my way. They looked like a unified front, which was telling, as Russ and Mitch didn't see eye to eye and at times were at each other's throats. I had never expected them to even tolerate each other, much less be buddies. Quite cute, actually.

Councilor Chang had informed us the bullet had been removed from Mitch, and Dr. Machine had cleared him, but to see him in person … my eyes pooled with tears.

Russ grinned, his green eyes sparkling like the sunlight reflecting on emerald stone. "Hello, Ava. You're looking well."

He had lost some weight, and his hair was shorter. But he looked rested and at peace.

I extend my arms to hug him, but dropped them instead. "I'm so happy to see you."

Mitch smiled, but something seemed off about him. His lips parted, closed, and parted. He had his hands inside his pockets, but he took them out, ready to …

"Oh, what the hell," Mitch said. His long legs covered the ground between us in a heartbeat. He squeezed me so tight I thought my chest would burst. "I'm an uncle. I can't believe it." He swung me around as he kissed my cheek.

I blinked when he set me down. With an infectious grin, he

looked at me like I had done something amazing.

"I saw my niece on screen. Avary is beautiful. She has your face, but she has Rhett's eyes."

She did indeed.

"Congratulations," Russ said, but he didn't sound as elated as Mitch. "I can't believe what Novak did to you. Regardless, I'm sorry about your father and your brother."

"And my mom …" I couldn't finish, nor did I have to. Mitch and Russ already knew my mother had died with Novak and Gene.

"Shall we?" Russ said. "Please follow me."

Russ led us through the double glass doors. Footsteps clacked on the white tile floor down the hallway. After rounding the corner, we entered a massive room.

A large screen hung on the back wall. Monitors beeped. High-tech equipment hummed. The setup reminded me of the laboratory at ISAN's secret base.

Cleo approached us with a smile. She had been standing next to Zen's medical pod. But when she saw Justine, she stopped. She ignored my sister and turned her attention to me.

Cleo's red hair was pushed back into a ponytail, revealing a thinner face. She looked pale and her eyes were puffy, like she had been crying.

At the facility, Novak had revealed that Cleo's father, also a scientist, had suppressed her power with a serum he had created—the same one in our protein drinks. And that Novak and Zen had been friends and had worked together.

Regardless of our past, we had to move on. Moving forward meant treating each other not by our parents' mistakes, but by our current actions.

"How are you?" I asked. "How's your father?"

"He's out of danger, but ..." She wrung a strand of hair behind her ear, her fingers trembling. "Thanks to Councilor Chang, he should be out of the hub soon." She lowered her gaze to her shoes, then looked at me again. "Congratulations. I heard about Avary."

Cleo would find out sooner or later, but I'd hoped it would be later.

"Thank you," was all I could say. I didn't want to talk about this subject, for she still had feelings for Rhett.

"Well ..." She crossed her arms, her gaze darting to Brooke, Tamara, and Justine. "I'm working on my ... It's not much. I mean, you have a team, but I'm willing to help."

Brooke's eyes grew wider. Tamara covered her mouth when a soft gasp escaped her. Justine kept her head lowered and said nothing.

In a roundabout way, it took guts to ask me. And I understood her need to fit in, to be wanted, to be useful in this crazy world. Cleo had desired to be a part of the resistance whether Zen approved or not.

I smiled. "I have a crew, but once I come back, you're more than welcome to go to the mountain base and keep training. Councilor Chang can direct you better, since she's heading a search unit for the specially gifted."

I hoped she didn't think I wanted to dismiss her. ISAN spent months preparing assassins in intense simulations. Teammates knew each other's weaknesses and strengths. The lead designed hand signals and body gestures, and my squad had plenty of practice with me.

I cleared my throat. "Can you direct me to Lydia?"

Mitch pointed to the first pod. My team and I followed him.

Lydia had her eyes closed while a machine inside her hub scanned her chest. Then a red laser silently went over her head.

"She's going to be okay, right?" I asked Mitch.

Lydia was one of my role models, and a great leader. Everyone respected her. No one had ever talked behind her back. I had to give her credit for hiding her true identity and working with Councilor Chang.

Mitch glanced at the monitor, the lines moving in a steady rhythm. "She's stable, but she's not out of the woods yet. We're trying to figure out why her fever spikes and why she hasn't woken up."

"I'm sorry, Lydia," I murmured, peering down at her pale face. "Novak is dead. He can't harm you ever again."

I had written Novak off as my father and no one judged me for his actions, but guilt continued to cling onto me like a plague. Clenching my fists, I thought back to when Novak had shot Lydia.

I'd wished I had taken the gun and killed him. Then my mother would be alive, and Lydia, Mitch, and Zen wouldn't have been wounded. My mind reeled in a vicious cycle of second-guessing.

I rested my hand on Mitch's arm. "Is there anything I can do?"

He offered a small smile and shook his head.

The door slid open, catching my attention.

"Welcome," a smooth, commanding voice said. Councilor Chang's heels tapped across the tile.

We said our greetings and sat on the sofas at the back of the room, except for Cleo. She went to the medical pods and spoke with the attending doctor.

Russ and Mitch went out of the room and returned with some

hot tea in recyclable paper mugs. They passed a cup to each of us. Tamara and Brooke drank, but I held on to mine. My mother had taught me to wait until after the elder had taken the first sip.

"Ginseng with honey." The Councilor placed the TAB—Technological Advance Board, a flat computer—on the sofa and raised her mug. "Good for your health." She drank and released a long sigh.

My mother used to serve me the same tea, and would say the same thing. I missed her. Seeing her again, even as a ghost of herself, had sharpened a longing that would dull over time.

"Why did you want to see us?" Brooke asked.

Chang set the cup on the glass coffee table. "I want to help you with your plan. Do you have one?"

I admired the Councilor, but sometimes she got on my nerves. Asking about the plan indicated that she didn't trust me.

I blew into the cup as I took a sip and said, "My team and I will arrive in Korea, and Justine is going to take us prisoner."

Justine's eyes grew wider, but she kept quiet as she drank.

"What happens if they decide to terminate you on the spot?" Chang leaned back and crossed her legs.

Tamara let out an audible breath. "They wouldn't shoot Ava, right? Besides, she can stop the bullets."

The Councilor raised an eyebrow and set the TAB on her lap. "How quickly you forget the sonic vibration that suppresses your abilities. Where do you think the invention came from?"

"Korea," Russ murmured.

"They've perfected it," Mitch said. "Not even Cleo can bring it down."

Cleo is an amateur, I wanted to say, but I bit my tongue. Chang had a point, but detailed plans never worked, from my experience.

I figured that once we were inside and had more intel, I would organize the rescue and destroy the lab that produced AVA soldiers.

"Do you have a suggestion?" Brooke flashed all her teeth and crushed the paper mug in her fist.

"Suggestion?" The Councilor sounded offended. She typed something on her TAB and a hologram of a formal letter popped up.

Mr. Park Ji Woo,

> As you've heard, Mr. Novak is deceased. East Sector received news from a source that Ava and her team will attempt to rescue the rebels you have in custody. I'm confident my unit will capture them. They are headed to Korea now. When Justine and Russ arrive, give them access to your data and do not harm the prisoners. I will send another squad to pick them up and deal with them under our restrictions.

Pierre Verlot

Russ twisted his body toward the medical hubs, avoiding my gaze. Had he requested to go with us? Or had Chang forced him? He shouldn't go back to ISAN.

Justine pointed at the hologram letters. "It's from Verlot? I thought he had a stroke and was in critical condition."

I raised a hand when the Councilor narrowed her eyes at my sister. "She's not aware," I said.

I didn't care what happened to Verlot, but I found it strange that a memo had been drafted and signed by him.

Chang straightened her spine and shut down the TAB. "I'm

going to tell you this because I trust you all. Do not disclose this intel to anyone. Mr. San is holding Verlot captive."

Gasps filled the room.

"We've been keeping him imprisoned to draw out information and use him when needed. And he'll be in prison for the rest of his life. But, whatever you decide, this memorandum should keep you safe."

Mitch scrubbed the back of his head. "In the message, it said, *I will send another squad to pick them up*. Which unit is going?"

The Councilor pulled up a portrait from her chip—an attractive man with dark eyes and squared jawline hovered in the air. "You remember Vince, right? And I'll appoint others. You attack when he gets inside the facility, not sooner."

She showed another photo. "This is your destination. We'll drop you off near Seoraksan National Park. And you'll have to find your way to Ulsanbawi Peak. Justine and Russ will be waiting for you there. Since Mr. Park has been warned, he'll station the assassin nearby."

"I worry about Russ," I said. "Why is he going?"

Russ gave me a sidelong glance. "I've been an agent long before I met you. I'll be fine."

I clenched my jaw. I wished he would stop being stubborn. "The new soldiers are faster than me. Stronger. They're—"

"Insane," Brooke cut in. "They're just like Gene. Maybe crazier. I agree with Ava. Russ should stay out of this one."

"It's up to him," Chang said. "I've already sent Mr. Park this letter. Let's not waste any more time. I have matters to take care of, so, Justine or Russ, one of you please keep in touch and let me know how things are progressing."

"I will," Russ said. "I mean, one of us will for sure."

The Councilor drawled up another hologram. A man in his mid-thirties, perhaps, with a pale scar from his left eyebrow down to his chin. He could have gotten that fixed. I'd met people like him who cherished their reminders of past tragedies. This man wore a gray suit—another Mr. Novak. I rolled my eyes. I was beginning to hate men in dark suits. "This is Mr. Park Ji Woo," she said. "He's the head of South Korean ISAN. He's just as ruthless as Novak, if not more. And this is Hae Jin." She flashed a photo of a girl. "She's one of the team leaders. I've been informed her power resembles Ava's."

Hae Jin's hair was tied back, revealing an oval face. She looked too angelic to be a deadly assassin.

I meant to sound matter-of-fact, but it might have come across as arrogant. "She doesn't have a map like I do."

"As I said, she mimics your gifts." She furrowed her forehead, annoyed.

Damn it, I'd thought I was unique. If she had similar DNA, it was possible. But I didn't have to like it.

"Your mission …" Chang said. "Demolish the AVA manufacturing compound and bring the rebels back home with you. Make Hae Jin a priority. I have plans for her. Then we'll take down one ISAN base at a time. Godspeed, and good luck."

"Who's taking us?" Tamara asked.

On cue, the door slid open.

"Hello, everyone. Have you missed me?" Zeke strutted in, a devilish grin playing across his face.

He wore all black, with his hair slicked back and tattooed dragon scales peeking out from under his sleeves. Thick silver chains garlanded his neck, and an onyx cross necklace hung between the unbuttoned halves of his shirt.

When Tamara sprinted toward him, Zeke opened his arms, ready to receive her.

"Tam—" He didn't get to finish saying her name.

She struck his cheek with a loud slap. The force of the motion followed through and he stumbled out of the room as the door slid shut.

CHAPTER ELEVEN—THE RESCUE

MOMO

The thick, cool air settled in Momo's bones as the night crept in. She shivered, sitting with her friends in a circle, the trash can fire giving them warmth.

Debra passed out packages of ramen she had taken from the rusty cabinet. "Sorry, but this is dinner."

Momo ripped the bag and took a bite. The crunching sounded louder in the quiet. "I love dried noodles," she said, between chewing.

"Me too," Coco said as she accidentally bumped her cap with Momo's.

Marissa licked her lips. "Such a yummy treat."

Jessa and Hector snickered. Debra and Jo laughed as they enjoyed their own.

Debra reached inside a drawer and tossed zip-up hoodies to everyone. "Put the hood over the hat." She flipped the material over her head to demonstrate. "The bill sticks out. We'll be able to identify each other faster in case we get separated."

Then Debra handed out small flashlights.

Jo held up hers. "Don't turn this on unless it's absolutely necessary. If we get separated, I'll click fast three times, like this." She pointed the light to the ceiling to demonstrate. "Respond back the same way. I'll find you in the darkness."

Momo crinkled the ramen wrapper and tossed it into the trash can and the flame rose higher, the stench of burnt plastic filling their space.

Debra clasped her hands, her features stern. "I think you're all wonderful and have great fighting skills, but don't underestimate ISAN CODE soldiers."

Jo flinched and pressed her thumb on her chip. She had gotten a message. After she read the hologram text, she said, "It's Vince. He asked me if we'll go to Korea after we finish our mission."

"Did you reply?" Debra asked.

"No. I wanted to ask you first, since you're the lead agent."

Debra met everyone's gaze and said, "If we were still in ISAN, we wouldn't have a choice. But we're no longer assassins. After we rescue Daniel and Pete, we're going to the mountain base." She released a long sigh. "I hope you understand my decision. I'm certain Vince can count on another unit."

"But what about never leaving anyone behind?" Marissa said softly. "Isn't that why we're risking our lives to save Daniel and Pete? We're all under the same rebel umbrella, whether they're part of our squad or our region."

Debra peered up at the ceiling and closed her eyes. She seemed to have some sort of brief, silent struggle. When she opened her eyes, she said, "We're not getting involved. Sometimes you have to look at the situation. To save one life by sacrificing ten is not the best plan. I'm closing this discussion."

No one said a word. Momo wanted to help Vince's quest, but she didn't want anyone else to go against Debra. They had lost many friends, and almost losing Coco had shaken her to the core. But she couldn't just stay put.

After they arrived at the mountain base, she would find a way to get to Korea even if she had to borrow a glider and leave on her own.

"Get ready." Debra stood and covered the trash can with a lid to kill the flame.

Without the fire to keep her warm, Momo shivered and rubbed her arms. Darkness surrounded them, and though they were safe, Momo's skin crawled.

Debra shoved the Taser behind her waist and zipped up her hoodie. "Keep tight, and use the same defense formation. Jo and I will take the front."

The small amount of light from Debra's flashlight guided them down the stairs and out into the street. Thunder roared and lightning arced across the night sky. Momo shuddered and swallowed hard. She hated the noise more than anything because, well, rain always followed.

Showers kissed Momo's cheeks as she flanked Jo, Coco and Marissa beside her. She held out her weapon. Luckily, they were rainproof. Pockets of flame in the distance indicated the homeless, also known as drifters, had come out. But, soon they would disperse.

The bill of her cap protected her eyes from the pouring rain and her boots gave a wet slurp in the mud. Momo wanted to lower her head to keep the water off her face, but she couldn't risk one moment of inattention.

She kicked a street sign pole and stumbled forward, swearing. She would have fallen flat on her stomach had Hector not clutched her shirt. Momo hated walking in the dark. If only she could turn on her flashlight. But seven ignited flashlights might as well be a sign that read, "I'm a target. Shoot me now."

"We're almost there." Debra halted under an awning at an old ice cream shop. Rain sluiced off the roof in steady streams. "The market is across the street. Once we get inside, we'll split up."

Thunder cracked and gave an echoing boom like an exploding bomb.

"Something feels off." Momo rubbed her arms. "I feel it in my bones."

"Everything will be fine." Coco's eyes flickered in silver as her fingertips sparked like the lightning arcing through the dark clouds.

For a moment, the ruined buildings and abandoned cars lit up through the sheets of the shower. A beautiful sight.

Another clap of thunder followed, and Momo came back to reality. The market was in one piece, except that jagged holes marred exterior walls that had been ravaged by time and neglect. She squinted, and could have sworn she'd seen a black cat dart over a delivery truck.

She blinked away the water coating her eyelashes, chiding herself for second-guessing every little thing. Momo knew better than to be distracted by feline apparitions. There was no room for error, and she couldn't afford any missteps. Not today. Not ever.

"Get ready." Jo raised a fist.

Debra craned her neck from left to right, then ran, the small light from the flashlight her only marker. They weaved around flipped shopping carts and parked cars. Water splashed each time they stepped in puddles. When they reached the grocery store, they pressed against the wall by the entrance.

Momo inhaled and exhaled as her pulse raced. She should be used to this kind of stress. She had been trained not to hesitate to kill, and not to fear. But as another round of lightning lit up the darkness, her mind played the image of Coco on the floor, bleeding, and Bobo dead inside the glider.

Stop. Momo gripped her head and focused. Jo had dashed inside, but she couldn't get her muscles to move. Coco yanked on Momo's shirt and tugged her along. It smelled like rotten produce and old socks. She wanted to gag.

"Are you okay?" Coco whispered. "You're acting strange."

Momo said nothing. She didn't want to share her gruesome thoughts, so she watched Debra's team head toward the produce section, then tailed Jo in the opposite direction.

The roof leaked in some places, leaving puddles scattered like land mines. No matter how quiet their steps, their shoes squeaked, but ISAN boots didn't make a sound, making it harder to detect the assassins.

Jo opened her flashlight and pointed it on a mouse running past them. Marissa covered her mouth to suppress a scream.

A clank startled Momo.

Jo lifted a finger to her lips, hushing them. "The noise is coming from the frozen food section."

"Maybe it's Daniel and Pete." Marissa sounded hopeful, her eyes gleaming. Leave it to her to be positive.

Jo inched closer, but stopped at the end of the aisle.

A crunch, as if someone chewed on chips. Then footsteps. Not one or two, but many. The footfalls became louder, as if they were deliberate.

Run, Momo wanted to say, but no words escaped. Was she the only one afraid of Davina? Momo felt like a coward. She had to gather herself, or she'd put her teammates in danger.

Thunder boomed and lightning flashed, highlighting the assassins sauntering toward them. They halted at the other end of the aisle as Jo's squad remained in the same spot. Davina was the only one without a weapon. Perhaps she didn't need one.

She wanted to grab the braid Davina had just flipped over her shoulder, and repeatedly slam her to the ground. Her heart pounded. She didn't like feeling scared. She recalled the words instilled in her as an ISAN soldier. *Chin up. Stand tall. Don't let your enemies sense your fear.*

Momo's face contorted in a furious grimace as she pointed her Taser, but she waited for Jo's order to fire.

"I thought I killed you all." Davina took a chip out of the bag and shoved it in her mouth. "No matter. I'll just do it again. Where's the other half of your unit? You should all die together."

"You crazy bit—" Momo began, but stopped when Jo held up her hand.

"Don't waste your breath," Jo said. "Repeat what we did on the last mission. Do you understand?"

She couldn't be happier to give Davina a surprise, but first the assassin's feet had to touch the puddle of water between them.

Just as Momo wondered about Daniel's and Pete's whereabouts, one of the assassins brought them forward, bound and gagged. Her instinct was to charge down the long aisle and Tase the terminator, but she hesitated. She didn't know the magnitude of her enemies' powers.

Jo extended her arms outward to her sides, a mama bear protecting her younglings. As if she'd read their minds, she said in a stern tone, "Coco. Momo. Stay. Don't you dare move."

Ten soldiers behind Davina formed a semicircle, aiming their gadgets at them.

"Surrender." Davina shuffled away from her team. "There's nowhere to run. Your pellets will bounce off us, and your weapons are ..." She laughed mockingly. "... nothing but toys."

Come closer, Davina. Step on the puddle three feet from you.

"You're fighting for the wrong network." Coco's sparkling electricity flickered between her fingers. "What they're doing to you is wrong."

Davina scoffed and took a few more steps.

Almost. One more step.

Davina's boots gave a wet slurp and splashed on the water. "I'm not your therapist, and I don't care about your reasons. ISAN made me who I am. I like being powerful. I'm done giving you a chance to surrender."

"Fine," Jo said. "Maybe this will wake you up a bit. Coco, you're on."

Coco clenched her fist, and a miniature fireball glimmered in her palm. She thrust out her arm and the spark grew brighter still before shooting a filament of light across the room.

Catalysts of electricity sizzled on contact with the puddle of water beneath Davina. The air crackled as blue and purple energy crawled up the assassin, electrifying her body until her hair rose tall, leaving behind a smell of smoke.

Coco extended the energy and zapped the other soldiers. While the electrical lights fizzled, keeping them immobile, Momo moved in with incredible speed and snatched Daniel and Pete, bringing them safely to Jo.

Marissa and Jo untied their bonds while Momo kept watch and Coco continued to unleash her light.

CHAPTER TWELVE—MISSION GONE WRONG

MOMO

Momo's eyes widened as Coco channeled her energy inside the abandoned grocery store like a goddess, conjuring up a deadly storm. The light in her eyes flickered and glowed with an otherworldly intensity. The electric energy emanating from her body crackled and hissed, illuminating the darkness in a riot of blue and purple.

Footsteps pounded as Momo and her squad sped down the aisles at the grocery store. Coco's display of power and the resulting yells had made enough noise to alert the whole neighborhood.

The light on the ceiling flashed three times, coming from the east. Jo halted by the cereal section and replied with her flashlight. Momo assumed that Jo waited for Debra to make a move, whether she'd exit the building or come find them. The beacon beamed again, closer: their answer.

Momo couldn't understand why they weren't exiting the structure. They had accomplished their mission by finding Daniel and Pete. So, why stay?

"You guys okay?" Debra's shoulders eased when Daniel and Pete approached her. Jo parted her mouth to speak, but she cut in. "We need to grab their weapons. Hurry."

Jo led the way back toward the frozen aisle.

Momo understood the importance of fighting on an equal

level, especially since the ISAN unit consisted of super-soldiers, but going back seemed like a suicide mission. Davina's team might have recovered.

She cursed under her breath as she sprinted next to Coco. Coco scrunched her face. She didn't agree with the decision either. "They're not there." Jo paled. "We should leave, now."

Momo had taken one step when a blast of air threw her and Coco up to the ceiling and scattered her teammates in different directions. She felt like she had been punched in the stomach, some form of vibration tearing through her bones. Momo landed with a hard thump, her chest flat on the damp tiles. Coco groaned beside her.

Pain seared through her muscles, but she had to get up. As her arms shook, she grabbed Coco. They stumbled down the aisle until a soldier stepped into their way, hands at her hips.

Pounding footsteps and crashing sounds echoed at the entrance, but Momo tuned it all out. She had to live before she could help anyone else.

"Where do you think you're going?" the assassin asked.

Coco took her friend's hand and ran, then skidded to a halt at the middle of the Italian section.

Davina smirked and raised her arm to show off her glove weapon as she strutted toward them, taking her time with an exaggerated sway in her hips. The soldiers tried to intimidate them, to instill fear. The tactic might have worked if Momo was standing alone, but having Coco by her side gave her strength. She wasn't only worried about her own safety, and she would do anything for those she loved.

"Let's make spaghetti," Momo said.

She grabbed vegetable cans from the bottom shelf and hurled

them at Davina and the other soldier on the opposite end, while Coco extended her electrical power to provide extra momentum to hit the targets on their faces. The CODE girls collapsed, knocked out, but Davina had ducked.

Davina had no idea she'd slipped beside her until she smashed a glass bottle of sauce on her head. Red liquid dripped off from her hair and splat on the floor. Then Coco sent the two shopping carts at her.

Momo clutched Coco's hand and dashed. When they passed the soda section, her teammate wrapped her lightning bolts around wine bottles and flung them at the two soldiers tailing them. The assassins slipped and collided with the wall.

The thunderstorm outside didn't scare Momo. In fact, it sounded far away. But her heart pounded, sweat beading on her forehead as they hid in a corner of the bread section. Hot air puffed out of her mouth as she panted. Where was their team?

"Coco? Momo?" Marissa sounded close.

"Here!" Momo covered her mouth when Coco widened her eyes. She had told everyone their location.

Coco tugged her to the produce area and hid behind a large wooden bin with Marissa and Jo. Jo extended a glove gadget she had taken from a fallen soldier, curled her fingers, and squeezed. A whoosh escaped from the weapon, pushing her back a step. The assassin flew backward as if punched in the stomach and shot through the broken wall into the rain.

"Grab the carts, Coco," Jo said, and squeezed again.

The powerful air slammed into a CODE girl. The assassin collided against the cash register. Coco's lightning bolts grasped the empty carts and she hurled those toward the soldiers by the bakery.

Jo said, "Push the carts to block the exit when we're out.

Hector will take it from there. Go now!"

Jo sprinted. Everyone followed suit and hid behind a truck, but Momo would not leave her best friend. She fired her Taser, even knowing it would do nothing to the assassins. She hoped to give her teammate time and distract the ISAN terminators.

The Taser pellets crackled and the red light sizzled around the soldiers' suits like thin ribbons. Davina dusted off her somewhat-scorched chest and smirked.

Unbelievable. Momo wished she had the same suit, but she couldn't help the giggle from the sight of Davina's hair drenched with spaghetti sauce.

"Go." Hector put up his hands and fire poured from his palms.

Momo crossed her arms over her head from the scorching heat. Coco dragged her away, but not a second passed before the flames died.

Hector collapsed. Blood dripped from his head, painting the concrete crimson.

She had a clear view of the assassin, who touched something on her wrist. A spinner, of sorts, came flying toward her. A bomb? She had to get Coco out of there and grab Hector.

"Jessa and Debra! Cover us!" Momo bellowed.

Her teammates were watching their every move from behind the truck, although Debra might not be aware that a bomb was headed their way.

Momo used her power of speed, shoved Coco toward the vehicle, and dashed after Hector. She hoped to save him before the explosion, but it was no biggie, Debra and Jessa would shelter them. When she lowered to Hector, fingers coiled around her neck and lifted her like a doll. She gripped the assassin's arms while her legs dangled.

Davina's cold killer eyes met hers as the shield kept them safe from the blast. Hues of red and orange coated the barrier, like the scene at the bookstore. The soldier's squeeze tightened, blocking her air. Though the edges of her vision became dark, she managed to peer down to Hector.

"Run." Momo's words came out through strangled breath.

"I caught a little mouse." Davina raised her higher, but loosened her grip.

She hated being called vermin. So insulting. They were the same height—probably the same age, too. But no matter how hard she kicked, the CODE girl smirked. Pain didn't faze her.

Smoke and ashes floated around them. The shield had been released. With no sight of the CODE soldiers, Momo assumed they had burned to the bones. Davina didn't seem to care.

"Any last word to your soon-to-be-dead friend, little mouse?" Davina let out a fake laugh.

"Run." Momo's voice projected louder.

Hector lifted his bloody head and pointed a shaky finger at the soldier. "You're. Going. To. Hell."

"You go there first." She stomped on his head.

Momo screamed, but no sound escaped. She slapped her flimsy arms, but she might as well have hit the assassin with a feather.

She closed her eyes as her heart shattered. *I'm sorry I couldn't save you, Hector. I'll see you and Bobo on the other side.*

Davina gave a sly smile. "Don't worry. You'll see your teammates soon. The blast killed everyone."

Momo wanted to believe she was lying, but the shield had come down too soon. And if Davina's squad hadn't survived the bomb, neither had hers.

Tears streamed down her face as her world went dark.

CHAPTER THIRTEEN–NEW TEAMMATES

HAE JIN

Hae Jin gawked at Sena and Min Hyuk after Mr. Park left. They remained standing in the middle of a room with gray walls and no door.

She dared not peer down at her friend, his blood pooling around him. All this time, she had thought Sena was the traitor. But Jung? Not possible. He had been on her team longer than her.

You shouldn't trust anyone. Sena's words rang in her ears.

Hae Jin didn't want to believe Mr. Park, but …

"Explain." She didn't mean to bark at her, but she didn't know who to believe. Could she trust Min Hyuk? Oh, God. What if they had been working together and Jung was the one who had been caught?

"I had to pretend to be the traitor," Sena said. "When the soldier was going to kill us at the lighthouse, I had no choice but to Tase all of you, or we would have all died. Bullets are permanent, you know."

Hae Jin didn't want to believe her, but she had heard from Mr. Park that Jung was the traitor. What if this was all a trick? Jung couldn't defend himself. She pressed her palms on her temples and lowered her chin. Her head throbbed, and Sena's story confused her even more.

Min Hyuk, who had been staring at his best friend's bloody

body, gripped Sena and slammed her against the wall. He clenched his jaw and hiked his eyebrows so high, his forehead creased.

"I don't believe you." He gritted the words through his teeth. "I knew him best. He would never betray me."

She craned her neck, avoiding his eyes. "I guess you didn't know your buddy well after all."

"You're lying," he snarled.

She scoffed. "Jung only showed you the side he wanted you to like. Had I not Tased him, he would have killed us on the spot."

He rounded a hand into a fist and punched the wall. "You have no proof."

Sena shoved him with all her strength and he stumbled back. "Maybe not, but I was going to shoot Mr. Park when he took the pistol and terminated your friend. But I guess that's not evidence enough that I'm no traitor."

Hae Jin paced, rubbing her arm. Why would Mr. Park kill Jung if he was loyal to him?

Min Hyuk gripped Hae Jin's wrist, forcing her to look at him. "I don't know what to believe, but let this go for now. We have other things to worry about." He pulled her closer and whispered, "Stop talking. We're being recorded."

She wanted to tell him about the cameras, but he was right. They shouldn't say too much.

The door slid open and Grayson entered. He shoved his hands inside his pants pockets and shook his head. Clad in a dark suit, not a strand of his sleek black hair was out of place.

The supervisors wore training outfits and sometimes formal attire, on missions. Where was he going?

"I'm very disappointed." Grayson tsked and kicked Jung's feet. "What a waste." He turned to face the group. "It's lunchtime. I'm escorting you to the cafeteria."

"Why are you dressed in a suit?" Sena asked.

Grayson dusted something off his lapel and raised his chin. "Your superiors are having lunch with Mr. Choi and Mr. Baek. They represent Korea in a team that runs ISAN headquarters."

Hae Jin hadn't known any names. She wasn't sure if the chain of command went beyond Park.

Grayson went out the sliding door, and the team followed him. While Hae Jin grabbed her food, Grayson made small talk with the assassins.

Her tray clattered on the table as she sat between Min Hyuk and Sena. The other twenty soldiers didn't engage in a conversation among themselves. She didn't recognize *any* of them. Where had the other teammates gone?

Hae Jin bit into a mix of rice and vegetables, a comforting dish known as bibimbap, and stole glances at the newbies.

None of them smiled or spoke. They sat with stiff backs and chewed in unison, more robot than human.

Sena nibbled on the beef and said, "They give me the creeps. What happened to the other girls?"

Grayson paced behind Sena and patted her shoulders. "Scattered throughout Asia. And these new soldiers have taken their places. Consider yourselves lucky not to be sent away."

"So, Sena, Min Hyuk, and I are from the original group?" Hae Jin asked, sipping her soybean paste soup.

"Yes. But don't worry." Grayson leaned over and whispered in her ear. "We won't send you away. You're valuable to us."

The mixed vegetables and rice, seasoned with a sweet-spicy sauce, stuck in her throat. Had the others been executed? ISAN would have terminated them rather than set them free.

Grayson stood tall and added. "Our intel informed us that Ava and her team are headed our way. I'll be sending the CODE girls to capture her. And if she dies in the process …" He shrugged. "…so be it"

Just like Mr. Park hoped. the reason he had kept them alive. Hae Jin's eyes lit up. She was sure Ava would prevail. Maybe, just maybe, she could help Ava and escape with her team.

A second chance. Hope bloomed once again.

CHAPTER FOURTEEN–NEW ROLES

AVA

Zeke's hand went to his face, his eyes wide with confusion when Tamara slapped his face. "What the hell was that for?" He was lucky she hadn't punched at full strength or body-slammed him to the floor.

"Geeze, I don't know." Tamara balled her fists, her nostrils flaring. "You left without a word, and you didn't even call."

Zeke flashed a fake smile. "Hello. Everyone, we'll be right back."

"Well, that was interesting." Josephine Chang rose from the sofa. "Make sure you keep me up to date. Before I forget, I was able to get my hands on some of ISAN's super-soldiers' suits. You can thank Mr. San from ANS. Please stay safe."

When Josephine left, I stepped in front of Russ, who remained sitting.

"You're not going," I said.

His eyes widened. "I'm the lead agent, remember?"

"We're not in ISAN," I said matter-of-factly.

Russ's lips curled, his green eyes gleaming. "That's true, but you don't tell me what to do."

"I can when it comes to your safety."

He stood, his face inches from mine. His heated gaze lowered to my lips and then back to my eyes. Russ cared about me more than as a friend, and at one point I'd had a crush on him, but I'd always known my heart belonged to someone else. So staring at each other seemed awkward, especially when our friends were in the same room.

"Hmmm ... that's funny," Russ said, "because I was going to tell you the same thing. Maybe *you* shouldn't go on this suicide mission." He poked my forehead and walked toward the medical hubs.

I rubbed at my brow and scoffed, going after him. "Were you not paying attention? Verlot wrote a memorandum. The rebel team is not to be harmed."

He pivoted so fast that I skidded to a halt and almost ran into him.

"You think that memo is going to hold?" Russ looked at me like I was an idiot, his green eyes darkening. "You think Mr. Park is going to be nice to your team?" He glanced at Justine and Brooke. They were watching us. "I guarantee he'll plan something to get rid of you." He leaned closer. "Remember: he's the one in charge of making and training CODE assassins. Coldhearted. Ruthless. They feel nothing. No fear. No pain. They do exactly what he tells them."

I shrugged. "Funny, that was what we were in ISAN. Sure, they're merciless, but they don't have unique powers. And they don't have friendship. Loyalty. Trust. These things are important to our success. And you think *you'll* be safe among the CODE soldiers?"

"Yes." He blew out a breath. "I'm an agent from the former United States. And we founded the International Sensory Assassin Network. They can't touch me. If they do, they'll be starting something they'll regret. Verlot has more power than you think.

And there is someone higher than him."

"But …" I held up a finger. "You're not part of ISAN anymore. What if they find out?"

Russ gave me a sidelong glance and then walked out the double doors. Something wasn't right—it wasn't like him to disrespect me so blatantly.

Mitch stood beside me and whispered, "There's more to this story. Make him tell you."

"Russ." I ran after him. "Russ. Wait." When he didn't stop, I sprinted faster and grabbed his arm.

"There's something I need to tell you." His eyelashes flickered and he pressed his lips together. "I'm not leaving the network."

I took a step back, my heart pounding. "What do you mean? Don't you want a new life?" The shock of his news turned into anger, and I socked his arm as my voice rose. "Are you crazy?"

Russ put up his hands. "Hear me out, okay? Novak informed his group about Mitch and Lydia being traitors, and they've replaced Novak with me. Though Justine doesn't know yet, she has been offered my title. So, this scheme of ours couldn't have come at a better time."

I blinked, confused. "You're not taking this position, right?"

Russ closed his eyes, and a muscle in his jaw flexed. When he opened them, the lines on his face eased. "I have no choice. If I do this, I can inform Councilor Chang of ISAN's activities before they happen."

"Then you'll be a double agent."

He hiked an eyebrow. "What do you think I've been doing all this time?" He caressed my face ever so gently. "You made me see the light. If not for you, I might have made wrong decisions."

I understood his reasoning, but that didn't mean I had to like it.

Russ gave a wicked grin. "I'm going to mold the assassins into my rebel team. The network won't have a clue."

I narrowed my eyes. "I love your plan. But Justine—"

"I'm going to convince her to take the position. We've won one battle, and when we take down Korea, the rebels in other countries will feel empowered. And there's another reason why I'm going with you."

Russ looked over my shoulder. I assumed that what he said next was something he wanted me to keep secret.

He lowered his voice. "I've been informed that Mitch's father might be there. I didn't tell him. I don't want him chasing after a "maybe" when he's worried about Lydia. If I weren't with ISAN, I wouldn't have gotten this information."

I wrapped my arms around his shoulders. "Thank you for all you have sacrificed and done for me. I'll never forget it. I'm indebted to you, so if you ever need anything, don't hesitate to ask."

His chest rose and fell and his warm breath brushed against my face. I'd missed his friendship. I'd missed our talks. I kissed his cheek and released him.

CHAPTER FIFTEEN–MEETING MR. PARK

MOMO

Momo moaned with a pounding headache, her arm and leg dangling from a mattress. Every inch of her body ached. Where was she?

She pushed herself up. The walls and the high ceiling spun and compressed.

"Whoa," she said, and pressed her temples.

No windows. No door. ISAN compound? Alone. No other furniture, aside from the cot. She closed her eyes to settle the acid sloshing in her stomach and fought the urge to vomit.

Nothing came to mind until she rubbed her hand on her thigh. Too soft. What had happened to her jeans, black hoodie, and cap? Someone had dressed her in the gray training outfit she hated.

Her chocolate bars were gone, though they'd probably all melted. And ... her coin. The old adage was stupid. Her penny hadn't given her good luck. She didn't believe it anyway. She had planned to take it to a pawn shop and trade it for some 4Qs.

Momo punched the mattress and wanted to scream. She curled into a ball and squeezed her eyes shut. She had no tears, even as her heart squeezed from the loss of her friends.

Empty. Cold. Alone.

Debra, Jo, Coco, Marissa, Daniel, Pete, Jessa, and, oh God... Hector. She'd tried to save him, but Davina had yanked her up with one hand like she weighed less than a bug. She'd rather die than be back in ISAN.

The hidden door slid opened and a tall, black-haired man sauntered in. A pale scar ran down the left side of his face, as if someone had cut him with a knife.

Momo set her clasped, trembling hands on her lap. His arrogant swagger and dark suit reminded her of Mr. Novak, but this man appeared younger.

"Hello, Monet. I'm Mr. Park."

She flinched. It had been a while since she'd heard her real name.

He took a step closer. "I'm interested in your gift, so I'm going to give you a new life. Either you cooperate and do as I say, or I'll erase your memory and turn you into one of my super-soldiers. Which one would you prefer?"

She clenched her jaw and tightened the grip on the edge of the cot. She didn't like her choices. All her friends were deceased, and when the rebels heard the news they might consider her dead, too.

No one knew that Mr. Park had locked her up in … where? She guessed Korea, but she didn't want to assume.

The man shoved his hands inside his pockets and rocked on his heels. "Before you decide, let me remind you that all of your teammates died in the blast. You are alone. Be smart, little girl."

Momo *would* play it smart. When the opportunity arose, she would kill him and take revenge.

"Where am I?" she asked.

"South Korea."

A twinge of excitement rushed through her veins, but she kept her expression neutral. Ava would be on her way soon.

"Fine," Momo said. "What do you want me to do?"

He walked backward toward the door. "You've made a wise choice. One of my girls will escort you to lunch, then we'll talk."

CHAPTER SIXTEEN—WELCOME TO KOREA

AVA

Russ and Justine plopped on the glider seats while Tamara, Brooke, and I situated ourselves across from them. The three of us wore the new battle outfits Councilor Chang had procured. The sleek, flexible material, cool to the touch, would protect us from Tasers and bullets.

"We're closing in on Seoraksan," Zeke said from the driver's seat.

Instead of taking one of Chang's gliders, he piloted his, and we arrived sooner than anticipated at the National Park. And we'd have to make our way to Ulsanbawi Peak. With my nerves on edge and too many emotions crowding my mind, I meandered to the door and pulled up my chip.

"Call Sniper," I said.

Rhett's hologram face appeared. Behind him was the orange tree in the mountain base's garden, near the carrot section. The screen panned down to show Avary, sleeping in his arms.

"Look who called us." Rhett's voice dipped softer. "It's Mommy."

My gaze shifted from Avary's beautiful face to his. "I'm inside Zeke's glider."

He snorted. "I'm not surprised he's there. Councilor Chang only needs to give him one name—*Tamara*—and he'll drop

93

everything."

I snickered. "Whatever happened before Zeke left, Tamara is not happy with him."

Avary opened her eyes and stared at the hologram me, and I could have sworn she smiled. Rhett sauntered toward the elevator, her irises sparkling golden against the sunlight, and she blinked.

"Zeke and Tamara are always hot and cold," he said. "I don't care why he's there, but one more person on your side works for me. Please be careful. Avary and I need you."

Something in my chest cracked. They were my life, my reason for living. My mom's request was the reason for the mission in Korea. Afterwards, Rhett and I would consider our next step as a family.

"I love you both very much. I'm going to shut down. We're close to our destination." I blew a kiss as my eyes damped.

The transporter took a quick dive and rocked to the side. I stumbled forward, and as I planted my hand on the door, I accidentally kicked a backpack with our change of clothes and weapons. I offered a reassuring smile to Russ, who had glanced back at me in concern.

"Turbulence," Zeke said. "This baby is invisible to the world, but not to Mother Nature. Get ready, ladies. I'm taking us lower."

Brooke and Tamara rose when their seat belts loosened. I pulled up a hologram monitor from my chip and pressed the green button on the app to start the navigation. Then I grabbed the pack and slung it over my shoulder.

"Be careful," Russ said.

"Go easy on us." I winked.

Justine paled and looked between Brooke and Tamara. "I'm not going to hurt you. And, no matter what, don't think I'm on their side. I don't ever want to go back."

"We know," I said. "You're undercover, like Russ. And if you're not sure what you're supposed to do, ask him. Our lives are in your hands. We trust you."

She nodded and eased her stiff muscles. Going back to ISAN after she'd escaped, even if it wasn't our homeland, couldn't be easy.

"We're here, ladies," Zeke announced. "Good luck."

The door slid open and the violent wind pushed us back. I held up a fist and pointed to the sky, and like the good old days, Brooke leaped first.

Zeke approached Tamara in a rush, just as she was about to jump. He gripped her wrist and swung her around to face him. She gasped, and her eyes widened in surprise.

"Be careful. I'll be waiting for you." He cupped her face and gave her a kiss she wouldn't forget.

Tamara watched Zeke return to his seat, a smile plastered on her face, then stepped out into the air like she was walking out a door. Easy. No fear.

I inhaled a deep breath and dove after her. We glided with the breeze, passing through clouds. Though I could see my teammates, the invisible parachute, shaped like angel wings, protected us from being visible from below.

The destination I had input earlier popped up in front of me with an "X" mark—a wide, grassy space in Seoraksan National Park.

We landed on the dirt with a thump. I rose and pressed the button to fold the thin material back into my suit, then took out the items for my team before finally hiding the backpack behind a bush.

I shoved my arms into the sleeves of the sweatshirt, adjusted the cap over my head, and pulled the bill lower to cover my eyes. Best not to look like assassins, and blend in with the citizens.

I drew up my cobalt-blue map of the park and waited. Red dots scattered throughout. Past the statues and shops—there. Found it. The six large white rocks clustered together, also known as Ulsanbawi Peak. Not easily accessible by foot.

My boots squashed the grass before I stepped onto the pebbled road. We passed under a grand wooden arch made with tiles and skirted around tourists gathered in clusters by a bear statue.

I admired the temples and peered into the gift stores with their traditional tile roofs curving upward. Not many original buildings had survived the meteor devastation.

Tamara pointed at the giant Buddha statue, sitting crisscrossed, hands across the knees in prayer. We passed the people taking pictures with families through the garden, and then I led them to a standing rectangular screen.

I punched in the number three and a code that Councilor Chang had given me. Using our own wouldn't be wise.

After we got access, we went through the automatic scanner and got in line for the cable car. Eight people rushed out. Brooke eased in, followed by Tamara and me.

The door closed and the tram lightly jerked. I gasped and moved to the corner. Not a good place to be when you are afraid of heights.

The cable went slow at first and then picked up speed. I didn't freak out, but as it rose over the trees, I gripped the metal bar and focused on the orange flowers on the hills. When the car angled and soared, the grandness of the mountain surrounding the park's perimeter came into view.

The giant Buddha statue shrank in the distance. People scurried like ants, finding their way to their transporters. A cluster of skyscrapers became visible, with gnat-sized gliders flying between the towers. Aside from the words written in Korean and the architectural and cultural differences, the city looked like home.

The meteors had devastated this country, as well as the rest of the world. And, like us, they had used the asteroids to advance technology faster than would have been possible. But some things, like this cable car, remained the same, to preserve the past.

The tram shifted in the wind and my stomach churned. *Don't vomit.* I glanced up at the ceiling and counted in my mind.

"Ava, you okay?" Brooke bumped her cap on my head.

"Don't look down," Tamara said. "It's kind of like flying, but not as fast."

Slow rides were the worst. But at least I didn't throw up.

The aerial tramway jolted and stopped. I walked out first when the door opened, and ducked my head lower. The freezing air brushed my face, but our suits kept us warm. There was no time to enjoy the view, but I admired the sunset casting hues of pink and violet across the sky.

We were instructed to go to the peak, where Justine and Russ would capture us. Cameras were hidden within the perimeter, so we had to be clever about the attack without hurting each other.

Ascending stairs led us higher into the mountains. The peaks seemed so close, and yet too far. And the higher we went, the thinner the air became.

A rustling noise stirred above me by the bushes and I halted, my team beside me. A trickle of dirt and pebbles fell from that very spot, and some landed on top of my cap. I peered up, but spotted no one.

"It's not raining sand, is it?" Tamara dusted dirt off her arm.

Brooke stilled and closed her eyes, listening. She flashed her eyes open, clutched Tamara's suit and mine, and shoved us back. Red laser beams skewered the spot we had stood seconds before.

Russ and Justine wouldn't fire at us, which meant he had been right. Mr. Park didn't care about Mr. Verlot's request, and had sent a unit to kill us.

Our plan had already taken a turn.

Shadows loomed, and an assassin landed in front of me with a thump from above, where the rustling had come from the bushes. Brooke, Tamara, and I parted and ducked for cover by the clusters of trees.

One of the CODE girls held out an arm. Something tied around her wrist and coiled her fingers. I had seen that weapon before. She fired and jerked back. A section of the mountain behind us exploded in a rain of debris. Dust coated the air, blinding us.

Brooke and Tamara dropped to their knees and coughed. Our caps had been tossed about and lost. A soldier grabbed Brooke and flung her over the rail.

The power and strength the assassins possessed were beyond imagining. These were CODE babies with AVA DNA. My DNA. Novak had taken so much from me.

I gripped the handrail, caught Brooke's leg before she fell off the precipice, and pitched her toward Tamara at the cluster of trees. *So close to losing my friend.*

I slammed my feet into an assassin's chest, who'd pounced on me. She collided with her teammate and then the second crashed into the third. Soldier three smacked into the rocky surface.

Another CODE girl somersaulted and landed in front of me. She threw a punch that hit air when I twisted to the side. She tried to sock me with the other fist, but missed again.

Her arms went faster, and I retreated as swiftly as she advanced. She put all her weight behind the last jab and stumbled forward, so I grabbed her hair. She didn't scream or show any sign of pain—rather, she clutched my arm and tried to shove me down.

Still holding onto her hair, I leaped up, planted my feet against a tree trunk, and used the leverage to fling her off the cliff. A nearby soldier watched her teammate fall to her death, but said nothing, betraying no sorrow.

I could have thrown others off, but I didn't want to hurt them unless it was necessary. Yes, they were ISAN terminators and they would kill me without a thought, but they knew no better.

A grunt caught my attention. A soldier had grabbed Tamara's leg and flipped her over. Tamara slammed to the pebbles and whacked her head. Blood coated her temple.

Brooke reached Tamara before I had a chance and Tased the assassin between the eyes at point-blank range. That soldier tumbled down the stairs and reached for the railing to pull herself back up. Even as she convulsed, she stood with no expression of pain—the result of being lobotomized. Though her movements were slow, she kept coming.

We ran as the five soldiers pounded after us. I twisted at the waist and shot my Taser. The pellets bounced off their uniforms. No shocker, but I hoped it would distract them and buy us time.

A click. Snap. Brooke looked at me as we sprinted. She had heard it, too. Some kind of high-tech weapon had cranked.

One of my arms wrapped Brooke's shoulder while the other went around Tamara's, and I flattened us, our faces kissing the concrete. A whoosh of hot air passed over our heads.

"They're crazy!" Brooke yelled over the roar of flames.

"Remind me to thank Councilor Chang." Tamara coughed. "The fire might have burned our skin off."

We jolted up and sprinted toward the six large white rocks clustered together. Justine and Russ came out of the shadows and pointed Tasers at us.

I skidded to a halt. Brooke and Tamara did the same. For a moment, confusion reeled my mind. I had forgotten they were pretending to side with ISAN, and I almost didn't recognize Russ.

Russ brushed off some ashes on his dark suit and ran fingers through his slicked-back hair. His resemblance to Mr. Novak made me shudder.

Justine's high heels clacked as she approached closer. She looked pretty, clad in black form fitted dress with her blond hair tied back and light makeup that accentuated her blue eyes.

He held up a hand. "You're surrounded, Ava. Surrender."

I scoffed at the CODE girls. They had their weapons pointed at us. Justine and Russ wouldn't shoot, but the soldiers would. Still, I had to pretend.

The Ava they knew would never surrender. So, to make the capture easier, Russ had devised a scheme, but hadn't told us the plan. We had to make it appear authentic.

Justine stepped forward and aimed a tool that looked like it would lob a cannonball. The barrel of her weapon recoiled slightly and a baseball-sized-something flew in our direction. As it arced overhead, it expanded into one giant net and the crackling blue web anchored on the ground in a dome of energy. When I edged closer to the electric light, a jolt of electricity flashed as it crackled.

"Do something!" Brooke shouted.

Even though she'd known she would be captured, fear showed in her eyes. Or, she was an outstanding actor.

Tamara stuck a finger through the sizzling energy and retreated with a yelp. "We can't get out. Why do they have the best gadgets?" Russ stood in front of me, his green eyes glaring. "You should have done this the easy way, but it's too late. When you wake up, I guarantee you'll have a headache. Good night."

"You are the worst kind of—" I began, but didn't get to finish.

He threw an object about the size of a golf ball through the electric net. It bounced and stopped under my leg, and smoke hissed.

CHAPTER SEVENTEEN–THE PENTHOUSE

JOSEPHINE CHANG

Councilor Josephine Chang sat at the mahogany dining table in her penthouse. She stared out the window at the multicolored skyline of the city below her, illuminated by twinkling lights from skyscrapers and the occasional glider soaring through the night sky. Despite the beauty, apprehension ran through her veins like a bad drug, causing an uncomfortable restlessness she couldn't shake.

She worried for Ava and her team. Would their plan work? What if Mr. Park dismissed the memo from Verlot? There were so many uncertainties, she felt like her head was going to explode.

A ping came from her chip. At first, she didn't recognize the caller, but remembered Russ's code name. Her pulse raced. She inhaled a deep breath and prayed he was sending her good news before reading the message.

> Brownies have been delivered. The lemon
> cookie did not crumble. Will let you know how
> the other tastes.

She let out a long breath and eased her shoulders. Lemon cookie—code name for Justine. Justine had been through so much. Chang worried she would fall apart during the mission

Finding out that Ava and Gene were her half siblings must

have been mind-blowing. Justine had also betrayed the father she worshiped, and had joined the renegades. She should be speaking to a therapist, not out on an assignment playing double agent.

Josephine closed her chip when the chimes rang from the monitor attached to the wall. The voice said, "You have a guest."

A hologram of an attractive, tall man with dark hair and beautiful eyes appeared. Vince had sent an email with a request to discuss the next plan in private. No one could see them together, so they met at a penthouse she rented under a fake name.

"Unlock," Josephine said.

The access gate at the entrance to the elevator released. While she waited for him, she put a few washed dishes in the cabinets, then stopped by the family room and straightened two oil paintings of palm trees.

"Guest has arrived," the voice announced.

"Open," Josephine said.

The door slid across the threshold, revealing a handsome man over six feet tall and muscular in build. Clad in jeans and a T-shirt, he appeared a bit more mischievous out of his uniform.

Her heart skipped, and the kiss they shared at ISAN's secret base replayed in her mind. Heat flushed her cheeks and a hint of a shy smile spread. Would he kiss her again? She shook off the thought. She had to focus on … she lost her thoughts again when Vince gave her a devilish grin.

"Hello, Councilor Chang." His voice dipped low and playfully.

Vince took his arms from behind his back and handed her a bouquet of a dozen red roses.

She gasped. "Thank you." Something inside her heart melted. She couldn't believe her eyes. She had never received flowers from a man before. "Please, come in."

"You look beautiful. "He pressed his lips against her cheek longer than necessary, and then entered.

Josephine didn't think her simple black dress warranted a compliment, but she thanked him anyway.

"Have a seat," she said, walking toward the kitchen.

Josephine should put the flowers in a vase, but she didn't have one, so she placed them on the counter. She would figure it out later.

"How's the special package doing?" Vince eased on the sofa.

"*My sister* is doing well."

She poured two mugs of ginseng honey tea and headed to the family room. She sat across from him and set her mug down to cool, a low table dividing them.

"Good. I'm glad to hear that."

Josephine pressed her lips together and rubbed her palms on her thigh.

"Are you nervous about meeting her?" he asked.

His heated gaze locked with hers and she forgot what they were talking about.

"No. Yes. I mean ... what if she doesn't—"

"Everything is going to be fine." He grinned. "I promise."

Josephine lowered her eyelashes, and then looked back up at him. "And if you're wrong?"

"You can punish me however you like." He winked

She giggled. "You're going to regret that offer."

Vince gave a half-hearted shrug, a mischievous glint in his eyes, and took hold of the mug. "Perhaps I won't."

Something about their conversation felt suggestive, though she couldn't tell who was initiating it.

"Thank you for the tea," he said, after he took a drink. "How did you know I needed this? And why are you sitting across from me?" He patted the cushion beside him.

Josephine perked her lips, trying not to smile. She wanted to sit next to him, but then she might not be able to control her desire. Their gazes met again and lingered, and she forgot where she was.

She picked up her cup to break the connection. They needed to get back to business. Lives were at stake.

"What information do you have for me?" she asked.

"I got a message from Jo." Vince took another sip. "They found the missing rebels."

Josephine gasped and covered her mouth. She was so happy, tears pooled in her eyes. "That's great news."

"But …"

Her breath caught. But, what? She couldn't bear it. Who else had died? Or who had gotten hurt?

"They ran into CODE soldiers." He rubbed his face and sighed. "I heard an explosion, and then we got cut off. I sent a unit to search for them, but we …" He cleared his throat. "I haven't heard from …"

Josephine sat beside him and grabbed his hand. "Oh, God. No." She nearly choked on her words.

Vince swallowed, his Adam's apple bobbing up and down. "I regret my decision. I shouldn't have told Jo. I sent them to their graves. These assassins are impossible to beat."

"Jo is not a child, and the children aren't helpless. Please don't blame yourself. If you never told them, you would regret that decision, too. We do our best, and we move forward."

Vince squeezed her hand. "I've lived through many battles, but it hurts more when the young ones' lives are taken."

She felt the same. It was the reason why she respected and cared about him. She had always put her people first, and had promised herself never to fall in love. But, the thing about love … there's no reasoning or predicting when and why it happens. Sometimes love happens when you least expect it.

CHAPTER EIGHTEEN–DINNER

AVA

I blinked and gathered my thoughts as I lay on my side on the cold tile floor, Brooke and Tamara knocked out beside me. Russ. Justine. The electrical net and the smoke. ISAN kept surprising me.

Someone's black shoes came into focus. Novak? Not possible. He was dead, and he better be in hell.

I pushed myself off the ground and pressed my back against the wall. No doors. ISAN compound, for sure. I tried pulling up my chip, then my map. A warm, tingling sensation coursed through my veins, but snuffed out. Just as I expected.

The stranger in the dark suit and gray tie came closer. The tall man had to be Mr. Park Ji Woo. He looked like the person Chang had shown us, right down to the scar.

It took every ounce of my will not to choke him with his tie. I had dreamed about doing that to Novak numerous times. I moved closer to my friends, ready to pounce if he tried to hurt them.

"Protective, are you?" Park said. "That's the difference between your kind and our super-soldiers. I wonder if I should fix them to care."

"I think …" I rose, looking squarely into his eyes. "You should stop controlling these children and give them back their lives, Mr. Park."

He rubbed his chin with one hand, the other balled into a fist, and then his expression eased. "You did your homework, Ava. You know who I am. I'm impressed."

"And you didn't do yours, because if you had, you wouldn't stand close to me."

I grabbed his wrist and swung his arm behind him in a lock. He bent forward and made no sound, even though he must have been in tremendous pain.

"Think about what you're doing, girl. Is this the right move for your teammates? You don't want their deaths on your hands, do you?"

I pulled his arm higher, my heart pounding. Had he poisoned them? I had wanted to be the only one on this mission, but everyone, including Councilor Chang, had gone against my suggestion.

"What do you mean? Tell me before I yank out your arm."

He groaned. "My voice activates this room. There's a gun pointing from inside these walls. Shall I tell it to shoot?"

Novak had shot our informant back in ISAN's secret base. The weapon had come out of the wall as she was trying to tell me that the baby was mine.

I couldn't kill Park anyway. Not yet, at least. I shoved him away from my still-unconscious team.

He stumbled and straightened his suit jacket. "Wise decision. Touch me again, and there will be consequences."

"What are you going to do with us?"

"That will depend on you." He headed toward the hidden sliding door, and then glanced over his shoulder. "A soldier named Sena will be stopping by with a change of clothing. You and your friends will join me for dinner."

When the door closed, Brooke and Tamara sat up, sitting cross-legged as if nothing had happened to them.

"Where are we?" Brooke asked, glancing along the walls. "Wait. Don't tell me. We're prisoners." She lowered her voice. "At least we're inside."

"When did you wake up?" I asked.

Tamara leaned closer and whispered, "Brooke and I were up not too long ago, but since she didn't get up, I didn't either."

I squeezed between them and plopped down. "At least you're up in time for dinner."

Brooke rolled her eyes. "He's crazy. Sure, let's all eat together like we're one happy family."

"It might give us an opportunity to do some digging." Tamara shrugged.

Brooke draped an arm around her shoulder. "We're prisoners, remember? We can't just demand answers."

The wall slid open, our conversation halting. A girl with a porcelain complexion and locks pulled back entered the room, carrying a pile of dark gray garments. She placed them on the floor by my feet, and then stood in a resting stance with her arms behind her back and legs apart—the pose of a perfect assassin.

She must be Sena.

"Please put these on," Sena said, looking at the wall, not even glancing our way. "Then I'll escort you to dinner."

"And if I refuse?" I asked.

"Mr. Park told me you might say that, so you're to be reminded that he can shoot your teammates." She lowered her voice. "Please believe him. He shot someone in this room recently."

Why did that not surprise me?

I picked up the bundle of fabric, tossed it to Brooke and

Tamara, then stripped and changed.

"I hate this outfit," Brooke hissed as she pulled the black sweatshirt over her head.

"What do we do with our clothes?" Tamara wiggled out of her pants.

I clenched my jaw. The combat suits Councilor Chang had worked so hard to get for us were back in the hands of our enemy.

"Leave them. Someone will come and pick them up. Come this way."

We followed her out the door. Our steps echoed on the white tiles and gray walls. The layout appeared the same as the ISAN back at home. After we rounded a corner, we passed the training facility.

CODE soldiers were practicing with each other. When I had trained with my teammates, we'd grunted or groaned, but these girls showed no emotion and no sound left their lips. So quiet and contained, like machines.

"This way," our escort said.

We rushed through the gym, empty of people but filled with weights, treadmills, and monitors that were only used in the presence of supervisors.

"Do you take classes?" Tamara asked.

"We did, but the new unit doesn't. I shouldn't be answering your questions. You can ask Mr. Park."

What the soldier said made sense. The CODE assassins were programmed to be fighters and nothing else. Were their ovaries taken out? The fact that I had such a question sickened me.

Sena halted in front of the double doors. "When you enter, bow to Mr. Park."

Brooke made a spitting noise. "You're kidding, right? I submit to no one."

Tamara released a long sigh. "It's an Asian tradition. You bow to your elders as a sign of respect."

Brooke stood face-to-face with Sena. "Neither Mr. Park, nor any other ISAN personnel, will get—"

I tugged at Brooke's sweatshirt. Now was not the time for an ego trip. "Do as I do, and that's an order."

Brooke's eyes grew wider and she frowned. "Fine."

Our escort shuttered a breath and placed a palm on the scanner. Red light crisscrossed over her hand and the door opened.

Park was seated at a large round table. His wide grin almost made me believe he was happy to see us. Russ and Justine stiffened. A few other assassins next to Park offered no greetings.

Sena bowed and then looked at me. She didn't say a word, but her eyes begged me to do the same. Would she get punished for my behavior? I didn't want to find out.

Park smirked as we bent at the waist and lowered our heads.

"Welcome." He waved to his left. "You know Russ and Justine." He swung his arm to his right. "This is Davina, Hae Jin, and Min Hyuk. And you already met your escort, Sena. I'm relieved you changed your clothes and that you're being submissive, or I might have shot Sena. Sometimes I get so angry, I take it out on my girls."

He might be worse than Novak. Unbelievable.

Hae Jin, the one with the angelic face, beamed with joy. She was as happy to see me as I was to see that she was alive. I would have to find a way to speak with her alone.

"Anyway, please have a seat," Park said. "Dinner will be served."

Glasses of water were already on the table. I sat and drank half of mine to avoid making eye contact with Russ and Justine.

An uncomfortable silence filled the air. The door opened and I flinched ... and *what*? An escort tossed Momo inside and left.

How in the world had she gotten to Korea, and why?

I had so many questions, but held them in. Momo wore the same training outfit, and her ponytail bounced as she hesitantly walked closer. She glanced around the room, holding up her chin and clutching her sweatshirt. When she met my gaze, her shoulders eased and her eyes glistened with tears.

She looked both relieved and like she wanted to cry. Had she been the only one captured? Where were Jo, Coco, and Marissa?

When Momo set her gaze on Justine, she scowled.

Momo hadn't been at the mountain when I had introduced Justine to everyone as my half sister. I had to bring her up to date as soon as possible—or maybe not. Perhaps it was best to keep secrets, for now.

"Monet ..." Mr. Park's voice rose in a warning. "Are you forgetting to do something?"

Momo let out a soft growl and bowed.

"That's a good girl. Now, sit next to Tamara."

Servers came with trays of food, placed one in front of each of us, and left. Before me was a bowl of hot white rice, stainless steel chopsticks, a spoon, and a plate of beef, bean sprouts, cold marinated spinach, and kimchee.

"Please enjoy your meal." Park picked up his chopsticks. "I had the cook make a special dessert. You're going to love it. But first, eat."

I had no appetite, but his words held a warning. And the smell of spicy tofu soup was delicious. It reminded me of my mother's cooking, twisting the dagger in my heart.

Utensils clinked against bowls. The warm tofu practically melted in my mouth and mixed with the fermented flavor, tasting heavenly. The last time I had tofu soup, I had shared it with my mother just before arguing with her and leaving the apartment. I would forever regret that day.

"What kind of beef is this?" Brooke moaned. "It's the best thing I've ever tasted."

Park laughed like he was genuinely amused. "If you'd like more, please let me know."

His politeness unnerved me. How dare he make us share a meal with him and pretend we were all friends? I curled my fingers tighter on my chopsticks and grabbed the spoon with my other hand. Novak, at least, had known better than to carry weapons during dinner.

How easily I could kill him. Leap over the table and drive the spoon into his jugular, or fling the chopsticks one by one into his eyes, and—

"Ava, you know Monet, don't you?" Park cut me off, as if reading my thoughts. "You should be her mentor when you join my international ISAN team. What do you think, Momo? I can call you that, right?"

Oh, hell no. He must be out of his mind.

Momo stopped chewing a spoonful of rice and furrowed her brow. She must be so confused.

Park cupped the bowl and drank some of the soup. "Maybe Monet needs more time. Joining a new crew is difficult when she was the only one who survived the explosion."

I accidentally swallowed an entire mouthful of cold spinach, devastated. It couldn't be true. What had happened?

Justine blinked and paled. Russ pressed his lips together and his spoon dropped with a loud clank onto his plate. Thankfully, Park didn't look Russ's way, distracted by Hae Jin's loud gasp.

Shouldn't Hae Jin be in prison? I had no idea why the girl I was supposed to rescue was sitting with us. He must be threatening her.

Momo lowered her head. Teardrops fell. I wanted to comfort her, but we were similar. We didn't want pity, or to be treated as weak. She would get through this.

She wiped her tears and raised her chin, meeting Park's gaze. She pushed back her shoulders and said, "I go where Ava goes. I'll do what she says. It would be an honor to work beside my mentor."

"Good." Park dabbed his mouth with a cloth napkin. "You made a wise decision. I knew you would submit." He turned to me. "Now, how to convince you to join our team? Perhaps after I show you something special, you'll reconsider. But after dinner, of course. And before I forget, I would like to congratulate Russ and Justine on their new positions."

Russ placed his spoon down and gave a curt nod. "Thank you. I hope to unite with the international groups and work together more efficiently. I'm excited for the arrival of the new crew in my compound."

Hearing Russ talk about these girls as if they were merely objects made my skin crawl, even knowing he didn't mean it.

Don't get too comfortable, Russ. And don't lose track of why you are here.

I trusted him, but he had gained so much power so fast—it could mess with a person who wasn't prepared, especially when playing double agent.

Justine, who had been quiet, said, "I had a chance to see your assassins in action, and they are remarkable. Your facility did a great job in creating the, as the rebels would say, 'super-soldiers.'"

Park grinned, and he looked very proud. "A perfect title, regardless of the over-simplicity. I wouldn't call them anything else. I'll be dispatching a group of my special soldiers, soon, all over the world."

CHAPTER NINETEEN–SUPER-SOLDIERS

AVA

After dinner, Mr. Park escorted me to the elevator alongside Russ and Justine.

"How far down are we going?" Justine asked.

"Not far. There's only one level."

I wondered if there was another way to enter the facility, or if anyone else had access. There had better be, or I'd have to take him hostage, and I'd rather not.

A rush of cool air greeted me when we stepped out. Park placed his palm on a scanner on the wall and then stuck his face in front of it. The laser, a red horizontal line, started at the top of his head and traveled down to his feet.

The door hissed and whooshed open. A few personnel dressed all in white sat at a desk, examining spiraling Helix strands and pushing on the hologram buttons. Behind the thick glass, a doctor in scrubs and a nurse attended to a patient.

I couldn't see what they were doing, but an IV was hooked to the patient's arm. And ten other children lay on gurneys, waiting their turns. None of them moved.

"What are you doing to them?" I asked.

"Lobotomy." Russ's voice was calm and measured, but his lips were pursed tight and his fingers clenched to his sides. "Isn't that right, Mr. Park?"

Park halted in the center of the lab, a gleam of pride in his eyes. "Our scientists have come up with a faster, more accurate, and less messy procedure. Laser lobotomy. We're enhancing them. They feel no pain. They don't feel fear. No need for mental missions. They obey without thought or question, but retain all their fighting skills and training. They are the perfect soldiers."

Justine moved closer to the glass, watching the doctor pull the sheet below the patient's navel and then mark her abdomen.

"He's going to remove her ovaries, isn't he?" Justine's fingers flexed and unflexed by her side, and her tone carried a hint of sadness.

The CODE army had so much harm done to their bodies and minds. Anger fueled my drive to bring this compound down, even more. I had to hurry. The longer it took, the more girls would be affected.

Park's bottom lip twitched, but he answered with a straight face. "Oophorectomy is necessary."

"But is hysterectomy necessary?" Russ's tone rose in challenge as he fidgeted with the top button on his suit jacket. "They'll have early signs of menopause, osteoporosis, mental health problems, and maybe heart disease."

Something had to be special about that button. I wondered what he was up to.

Park let out a mocking chuckle. "Mental health is not one of our concerns. And, as for the other stuff, I doubt most of these girls will live long enough. Anyway, come along. I'm on a tight schedule."

No monthly periods got in the way of their duty. But these girls had no say in what they wanted. They were disposable.

I could spit in his face. He was a monster. No, worse than a

beast. It took every ounce of my will not to kill him on the spot.
Hold on. Be smart. You need answers.

We exited the lab and entered another room, but this one was empty and circular. No equipment. No monitors. Not a single sound. Only glass walls that showed … oh God. There must have been a thousand of them. Row after row, super-soldiers lined up with chins up and arms to their sides.

"Incredible." Russ's eyes grew wider. He pressed his palms to the glass, then lowered them and shoved them inside his pockets.

He hid the fear from Park, but not me. I knew him well. Justine had never been good at concealing her anger, so giving her back to us was the right move.

"They are indeed," Park said. "And they're under my control. Many of them will be shipped to different countries. It won't be a country that takes over the world, but an organization founded by individuals. International Sensory Assassins Network will govern citizens from all nations."

"You're planning to start a war?" I shivered, trying to tame my fury.

He scoffed. "Planning? The war began the day a scientist created HelixAVA."

There was so much more I didn't know. When my team and I had assassinated political figures whom we thought were criminals, we had actually been killing off the good people who were trying to stop the network, along with any competition.

I winced and my stomach somersaulted. I'd had a hand in terminating those who assisted Councilor Chang and the rebels.

I paced before Park and examined the girls closer. They all wore identical black jumpsuits, and their hair was tied back.

These soldiers were all nearly the same height and didn't even flinch. Frozen in place. No chest movement to show they were breathing. I continued to circle the room, staying away from Russ and Justine. I had to keep up the façade that we were enemies.

"Do they stand all day?" Justine asked.

Park raised an eyebrow, looking at her as if she had asked a stupid question. "Of course not. It's time for their dinner." He pressed a hand to the glass. A hologram screen appeared, and he spoke into it. "Stand at ease."

The countless girls in rows stepped one leg to the side and placed their arms behind their backs. Not a single noise came from their movement. It happened all at once and in sync. It would have been admirable, except nothing in ISAN was cool without also being horrible.

Russ inhaled deeply. He must have had the same thought as mine. They were too stealthy, and that made them even more dangerous.

Park continued. "Attention."

Boots hitting together echoed as one loud thump and two fingers went to their heads to salute. Again, precisely in sync.

"Pivot and march to the dining room," Park said, then he put away the hologram screen. "Almost perfect. I just need an experienced agent to lead a team in Korea. That's why I want you, Ava."

I furrowed my brow.

Justine's heels clicked, reminding me of someone I loathed. "Why Ava? She doesn't care about your soldiers, but I do."

She was acting and staying in character, but goose bumps rose along my arms.

Park raised an eyebrow. "Don't you need to get back to your country, to *your* team?"

Justine bristled. Perhaps she'd realized her mistake. "Yes, but I'd thought you could send them to me, and I would train them."

"Thanks for the offer, but ..." His lips curled upward. His voice was full of assurance and power. "Ava will lead a team on a mission tomorrow. Because if she doesn't, she won't like the consequences."

I might as well have swallowed a rock. I had a feeling he wasn't just threatening my squad. Something much worse.

"She'll agree." Russ narrowed his eyes at me. "I'll make sure she does."

Russ's gesture told me to stop taunting Park, shut my mouth, and get to know the soldiers' weaknesses and strengths. Who better to learn more about them than their leader?

He was right, but that didn't mean I had to agree right away. I'd be expected to put up some resistance. Park didn't want to kill me. And that alone gave me the upper hand.

CHAPTER TWENTY-VINCE

JOSEPHINE CHANG

Josephine paced in Mr. San's office as she anxiously waited for him. She'd flown to the ANS base to get some answers regarding CH20, which stood for Counter Helix—a serum that inhibited all forms of Helix.

HelixB77 gave the girls the ability to move faster, be stronger than an average man, and see and hear beyond human capability. Currently, ISAN was using HelixB99, which worked for both male and female assassins without major side effects. As for the super-soldiers, she didn't know.

When the door slid open, Mr. San strolled in and she planted herself on the sofa.

"Sorry," San said, taking a seat across from her. "I was in a meeting. How can I help you?"

Josephine flinched when the sound of chimes rang in her ears. A message had come through from Russ. "Please give me a second. This is important."

> I'm sending you a recording of the CODE army. Also, Mr. Park wants Ava to lead the international team, and he wants to send her on a mission. I'll send the details soon. Please respond with instructions.

Before Russ had left with Justine for South Korea, Josephine had one of her assistants implant a device inside his pants pockets. All he had to do was shove his hands inside to trigger his chip to record and save from its position on the top button of his suit jacket.

She downloaded the video and gasped. San scooted closer to her and bristled. There were more soldiers than she had anticipated. She couldn't believe all these girls had been lobotomized.

"My God." He clenched his teeth. "How can they get away with this?" He stood and pushed back his hair, anger pouring through his tone. "We might win some battles, but we won't have a chance at winning this war if we don't find a way to … but they are just children. We can't kill them. What do we do?"

Josephine stared at the space where, a second ago, countless girls had been projected. If it hadn't been for Ava's mother, they wouldn't have known where to look.

Once Chang had learned of the CODE soldiers, she funded research only Vince knew about, to find a way to stop them without killing them. But the researchers needed time, and time was running out. She had to get help from other trusted sources.

"By any chance, do you have ISAN's newest CH20?" she muttered. "I don't know if the number is correct, since they are always perfecting their serums."

"I do," he said, a hint of mischief in his tone. "What do you have up your sleeve, Councilor Chang?"

She threw back her head, laughing. "You always assume I have an agenda."

He plopped back on the sofa, his knee almost touching hers. "Don't you? It's what I most admire about you."

Josephine crossed her legs. She caught San watching her skirt rise along her thigh. She hadn't meant to show off her long legs, but his gaze broke when she reached inside her jacket pocket and pulled out three tubes wrapped in fabric.

"Here." She handed them to him. "Can you have your scientist confirm what the labels say? Then compare them to CH20. If the tests come back with a positive result, then we may have a solution to stop the CODE army."

He shuffled the glass tubes in his hand and then looked up at Josephine with admiration. "I'll get back to you as soon as possible. You are a remarkable woman."

She offered a coy smile. "I've been told that a few times before."

He chuckled. "I love how modest you are."

Josephine rose. Enough banter. She had to get busy.

"Leaving so soon?" He stood and wrapped his fingers around her elbow. His eyes hinted at something intimate.

She had vowed to never engage in anything but business with the men she worked with, no matter how persuasive, handsome, or charming they were. Vince was a different story. He'd been her best friend since her career began.

"How am I supposed to impress you if I don't get to work?" She hoped he would take the hint. And, as she'd assumed, he lowered his hand.

"Then you'd better get going." He gave a curt nod.

The door slid open, and before she walked out she said, "I'm curious. Do you know what serum they use for the CODE soldiers?"

"You're sending a team to get a sample of it, aren't you?"

"We don't have time to recreate it, and we need the exact formula. Either we'll steal some or capture a soldier."

He walked closer, but gave her space. "I've been trying to get my hands on it, as well. The serum you are looking for is called HelixAVA."

"AVA?" Josephine felt foolish for raising her voice, then it softened as the door closed. She didn't exit, as she had more questions. "I mean—"

"I said the same thing." He chuckled. "It's to differentiate from the other serum. It's a death sentence, if given to the wrong soldier."

She stared at him as she processed his words. He seemed to be always one step ahead of her. Where was he getting his information?

"How do you know?" she asked.

"Verlot, of course. It's amazing what that man will do for food."

Josephine laughed, but she hoped San was genuine. Trusting him completely wasn't an option when so many lives depended on her. However, he had helped her every step of the way so far. But still, he would have to move mountains before she would trust him with her life.

CHAPTER TWENTY-ONE–THE MISSION

AVA

"What did you just say?" Brooke paced, her shoes squeaking against the polished tile floor.

After I'd returned from the CODE army tour, Sena had escorted me to a clean room with cots and a toilet.

Sitting on a mattress, Tamara folded her legs and wrapped her arms around them.

I grabbed Brooke's wrist and whispered in her ear. I didn't know if someone was watching us. "I don't like this either, but this is how we learn about these soldiers. You don't have to come."

Brooke shoved me. I stumbled backward. I didn't know if her violence was for show, or if she was upset.

"Of course I'm going, Where you go, I go. Who's going to watch out for you?"

Tamara released her legs and raised an arm halfway. "I'm going too."

"I love you both, you know that?"

"Yeah, well ..." Brooke tossed her hair and leaned into her hip. "Next time, though there better not be a next time, you should start with 'Mr. Park is forcing me to go on a mission with the CODE soldiers.' I thought you were out of your mind when you said you're leading the international ISAN team."

"You could have told us yesterday," Tamara said. "Why now?"

125

I sat on the cot beside her. "I didn't want you to worry. I didn't want—"

Brooke plopped down next to me. "For us to think about it so we could get some decent sleep." She rested her head on my shoulder, one arm behind my back. "So you can take the burden on your own."

Tamara planted her head on my other shoulder. "That's what a true leader does."

My breath caught in my throat, and I choked up. "This feels like old times, doesn't it? We had a lot of talks in my room in ISAN."

"But this time we have more people we care about," Brooke murmured.

"We have a larger family now," Tamara said. "I miss everyone at the … you know where."

"How did we get so emotional?" I laughed. "We really have changed."

They chuckled and squeezed me tighter.

We'd come a long way, and our lives were richer. I wanted that for the CODE assassins, too. We could make a difference. My mother had believed I could. I had to believe it, too. She'd saved my daughter, and so I must do the same for those girls.

The door slid open. We parted ways. The cold replaced the warmth from my friends' embrace.

Davina strutted in, her braided hair bouncing against her back. Behind her Momo grudgingly walked in, carrying a pile of suites. She looked at me as if waiting for direction.

"Aww." Davina gave a fake smile. "Did I break up a moment?"

"How about I break you?" I smirked.

"Put those on," Davina snarled. "Then come with me."

"What do you want from us?" Brooke grabbed one from Momo.

"It's not what I want. If I had it my way, you wouldn't be a part of my unit."

I shoved on the uniform. "You mean *my* team. I'm the lead."

Davina's nostrils flared, baring her teeth. "For now. But you should hurry. Mr. Park doesn't like waiting."

Cool to the touch, the flexible uniform hugged every inch of my body. It was the same as the ones Davina and Momo wore.

Davina walked away without a care, trusting we wouldn't do anything behind her back. But then again, if we brought her down, where would we go? I had no idea how to leave this place.

I lagged behind and yanked Momo beside me. "What happened?"

Momo met my slow pace, but she kept her gaze rooted ahead. "First, tell me when and how we are getting out of here."

I trusted Momo, but she might accidentally say something if I told her my plan. And her uniform might be bugged, so I ignored her. But I had to tell her to trust Justine and Russ.

"Fine." She stomped her feet. "No one tells me anything anyway, but I'll answer your question." I expected her to whisper, but her voice kept growing louder. "It's a long story, but ..." She pointed at Davina. "She killed Coco, Jo, Marissa, Debra, Hector, Jessa, Daniel, and Pete." She said their names as if she never wanted the assassin to forget them. "She captured me and brought me here. I'm going to—"

The soldier grabbed Momo and slammed her to the wall. I placed out a hand to stop Brooke and Tamara from intervening. I wanted to hear what Davina had to say. She wouldn't hurt Momo when we were on our way to meet Park.

"You little punk," the assassin growled, shoving her arm against Momo's neck. "You only think about what I did wrong. What about you? This is war, kid. Stop whining. Either join the winning team or die."

"Let go of me, you piece of …" Momo's voice was muffled.

Davina leaned harder on Momo's throat.

Momo acted out of character, but I knew why. Her friends had died in front of her.

The ISAN secret base blowing up, my mother trapped inside, kept playing in my mind. I even had nightmares about it. I understood what she was going through.

"I could end you right here." Davina gritted the words through her teeth.

"Go ahead. I dare you." Momo's eyes darkened.

"Nah." Davina dropped her arm to her side. "I think I'll let you live so you can suffer."

With those words, Brooke and Tamara backed away, relaxing their fists. They had been ready to pounce on Davina, who strutted away as if nothing happened.

Momo straightened and rubbed her neck. "Well, that went very well." Her fierce gaze followed Davina. "Join the winning team. Huh!" She blew out a breath. "I'll show her."

"Come on, kid." Brooke grabbed Momo's earlobe and dragged her down the hallway. "Don't do anything stupid. You won't get your revenge that way."

"Ouch. Ouch. Ouch." Momo grumbled all the way to the meeting room.

Russ and Justine found their seats next to Park at a long table. Hae Jin, Min Hyuk, and Sena sat on the other side of him. While the three rebels remained standing in front of the table, Davina joined Sena, standing by her side. None of us greeted one another as we got down to business.

Park waved a hand and pulled up a hologram image of a beautiful city gleaming in all the hues of the rainbow. "This area is called Itaewon. It's known for its nightlife, shopping, tourists, and young crowd. And the underground market with loan sharks, illegal drugs, and prostitutes."

"Oh, wow." Momo's eyes grew wider. "I've always wanted to go there."

"Don't tell me we need to …" Tamara swallowed. "The last time we dressed as hookers, it didn't go so well."

Brooke covered Tamara's mouth with her hand and whispered, "Don't tell him anything." She met Park's gaze. "She doesn't know what she's talking about."

Russ closed his eyes and shook his head. I knew what he was thinking. This was our team. We talked too much and said unnecessary, stupid things. If Mitch were here, he would be laughing.

Justine must have had the same thought. Her lips twitched, hiding a grin. Meanwhile, the Korean assassins remained motionless and didn't say a word.

Park folded his fingers and growled, annoyed he had been interrupted. "Your mission is to capture Lee Joon Soo."

He pulled up a hologram image of the target. Middle-aged. Pale skin. Hair parted in the middle.

"Why?" I asked. If Lee Joon Soo were important to the resistance, I would sabotage the operation. But I needed a clear answer. No more killing the good guys for ISAN.

"The reason is not important," he said, and turned to Russ. "Did your leaders not teach these girls manners?"

I slammed my hand on the table. "I'm not one of his girls. I belong to no one. And I never said I would be joining your team. You only assumed."

Though I had already made up my mind to go, I wanted to give him a difficult time. Why should I make anything easier for him?

Park leaned back into his leather chair and scrutinized me from head to toe. He inhaled a deep breath. "You will do as I say. You do remember that I said there would be consequences if you didn't? Let me show you something."

He called up a second hologram with a wave of his hand and I nearly dropped to my knees, but managed to keep a neutral expression. Brooke kicked my boot and Tamara and Momo let out a whimper. Justine stiffened and Russ clenched his jaw. But the Koreans furrowed their brows.

Park couldn't possibly know about the secret base. It wasn't even on the radar.

He shut down all the 3D images. "Before you say you have no idea why I've shown you this image, let me tell you something. Your father forced it out of Zen's memory and sent me the location before he died. I had my team locate and scout the area to confirm, and to our luck, a glider happened to slip through an opening in the mountain. So, if you ever want to see Rhett and your little family again, you *will* obey, Ava."

I'd thought he was bluffing, at first, and that he had gotten lucky by choosing a mountain that resembled our base. But, to be honest, I couldn't distinguish one from another, except that ours had a flat surface that opened and allowed the gliders to enter. But if he had taken it out of Zen's memory, there was no doubt.

Novak continued to hunt me even after his death.

Park's words went in one ear and out the other. I had to find a way to tell Rhett. If Park knew, then everyone else in ISAN might know—or, maybe he had been keeping this information for himself to control me and outmaneuver other directors. Regardless, it was only a matter of time before they attacked the rebels in the mountain.

Oh, God. Rhett. Avary. All those people. Stay calm. Just do as he asked.

I looked at Russ. He was the only one who could get word to Rhett. As if he understood what I was asking, he gave me a slight nod. Still, I would be on edge until I knew everyone was safe. But what if Park had a team waiting for them if they tried to leave?

"Fine," I ground out. "As long as you don't touch that mountain, I'll bring you your man. But, why me? Why can't you send your loyal assassins?"

He pushed out his chair and rose. "My girls are too young to enter a bar, and they don't have the charisma to seduce a man. Let me show you something. Davina, come."

She got out of her seat and stood in front of him. While Davina ran her fingers through his hair, he jerked to the side. She had been too rough—enough to pull the strands out.

Brooke, Tamara, and Momo spat out a laugh while everyone else remained silent.

"See what I mean?" Park rubbed his temple.

"You made them that way," I said.

Park's chair grazed the tile floor and he sat back down. "It's a simple job. Either knock out Mr. Lee with a Taser, or put sleeping medicine in his drink. I prefer the latter, but whatever makes it the most feasible."

"How do we get a Taser?" I asked.

"The location of the meeting and the room has already been determined. I'll have someone attach one weapon under the table, and I'll provide you with the medicine. I'm sending my unit, but only Brooke and Tamara will join you inside. Mr. Lee will have a friend, so you'll have to entertain them until you get the job done."

Entertain. I'd rather not. "Then what?"

"The rest of the team will deal with his bodyguards." He glanced at Hae Jin with a stern look. "Don't do anything you'll regret, and I'll let you know when it's time."

I had no idea what he meant, but those coded words sounded like he was telling her to stand down on assassinating someone.

"Don't fail me, Ava." Park's voice punched through the air. "Lives are in your hands."

That's nothing new.

Who are you, Lee Joon Soo? And why are you important to ISAN?

CHAPTER TWENTY-TWO–LEE JOON SOO

JOSEPHINE CHANG

Josephine had just finished a meeting with the other two Remnant Councilors of the former United States. Sylvia Martinez from North and Timothy Jones from South agreed they would announce Verlot's death soon. It had been too long since he'd made a public appearance, and people were going to wonder.

As for the right candidate to replace him, she would worry about that later. Chang had to deal with the matter at hand, first.

Instead of leaving her office, Josephine remained seated at her desk, one hand on the mug of cooling tea. She was expecting a call from Lee Joon Soo, and she didn't want to miss it.

Russ had informed her Ava and a team would be heading to Itaewon soon, searching for Lee Joon Soo. How did Mr. Park know of him?

Joon Soo owned a pharmaceutical company that manufactured beauty pills and a skincare line. Korea was known for the best skincare, but he'd gone international and had made billions.

He had access to the top scientists worldwide and had begun working with private companies. What he did for them was not disclosed.

Joon Soo had worked with Zen before, so she trusted him. While she'd met him once, she had recently reached out to him again.

Josephine took a sip of her favorite tea, and then her chip chimed. She placed down her glass with a hard thud and answered.

"Councilor Chang." Joon Soo's lips curled into a devilish grin and his tone became playful. "You're as beautiful as I remembered. How are you?"

He hadn't aged, even with more white strands in his dark hair, which was parted down the middle.

She didn't want to do small talk, and she had no time to humor him. "It's been a while. You look just as handsome."

Okay, perhaps flattery would get him to answer faster.

"How's the old man?"

"He's out of the medical hub and doing well. He sends his regards and told me to tell you to trust me."

Zen hadn't, but what the hell. She might as well add a twist to their conversation.

"Did he, now?" His tone dropped and an eyebrow rose. "So, how can I help you?"

"I'm confirming our meeting. Did you get a hold of the counterserum?"

He leaned back into his chair, holding a glass, and twirled the ice inside a brown liquid.

"I did. That's the reason I messaged you. I'm going to Itaewon to see an old friend, first."

Meeting a friend first? Did he not understand the word "urgent" in her email? Her heart pounded. Time was running out. Every second of delay meant possible deaths.

"Don't worry." He chuckled. He must have seen her scrunched features. "I told him to meet me at the location of our meeting. That way, I won't be late."

Josephine debated whether to say anything to him about Park.

If she didn't and something happened to him, she would never get that serum. She had to trust her instincts.

"I need to warn you about Mr. Park, who works for Korean—"

"ISAN." He took a gulp of his liquid and sighed. "Don't trust anyone from that network."

Joon Soo knew Josephine was on one of the Remnant Councils, but he didn't know she had been at war with ISAN.

"His assassins are coming for you at Itaewon," she said. "I don't know how he knew—"

"That bastard!" He slammed his glass on the desk. "The client I'm meeting must have told him. He might be an ISAN agent. I knew there was something fishy with him when he didn't wire the 4Qs, and wanted to meet me first. Thank you for the heads-up."

"Of course. Mr. Park is holding some of my people captive. It's a complicated story, but the lead's name is Ava. Do not hurt her or her team. Also, I have an escape plan for you, and I'll send you the address of where to meet me."

He stared at something in his office that was off camera. He seemed to be a world away.

"Joon Soo?" She said his name three times.

"Oh, sorry. I was thinking." He crossed his arms on the desk and beamed a wicked smile. "I just thought of something. And please give me details regarding my escape plan."

CHAPTER TWENTY-THREE–ITAEWON

AVA

T he Korean ISAN transporter took us to Itaewon. Once we landed, Davina and her crew took a route different from my team. Too many of us would cause attention.

As I blended in with the crowd, I admired the city lights. The skyscrapers and the advertisements on the buildings were nothing new, and I felt as though I was back home, except for the foreign characters flashing on the screens and the language spoken on the loudspeaker.

I couldn't turn on an app to translate. Park had blocked our chips, and we couldn't communicate with anyone.

The night sky glowed with colorful gliders whooshing above the cityscape. Kids scampered about on anti-gravity boots, their feet hovering inches off the ground, laughing and spinning in circles around the illuminated park.

Families filled the sidewalks with chatter as they strolled along the street markets. Farther up ahead, music drifted out of clubs and bars, punctuated by wild cheers.

"Wow. Look at all these people and shops." Momo couldn't stop staring.

Brooke grabbed Momo's shirt and yanked her away from a passing motorcar. She would have been hit head-on had it not been for Brooke's fast reflexes.

We moved through the shoulder-to-shoulder crowd and passed a line of shops. So many food carts, and each vendor had an electronic display of what they sold.

I inhaled the sweet-spicy aroma of the stir-fried rice cakes. The word *Tteokbokki* flashed on the panel, then in different languages.

"I want some of that." Tamara pointed to the cart selling stir-fry.

"Looks good," Brooke said, still holding on to Momo. "It says 'kimbap.' What is that?"

"Seaweed rice rolls," Momo said. "Want me to steal some? I like the one with beef called bulgogi."

"Maybe on our way home," Brooke said.

The only ones not drooling were Hae Jin, Min Hyuk, and Sena. This was their country. It was nothing new to them.

We exited the alley of restaurants and stores that sold cheap clothes and skincare and rounded the corner of a tall building. This section of Itaewon was just as bright and loud, but with mature crowds.

Men and women displayed more skin than they should. Their suitors in ground transportation parked in front of them. Brooke covered Momo's eyes and tugged her along.

"Hey!" Momo squirmed, trying to get out of her grasp. "I've seen a lot more."

I had, too, when I had been on the run from my foster father. Good riddance. He was locked away for life.

Brooke halted when we came upon a barbecue restaurant. The customers sat at the round tables, frying beef and chicken. Kimchee, seaweed, fishcakes, and glass noodles were set in small bowls. I wasn't hungry, but I drooled and my stomach rumbled.

I missed eating out—something that people with normal lives

did. I wondered if I would ever be able to, in the future.

"We should go," Hae Jin said, snapping us out of a daze.

Hae Jin and Min Hyuk went ahead of us. Sena lagged behind them, alone, like she wasn't a part of their team. Perhaps they didn't trust her.

Min Hyuk and Hae Jin whispered into each other's ears. I hadn't known them long, but they seemed to be close. They reminded me of Rhett and me. I pushed back the thoughts of Rhett and Avary. Distractions would lead to mistakes.

Min Hyuk halted in front of a traditional Korean house, our destination, which had been converted into a bar and nightclub.

"It looks so cool." Momo rounded the back of the structure into the dimly lit area.

"These hanok are rare," Hae Jin said. "Many were destroyed by the meteors. They were first built in the fourteenth century during the Joseon Dynasty."

"That's too bad." Brooke shook her head as a group of CODE soldiers marched beside the clusters of trees.

Davina jerked her chin. One of their girls tossed us a duffel bag. Then ten assassins made a half a circle, blocking any view of us from outsiders. I pulled out clothes, tossed some to my unit, and then took out the rest of the items.

We changed into formfitting black dresses and put on dark, long wigs. Then we stepped into high heels. I handed Tamara the sleep medicine, and she shoved it inside her bra.

"Okay, let's do this," I said. "Brooke, Tamara, and I will go in, and you two wait out here with Momo and be our lookout. Hae Jin, find us if anything seems suspicious."

"You three are gorgeous." Momo let out a soft howl.

"Momo …" I began. "Stay close to Hae Jin and don't do

anything without her permission. Got it?"

She slumped her shoulders and pressed her lips together. "Fine. But hurry. These robots give me the creeps."

Someone gripped my wrist and I jerked.

Hae Jin whispered in my ear so only I could hear, "If we take Joon Soo as a hostage, then ISAN will have the upper hand."

I had questioned if I could trust her, and there was my answer. "I'm trying to keep my people safe. I have no choice."

"If you bring in Joon Soo, you have to find out what Mr. Park wants from him, and you have to get him out before he's terminated."

The CODE soldiers glared at me, likely wondering why we were holding a conversation instead of heading to the nightclub.

I needed to buy time, so I grabbed Hae Jin's hand and placed it on my wig. She caught on.

"Let me fix that for you," Hae Jin said.

I whispered, "A team was supposed to pick you up. What happened?"

"I'll explain another time. When you leave, don't forget to take us with you. It's only the three of us, now. Well, maybe two. I don't know if you can trust Sena. Don't tell her anything."

Her somber tone broke my heart. "I'll find a way, I promise." I glanced over my shoulder to Momo and gave her a thumbs-up before heading to the flashing blue neon Korean characters.

Guards scanned our bodies with a tool the size of a flashlight.

"You're safe to go," one of them said, and opened the double doors to a grand patio.

The structure wrapped into a large square space with many chambers that had been turned into private VIP rooms.

White lights hung from the branches and along the rooftop.

Music blasted, and people danced around the band set in the center of the patio. A bartender poured beer for his clients, who sat cross-legged on red cushions, then he slid the cups of rice wine down the table to the customers, garnering a cheer from them.

Tamara grabbed my arm and righted herself. Her heel had caught in the crack of the stone floor.

"Damn heels," she grumbled.

I felt the same way as I wobbled across the courtyard to the VIP rooms and searched for the only hanji paper door. There ... in the center. I slid the door open and closed it behind me after my squad entered.

Two middle-aged men with alcohol flush sat on cushions, a table between them. They each held a small white cup in raised hands, but halted before they could toast.

Both had their dark hair slicked back, and they both wore the same black pants with a white, long-sleeve dress shirt. You couldn't tell who was who from a distance, but up close I recognized Joon Soo's pale face from the hologram image Park had shown me.

We took off our heels and walked across the wooden floor barefoot.

"Ah," the man said, slurring his words. "You must be the entertainment I ordered. Don't just stand there. Sit."

Joon Soo raked his gaze over my body and then pointed at me. "You, come ... to me."

His friend waved a dried fried octopus leg and bit into it. "I'll take the other two," he said around a mouthful.

When we took our places, I grabbed the cups from a tray and handed them to Brooke and Tamara. I poured a little bit of rice wine as I faked a smile and then felt under the smooth wood surface for the Taser. There. Where I had been told it would be.

"Let's toast." The friend raised his cup, nearly spilling the liquid. "To the beautiful ladies and our new business deal."

What business deal? After I kidnapped Joon Soo, I would have to pry it out of him.

Glasses clinked. I downed the rice wine. It was my first time drinking it. Sweet, tangy, and bitter-tasting.

"Have more." Brooke poured wine with a high-pitched laugh.

Tamara ran a hand along the friend's arm, giggling. "You have lots of muscles, Mister."

His lustful gaze made me worry, but she knew how to handle a man. Tamara leaned closer, teasing him by licking her bottom lip. She was shy, but when she was on a mission she played her part well, especially the game of seduction.

The friend's hand went to the back of Tamara's head and he pulled her in for a kiss. Brooke stiffened and made no sound, but she tightened her grip on the jar of wine, ready to use it as a weapon.

"You can kiss me later, when we're alone." As Tamara pushed him back, she slid a hand down his arm.

A hologram of the friend's face, and his information, popped up. She had managed to release his chip. *Good girl.*

Name: Bae Young Gil
Age: 40
Occupation: Unknown

"What did you do?" he yelled at Tamara, and slapped his wrist to close his personal information.

Tamara batted her eyelashes and clasped her hands under her chin, feigning innocence with a coy pout. "I didn't do anything. Don't be mad at me. I'll make it up to you."

"Don't be upset." Brooke pinched Young Gil's cheek. "Let's dance."

Brooke gently tossed her wig hair and shimmied her shoulders. Her bouncing cleavage made it impossible for him to look away.

His lustful eyes grew wider and he mimicked her wiggle.

"We should do the same," I said to Joon Soo.

Brooke and I distracted the men while Tamara released two droplets of sleeping medicine into their drinks. If Rhett could see me, he would die from laughing. *Stop thinking of him and Avary.*

I held up my cup. "Let's toast. To a night we'll never forget."

We downed the rice wine and thumped the glass on the table. Young Gil collapsed a few seconds later, his cheek kissing the bowl of dried octopus. Joon Soo gawked at his friend, but remained upright as he yanked a leather briefcase closer to him.

Something important must be in that case. A weapon?

My team and I exchanged wary glances. Why was Joon Soo still awake? His cup was empty.

This wasn't going according to plan. *What do I do?* Pulse racing, I curled my fingers into fists.

The lines across his forehead eased. "Tell me which one of you is Ava?"

I grabbed the weapon under the table and then aimed it at him with steady fingers. "Why do you care?"

He put up his hands. "I'm working with Councilor Chang."

"Why should we believe you?" Brooke raised the wine bottle like a club and then shoved an octopus leg in her mouth.

He scoffed. "Do you know who I am?"

"We don't care," Tamara said, pouring wine into her cup.

I jabbed the Taser to his temple. "Do you have any idea how much this will hurt? Answer her question."

He released a sharp sigh. "Councilor Chang told me that a network called ISAN would be coming for me. My client ratted me out to Mr. Park. So, to make a long story short, you'd best not kidnap me or you'll never win the war."

I lowered and eased back to my seat. "We have no choice but to take you with us. Park will kill our friends if we fail. CODE soldiers are our backup in case you escape."

He winked at me. "Ava, right? Councilor Chang's men should be here by now, and I have my bodyguards throughout the nightclub. And I also have a plan. Let me tell you all about it. But first …" He hiked his long leg over the table and put his face near Young Gil's. "I'm going to make you regret stabbing me in the back, asshole." He pulled out a flat metal box from his leather briefcase and showed us the contents. "This should do the trick."

Brooke gasped. "As Ozzie would say, holy mother of all mothers."

Tamara gave a wicked smile. "Brilliant."

Genius. I wished I had thought of it.

Joon Soo placed a thin polymer skin over Young Gil's face. The layer molded perfectly, making him his twin. Then he shuffled by the back wall and knelt, running a hand over the wooden floor before lifting up a section big enough for one man to drop. His escape route, I assumed.

"Now I'm ready," he said, and gave us the details.

CHAPTER TWENTY-FOUR–THE ESCAPE

AVA

Joon Soo made a call to his men from his chip, and then injected Bae Young Gil with a serum to wake him up. Just as he put the metal case and syringe in his briefcase, screams outside the room rent the night.

A bullet pierced the hanji paper door and hit the wine bottle. Shards of glass blew outward like mini fireworks. Gunfire echoed, shattering windows with every shot in rapid succession. Light streamed into the room from the holes, casting strange shadows on the floor and the walls.

I dashed for the corner of the room and curled into a ball, my heart pounding. Tamara and Brooke scrambled beneath a low wooden table.

The tattered door hung open and Young Gil was gone. As Joon Soon had pointed out earlier, he had escaped through a secret door on the floor.

I grabbed my heels and rushed out, barefoot, to the patio to the madness, and sprinted past the flipped tables and chairs. Customers continued to scream, and shoved against each other in their rush to the exit.

Chang's men and Joon Soo's bodyguards were firing at the CODE soldiers. Bullets and Taser pellets flew in every direction, creating chaos and destruction. Several diners wailed, clutching wounds. I wished Chang hadn't sent her troopers. More lives would be sacrificed.

"Joon Soo!" Momo pointed toward the back door and ran after him.

Not Joon Soo, but, rather, Young Gil. But she didn't know. A few CODE assassins nearest to the back door tailed them.

"This way," I said to Brooke and Tamara, but Momo came running back and nearly bumped into us.

"He's gone," Momo said. "I'm going to the roof."

Good idea. I tossed my heels into a broken chair, Brooke did the same and we followed Momo, hauling up into a branching tree, then climbed higher and hurried across a limb thick enough to hold our weight.

I leaped to the rooftop next to Momo, the tiles cool and smooth under my feet—a relief from the scratchy surface of the limbs.

My team, Hae Jin, and Min Hyuk scrambled up after us. Sena remained on the ground with the CODE girls.

Brooke almost tripped from the slippery tiles, and I clutched her arm and yanked her next to me. She gave me a curt nod and peered down at the crowd.

"This is almost comical." Tamara twirled her high heels as she would have her pocketknife.

Citizens ran in a mad dash for cover. Some sprinted inside the surrounding shops. I felt sorry for the food stand owners as bullets pelted the wood and steel. It was difficult to tell who was who since, everyone wore black, but one figure with long braided hair stood out, crouching by a skincare shop.

I remained on the roof with my team and focused on Young Gil with Joon Soo's face who was hiding behind a tteokbokki cart, the owner down on his knees with him. A few CODE soldiers and Councilor Chang's guards passed by. Young Gil reached over to scoop some rice cake and proceeded to eat while in hiding.

Enough of this. I placed a thumb and forefinger in my mouth and blew loudly over the screams and people scrambling to escape the crossfire, to get Davina's attention. She and the two CODE girls next to her peered up.

I pointed at the tteokbokki cart across the street from her. Just as Davina pulled out a Taser, Tamara flung her high heels in quick succession, hitting Davina and one of her crew on their heads. They growled, but could do nothing. So satisfying.

Despite the chaos and danger, Momo and Brooke erupted into snickers.

Tamara's aim was as precise as Rhett's with a gun. I wished I still had my shoes. I would have thrown them at her, too.

No warning for Young Gil. As the assassins moved with grace and speed, he never heard or saw them as Davina wrapped her fingers around his neck and yanked him up. The food cart owner scrambled away.

Young Gil didn't move. His arms flopped at his sides. She must have pressed on pressure points that would cause pain with any movement. Then the CODE girl Tased him. He convulsed and then slumped, knocked out cold.

Davina spoke into her chip to inform Park while hauling Young Gil into the open, his dark socks dragging on the concrete. Too busy escaping, he had forgone his shoes.

Joon Soo must be long gone, explaining his and Chang's guards' absence on the street.

My unit and I jumped down from the roof and rounded the corner to the back of the restaurant where Sena waited with the duffle bag. We changed into the training outfits and comfortable shoes and then got inside the glider.

After we landed at the Korean base, one of the soldiers hefted Young Gil over her shoulder and the rest of the assassins sauntered to the training facility. Davina, Hae Jin, and my teams headed to the meeting room.

Park sat in his usual center spot at the long table, Russ and Justine on either side of him. We didn't sit, but stood in a resting stance.

"Good job on accomplishing your mission." Park said it to his team, but he looked at me. "That wasn't so bad, was it?"

I wanted to tell him to go to hell, but now wasn't the time. "I brought you Joon Soo, and if you want me to continue to lead your international troop, have Russ take Brooke, Tamara, and Momo back to the US ISAN base. I don't need them."

Brooke bumped her shoe into mine and Tamara elbowed my side. They disagreed with my decision, but I wanted to keep them safe. And I needed them to go to the mountain base and alert Rhett.

Park regarded me for a moment and said, "Very well. Brooke and Tamara can go with Russ when he leaves. But, *after* I extract the information from Joon Soo. I'm sure Russ would want to be here. But ..." His gaze shifted to Momo. "I'm going to hold off on her. I have a task for the little one." He pressed his chip on his forearm and spoke into it. "Send a couple of my girls."

A task? My stomach lurched with Park's directive.

Momo shoved her hands inside her pants pockets just before two soldiers entered and grabbed her by either arm. My heart palpitated, and chills ran down my neck.

Momo met my gaze. Her eyes widened with fear, and then she looked at Park. She wiggled and tugged against her captors, but she was no match for their strength.

Brooke rounded her fists by her side and Tamara tapped her foot, anxious and worried. Min Hyuk's shoulders tightened and Hae Jin's teeth clenched. They didn't know my little friend well, but I appreciated their concern. But Sena and Davina kept quiet, stone-faced.

"Stop," I said as the door slid open. I put every bit of the authority of an ISAN team leader into my voice.

Momo stopped kicking, glancing over her shoulder to me. I hated this feeling, like she was being sent to her death.

Park furrowed his brow, irritated at the hiccup. "What's so imperative?"

I gave him a heated stare, then glared at the two soldiers. "I know what you two look like, and I swear, if you hurt her, I'll tear your limbs off one by one. They say you don't feel pain, but I promise you, you will."

Mr. Park smirked. "There's the Ava I've heard all about." He waved a hand at the assassins. "Take Monet to the training facility and let's test her survival skills."

"Ava, I have something!" Momo shouted. "I got it from—" The door shut before she could finish.

What something? In her pocket? Why hadn't she given it to me earlier?

I growled and my leg muscles tensed, ready to pounce on Park.

Russ brought his curled fingers down to his lap, hiding his rage.

"Don't get upset, Ava." Park pull up a hologram image from his chip. "I'll let all of you watch. It's the least I can do."

Momo appeared in the grand training room. The tables toward the back wall had weapons like the glove. She paced the large square mat inside the center of the room. Two assassins stood in the middle of the mat, clenching their jaws.

I smacked the table inches from Park's crossed arms. "Are you crazy? Stop this right now, or I won't cooperate."

He let out a long sigh and ran a hand down his tie. "Don't forget about the mountain base. You shouldn't threaten me. I might get angry."

I took a step back and shuddered. Momo better not die. He better stop the fight before they ... I couldn't think about it.

"Don't worry," Park said. "I have faith in her. I dropped the inhibitor soundwave in that room. She can use her power. If she survives, I'll let her lead my youngest team."

He made me sick. Acid bubbled in my stomach and rushed up my throat. I kept seeing my daughter's face.

Avary is safe. She's with Rhett. My daughter will never become an assassin.

Park barked an order at the hologram. "We don't have all day. Get her."

The soldier with blond hair rushed to Momo. Momo swung her leg and knocked Blondie on her back. The soft mat cushioned her fall and she rose with ease.

Momo ran, but she didn't sprint at her full speed. She didn't know she had her powers back, so she didn't even try. As she dashed toward the table with weapons, the sound of a cracking whip split the air.

She flipped backward like an acrobat and grabbed the glove from the table, then jolted forward to escape the whip coming for her from the CODE girl with curly hair. Momo turned on the gadget, pointed it at Curly, and squeezed, but she dodged to the side and Momo missed.

"Damn it!" Momo crawled under the table, but Blondie must

have anticipated her move.

Blondie grabbed her feet and dragged her across the tile floor as Momo kicked and screamed. Then Blondie hauled her up by the neck, feet dangling three feet off the floor.

"Get off me, you machine." She pounded Blondie's arm, but she wouldn't let go.

Blondie curled her lips—not a smile, but something evil. "Little bug, you're so easy to catch. I think I'll play with you first before I rip out your heart."

She punched Momo's chest. Momo went flying and landed on the mat in front of Curly. That soldier kicked her in the stomach, tossing her back to Blondie. Blood seeped from Momo's mouth.

Gasps filled the room, but Park laughed.

"That's enough!" I flung myself over the table and gripped Park's suit jacket as I pulled him to his feet in one swift motion.

He didn't fight back, nor did he say anything. His gaze was focused on Blondie on top of Momo, punching her face. Momo put up her fists to block the blows, but with one of her hands, she took out something from her pants pocket and then she crossed her arms again.

Why would she risk a punch to her face? She had said … "*Ava, I have something.*" Those words kept playing in my mind. A bomb? Whatever she had, would it kill her? Oh, God! I'm going to puke.

I shook Park, his jacket still in my grasp. "Stop them right now!" I grabbed his tie and tightened it around his neck until he gave a smothered gasp.

"If you kill me, my soldiers will blow up your mountain base," he said through his strangled breath. "It has been installed in their memory. So, what's it going to be, Ava? One life, or many?"

Please be strong, Momo. I can't help you. I'm so sorry.

150

I released Park, though I wanted to slam him against the wall. As he straightened his tie, his smirk disappeared and his eyes grew so wide, his eyebrows arched like crescent moons.

Momo was on her back. Her chest rose and fell. On either side of her lay two motionless soldiers. Had she killed them? How? I had been too busy attacking Park, I hadn't seen what she did.

Park's face reddened—from fury or fear, I had no idea. Maybe both. He said something into his chip in Korean, and then a warning shrilled outside the meeting room. Momo jolted up, grabbed her head, and stumbled forward. Then she rushed out the exit.

Good girl. Find a place to hide until I find a way to get out.

"What did she do to them?" Park growled.

"How is this possible?" Russ said. "You can't let her get away. Justine, come with me."

"Wait." Park grabbed Russ's arms. "My girls are looking for her. She can't escape. There's only one exit, and it's heavily guarded. We're underground, remember?"

Russ yanked his arm back. "At this point, I don't trust anyone to get the job done. Stop playing games."

"I was merely testing Monet's limits. Isn't that Novak's style? You worked under him, did you not?" He didn't wait for an answer. "Anyway, I'm on my way to interrogate Joon Soo. You should come with me."

It was an offer Russ couldn't let pass. He needed to know why the prisoner was important to ISAN.

"Fine, but I want Justine to look for Monet. After she's found, I'm taking her with me. She's ours. Don't forget that. And next time you want to 'test her limits,' I suggest you ask me first."

Park dipped into a quick bow, but I wasn't sure if he was being respectful, or mocking Russ.

CHAPTER TWENTY-FIVE–THE SEARCH

JUSTINE

Justine rushed out of the meeting room, nearly tripping on her feet. She had to find Momo before the CODE girls did. Momo fighting the super-soldiers had her on pins and needles, and she wanted to puke. Justine didn't know her well, but the little girl was part of the resistance.

Act like an ISAN leader. Basically, be a bitch. Head up. Shoulders back. Don't smile. Bark orders and don't take shit from anyone.

The old Justine wouldn't have cared if Momo died, but the new one did. Her heart had softened when her team had welcomed her back with open arms. They'd protected her when the other rebels gave her dirty looks and spat on her.

Yes, she deserved the hostility. After all, she'd tried to kill some of them. And even if she'd never met most of the resistance, they knew of her, or at least her name.

As she strutted down the gray hallway, she placed a hand on her Taser. Faint footfalls echoed. Momo?

Once she found Momo, they'd together search for the lab Russ had informed her about—the lab where he thought Mitch's father might be.

Justine would do anything for Mitch. Not because of her crush, though she still had one, but because she respected him. He was one of the few who believed in her, and after a lifetime of ridicule from her father, a little faith meant everything.

She also owed Mitch her life. He hadn't left her to die when she had been attacked by the giant spider, even though he had been a double agent at the time.

Justine passed a few CODE soldiers in the hall, sprinting the opposite way from the direction she was headed. She didn't know where she was going, but she followed the layout of the compound back home. All the sectors she had visited had a similar blueprint.

Momo would likely hide somewhere secluded—something Justine would do. Somewhere that said *Keep Out*, like the sign flashing in bold red letters on the wall in Korean, then in English and other languages. She ignored the warning and approached the door.

So quiet. Only the thudding of her heart in her ears. Just as she twisted the doorknob, pounding footsteps resonated. She gasped, surprised that the door was unlocked, but she supposed Park didn't have to worry about the assassins entering a restricted area.

Three soldiers came around the corner, Tasers out, and headed straight for the door she wanted to enter. Justine thought of leaving. Why should she care about Momo? Who was this girl to her? But then a little voice inside said, *You're the only one who can save her. You're a rebel, now.* And maybe if Momo told her friends that Justine had helped her, they would treat her like one of their own.

She just wanted to feel like she belonged.

Don't let them inside. Momo can't fight five super-soldiers.

Justine pointed at the *Keep Out* flashing sign and raised her chin. "What are you doing?"

From what Justine had observed, the soldiers didn't ask questions. They followed commands.

"We believe Monet is hiding in there," one of the girls said.

"She's not. I checked. She was spotted by the dining area. You should go there."

The soldiers exchanged glances, confused.

Justine shifted on her feet, trying not to hold her breath. What if they didn't listen? She used the same commanding tone Ava used in ISAN.

"You know who I am, right? I'm giving you an order. Do as I say, or I'll report you to Mr. Park."

The girls dipped into a bow and left. Justine waited until they were inside the elevator, then eased her shoulders through the door. She flinched when a faint beeping and hissing sound filled the room. When she did a quick glance about the dimly lit large space, she couldn't figure out where the noises had come from.

As she walked toward the back, she bumped into a desk with monitors and cringed. No soldiers jumped in front of her, so she exhaled a breath.

"Momo, are you in here?" Why was she whispering? Because the little girl might think of her as an enemy.

Momo hadn't been at the rebel base when Ava had announced the news about Novak being her father and Justine her half sister. So she had to think of something wise to say.

She held out her Taser, careful not to make a sound. She slowly pushed on the gurney in her way.

"Russ sent me to find you. Can you come out? It's just you and me."

No answer. She would try one more time and leave.

She weaved around large crates and sauntered toward the corner, where a shadow caught her eye. "Momo, I'm here to—"

Lights came on. She blinked in the brightness. Someone

grabbed her arm and yanked her down behind the crates. Then a hand covered her mouth and Justine was face-to-face with Momo.

Momo pointed to the thick glass that took up the space of the back wall where the light came from. Justine couldn't hear anything, but Momo's expression told her to be afraid. Justine's stiff muscles relaxed when the rebel girl appeared to trust her.

"What happened to those super-soldiers in the training room?" Justine whispered. "Did you kill them?"

"I knocked them out," Momo murmured.

Justine had seen her reach inside a pocket, but then one of the CODE soldier's arms had gotten in the way of the camera. Justine didn't want to point out what she had seen. It might be nothing, and maybe she had imagined it. It had happened so fast.

Momo rose and peered toward the thick glass. Justine did the same, but what she saw next flipped her stomach.

Middle-aged men and women lay inside individual medical hubs. Tubes came out of their noses, mouths, and arms, feeding into attached bags. One of the tubes was red. A monitor on each hub beeped and flashed in green, red, and yellow lights. The subjects were alive.

This must be the lab Russ had been hoping to find. And Momo had found it by chance. What were the odds? Sometimes fate was kind.

A woman in a white lab coat on the other side of the glass walked toward the two female assistants checking the monitors on the first pod. The lady in white held up a TAB and read a message.

"Mr. Park said to terminate those we have exhausted," the woman in lab coat said. "I'll decide within a few days who will be moved to another facility and who we'll cremate at the designated funeral home."

A monitor beeped rapidly, and the body inside the second hub jerked and bounced. Momo gripped Justine's arm. Justine flinched, then stiffened, but she understood how Momo felt.

The rebel girl trembled as the three ladies surrounded the convulsing woman. They didn't try to revive her. Instead, the woman in the lab coat shot something in the IV and watched until the rapid beeping became one long tone.

Momo lowered her head to Justine's shoulder. Something melted in her heart. She didn't have a younger sister, but she did have an older half sister. What would Ava do?

She wanted to show the girl she wasn't heartless. Justine patted her back in a steady rhythm like she had seen Ava do when burping Avary.

Should she lean into Momo's body, too? She resisted the idea of even more physical contact. Expressing affection wasn't her thing. She'd never been on the receiving end of it, so she didn't know how.

Momo planted her fingers on her shoulders and shook her, forcing eye contact. "Rhett's father is in there. I know he is."

Justine lowered her voice. "I agree. Mitch has been looking for his father for a long time."

"Rhett's father." Momo frowned.

Justine snorted. She hadn't known it before, but the girl had a crush on Rhett. It was nice to have a short reprieve, thinking about crushes and boys, but she needed to get back to the present.

The lights turned off. When the ladies left through the door on the other side of the glass, Justine pushed the door on her side. She didn't know if she needed a key card to exit through the same door, so she felt relieved when Momo wedged a foot in it to keep the door ajar.

"Hurry," Momo said.

Justine went to each medical hub, checking first to see if the patient was a male or female. If female, she passed, but if male, she read their profile.

No names were displayed, but each had an ID with letters and numbers on the side of the pod. She moved on, finding no one who could be Mitch's father. She didn't know if that was a good or a bad thing.

She skipped over a woman, and the next occupant was male. Salt-and-pepper hair. His eyes were closed and his sharp features, high cheekbones, strong nose, and a nice set of lips were similar to Mitch's.

Name: XYM76.
Age 55. West Sector.
Occupation: Council Guard.
Children: Mitch and Rhett.

Justine's heart thundered and she couldn't move, terrified she would trigger an alarm with the power of her emotions. Silly thought. They had to get out of there fast. She tugged Momo through the door and back to the storage room as the door sealed behind them.

"Hey, what are you doing?" Momo pulled away. "Did you find Rhett's father?"

"Yes, but don't tell anyone. Russ will tell me what to do."

The girl's eyes widened and she clasped her hand over her mouth. Did kids scream from being happy? Justine had no idea, but she seemed stunned and ecstatic at the same time.

"Listen, Momo. I'm sorry, but I will have to take you as a hostage. Park was there when Russ gave me the order to find you."

She reached to grab Momo and drag her out, if she had to, but the girl stuck out a hand.

"Or …" Momo began. "You can tell them you couldn't find me. That way, it will give you an excuse to wander the halls."

The old Justine would have stomped on her idea because of her ego, but the new Justine said, "Good thinking. I'll be back to bring you food when I get a chance. Stay hidden, and be safe."

The girl gripped Justine's arm as she turned to leave. "You're not so bad."

Warmth spread in her chest. "Thanks, kid. I needed to hear that."

"Sometimes all it takes is having someone believe in you, and you flourish with kindness."

Perhaps that was what had happened to Justine. Her team—Ava, Brooke, and Tamara—believed there was goodness in her.

CHAPTER TWENTY-SIX—DISGUISE

AVA

After Mr. Park sent his CODE soldiers to find Momo, we were escorted back to our cell. Brooke and Tamara slumped on their cots and I did the same as thoughts of Rhett, Avary, and my mother came to the forefront of my mind.

"Did Momo reach inside her pocket?" Brooke murmured. "Or was it just my imagination?"

"She has something," I said.

"How did she get it, and what is it?" Tamara laced her fingers through her hair and let out a deep breath.

I didn't share my theory. Not because I didn't trust my team, but because I didn't want anything to happen to Momo if we were being recorded.

Momo had followed the wrong Joon Soo out of the restaurant. She had been in my blind spot, so I hadn't seen either of them. Young Gil must have handed something over—or she'd stolen it from him. But, why?

Brooke sat tall, clutching the blanket. "When Mr. Park finds out what Momo did to his girls, he's going to interrogate her. She's good at lying, but Park will beat it out of her."

Tamara jolted up. "I hope Justine doesn't find her. Or keeps her hidden. Justine will do the right thing, right, Ava?"

"She's good at pretending to be on ISAN's side," Brooke said,

159

her voice low. "But sometimes I wonder. I hate to admit it, since she's your half sister and you want to trust her, but she's moved up the ladder. What stops her from going back to her old self?"

"For now, I'm going to trust her." I'd questioned whether Justine would turn her back on us if she had the opportunity, but she had seen the worst of ISAN—had seen what they had done to the girls. And she'd had a taste of what we could offer: the kind of acceptance she craved. Unless she were a monster in a mask, she would remain loyal.

The door slid open. Hae Jin and Min Hyuk entered. *Are they always together?*

"We're here to escort you," Hae Jin said.

"Where are we going?" Brooke sounded annoyed.

"Mr. Park has questions," Min Hyuk said. "He's in the holding cell with Russ and Joon Soo."

Sooner or later Park would find out the prisoner's real identity, but I had been hoping to buy more time.

We followed Hae Jin and Min Hyuk down the hall and then took the elevator one floor up. We turned right at the exit and entered a room. The cool air and eerie quiet reminded me of ISAN back home.

Young Gil sat in the center of the room, his arms bound behind him. His head slumped to the side, revealing puffy, bruised eyes and cheeks. Blood stained his cut lips. I kind of felt sorry for him.

Who had hurt him? I got my answer when Park unrolled his button-up shirt sleeve and wiped a set of stained metal rings with a towel. Then he set them on the tray.

Russ pinched his eyebrows to the center and curved his lips downward. He looked concerned, but he was always worried. Did something happen to Momo?

"Why are you beating the prisoner?" I asked Park as I remained by the door with my team. Hae Jin and Min Hyuk stood behind us.

Park growled and slammed a fist on the tray, and the metal rings jumped and clanked. "He's telling me he's not Joon Soo. He's telling me he is Bae Young Gil, my source." He marched up to his prisoner and grabbed his chin. "I know what my guy looks like. You better tell me where you hid the serums, or I'll kill you with my bare hands."

"For the last time, I'm not Joon Soo," he said through gritted teeth.

Park narrowed his eyes at me. "What happened in that room?"

I raised my chin, confident. "They were in the process of making the transaction, but your idiot girls fired at us through a closed door. We had to duck for cover. Both men ran out. It was chaos, and then we captured Joon Soo."

"I'm running out of patience and time," Park said to Young Gil. "Tell me where it is, or I'll have to pry it out of your memory. It won't be pleasant."

Young Gil dipped his head. Blood dripped from his cut lips and splashed on the tile floor. Exhausted, even his voice had lost its strength.

"Pry it out of my memory. I don't care. But when this is over, you and I are done doing business and I'm going to sue your ass."

He shouldn't have threatened Park. Now he was as good as dead. But it didn't matter, I suppose. Park would have disposed of him anyway, as soon as he got what he wanted.

Park shuddered. His face flushed with anger. He wrapped a fist in the prisoner's shirt and yanked him out of the chair.

"You ... you ..." Park snarled.

He stared at the prisoner's face and then shifted his gaze lower. Finally he released the man, let him fall back to the chair, began to unbutton Young Gil's shirt, then lowered it off his shoulders.

"What's he doing?" Brooke whispered in my ear.

Park spun toward us, exposing a dragon tattoo on Young Gil's arm. The same tattoo we'd seen on Zeke. This man belonged to Imugi, an underground faction.

I lifted my hands. "Is he a double agent? And, if so, how many more are you dealing with?"

Park clenched his teeth. "Where is the real Joon Soo?"

Far away from you and with Councilor Chang, by now.

"What do you mean?" I blinked, dumbfounded. "Look at his face. Didn't you say you know him? You didn't tell me to strip him and look for a tattoo. This is your fault. You should have trusted me and given me more details."

Park slapped his forearm and pulled up his chip. He moved his finger along the hologram keys. A red light scanned the fake Joon Soo's face. After he shut down his chip, he began to peel a thin layer off the prisoner, starting from the hairline on the forehead and down to his chin. Then he tossed the skin-like material on the tile floor by my feet.

Brooke, Tamara, and I gasped hard. If I didn't sell my performance, Park would bomb everyone I loved at the mountain base into oblivion.

"What *is* that?" I sounded horrified, pointing at the polymer skin. "This man double-crossed you?"

Young Gil raised his head and one eye grew dark and sinister. "Those girls drugged me. Something happened in that room."

"Liar." Brooke huffed out a breath. "He tried to kiss me."

"He's the one that tried to drug *us*," Tamara said. "If I hadn't seen it, our mission would have been botched."

"And if we drugged you," I said, "how did you escape?"

"There's an antidote." The prisoner snarled at Park. "What kind of business do you run? You sent these whores to spy on me?"

Sorry, dude. He had been the only means for Joon Soo's escape, and I didn't help anyone that did business with ISAN.

Park didn't look at us, nor did he say anything to his source. He turned on his chip. "Davina, did Justine find Monet?"

A heartbeat later, he pressed his lips together and a hard line crossed his forehead—an indication he'd gotten the answer he didn't want.

Had my team and I told a believable story?

Park gripped the tray, his knuckles turning white as he turned to me, and said in a steady, calm voice, "Tell me where Lee Joon Soo is."

My skin crawled. I had no idea what Davina had told him. She might have made something up. I had to maintain my usual attitude to show him nothing was off.

"How the hell should I know? I thought he …" I pointed to the prisoner. "… was Joon Soo. We all did. Davina was the one who brought him in."

"I'm giving you one last chance, Ava. And whatever happens next, it will be on your hands."

I didn't like his threat and the way he spoke to me, an eerie echo of Novak.

I took a step toward him and looked squarely in his eyes. "I've told you already, and I'm telling you again. I don't know where he is."

And that was the truth. After we changed the plan and the bullets started flying, Joon Soo was nowhere to be seen. He had escaped through a secret hatch in the room.

"Very well." Park turned to his chip. "Girls, come in."

Footsteps pounded. The door slid open and CODE soldier surrounded us, standing too close for comfort.

Park spoke into his chip again as he met my gaze. "Davina, send your troops to the mountain."

"No!" I rounded my fists, anger surging through my veins. "We had a deal. I brought you Joon Soo. Call off your dogs now. I swear: if you don't, you'll wish you'd never met me."

He gripped my hair, then, with the other hand, he ran a thumb under my nose so fast, I didn't have a chance to stop him.

"I already wish I'd never met you. Sweet dreams, Ava."

The acrid smell stung my nostrils and I stumbled backward. The walls spun and Park swayed as his lips opened and closed, saying something I couldn't hear.

No. Oh, God. I had to ... Russ ... but he couldn't help me, at least not yet. He had to warn Rhett.

Please, Russ. Help ...

CHAPTER TWENTY-SEVEN–CHAVA

JOSEPHINE CHANG

"**W**hat if something went wrong?" Josephine said to Vince, who sat across from her at her office meeting room table.

She had just come back from announcing Verlot's death to the world, and news of a temporary replacement who would be voted in by the three council members. Martinez and Jones had already approved Josephine's request. She just had to convince the candidate to accept the position.

"Joon Soo is coming here, right?" Vince asked.

"Yes." She pushed out of her seat and paced from the kitchen to the living area. She didn't know if Ava and her team were safe, or if Joon Soo had made it out alive from the nightclub at Itaewon. The waiting was killing her.

Joon Soo had informed Josephine of his plan. He would inform the girls about tricking everyone by placing a false face made with polymer skin on Young Gil. This would buy him time to escape and give Ava and her team a captive to hand over.

A chime rang on her desk. Josephine pressed the button on the panel. "Yes," she said to her office manager.

"Mr. Lee is here to see you."

"Thank God! Let him in."

The door slid open and Joon Soo raised a hand in greeting.

The other hand held a leather briefcase.

"Councilor Chang." He gave a curt nod. "Sorry I'm late."

"Please, have a seat." She led him to the chair and introduced Vince.

Joon Soo set the briefcase on the table and unlocked it.

She intertwined her fingers. "Before we begin, can you tell me if Ava and her team are safe?"

"Yes," he said. "I told my guards to come at a designated time. They fired bullets through the upper half of the door to cause a commotion and to draw out the CODE soldiers so I could escape. Afterward, I made my way to safety and waited until Ava and her team got on the ISAN glider. Please thank Mr. San for me. Does he have an escape route in all the facilities he owns?"

"I wouldn't know." She shrugged and thought about the secret medical base with an underground tunnel where they had hid Verlot when he was shot.

"I felt like a spy, like James Bond." He snorted as he grabbed a container from his briefcase and opened it.

"What is that?" Vince asked.

Joon Soo took out one capsule and placed it on his palm. The capsule was about the size of a bullet, and the liquid inside glowed neon blue.

"This is CHAVA …" Joon Soo began, his eyes gleaming. "The counter for HelixAVA. Not only will it heal the wound, once penetrated, but it will also repair parts of the brain affected by the lobotomy. This is the miracle you've been praying for, Councilor Chang. Young Gil wanted to purchase it from me. This is what ISAN wanted, but they'd heard only rumors. When they find out what it does, they'll do anything to destroy it."

She released a long breath while Vince pounded once on the

table with a fist, grinning. What Joon Soo said sounded too good to be true. She wondered if this counter-serum could heal other kinds of wounds. She would ask later. CODE girls had to be brought down, first.

"May I?" Vince picked one up from Joon Soo's hand. He held it between his thumb and forefinger and examined it. "It's so small."

"It's concentrated." Joon Soo sounded offended. "It's a perfect fit for the Taser, and sharp enough to penetrate through skin and the toughest combat suit. I assure you that the potion works fast. The capsules can even be swallowed."

"What happens once the remedy is in the body?" Josephine asked.

"The subject collapses into slumber instantly, and the serum works its magic. My workers are bringing up the amount you asked for as we speak. So, will you be wiring me directly?"

Josephine smirked. "Verlot will. It's the least he could do. He had to make up for his crimes. No one but Martinez and Jones knew Verlot would be providing funding to destroy what he helped to create." She couldn't wait to tell him. It was going to be so satisfying.

Vince gave Joon Soo the capsule. "Can we trust your word? How do we know it's successful?"

Joon Soo placed the container inside the briefcase and locked it. "We captured a few CODE soldiers and tested it out on them. I have data and results of our tests, which I have sent to Councilor Chang."

She nodded. "I have it, and I'm impressed. Let's get this shipment to the rebel units."

Time was running out. She had no choice but to trust his

data.

Her chip chimed. She was going to ignore it, but Russ had left a message.

"You need to hear this," she said, and read it out loud. "Mr. Park found out the real Joon Soo escaped." Josephine had known this would happen, so she wasn't shocked. "Monet might have found a solution to bring down the CODE army."

Joon Soo scrunched his features, confused, and then snorted. "I gave Young Gil a few samples before Ava and her squad entered our private room. I didn't get a chance to take the capsules from him. While I hid beside a tree, a little girl came from behind him and stole them. She moved fast."

"That's Monet for ya." Vince grinned, his eyes beaming with amusement. "Atta girl."

Josephine smiled, but as she continued to read out loud, her heart dropped to her stomach. "Please inform Mitch and Rhett that Mr. Park sent CODE soldiers to the mountain base. They have been found. They need transportation now."

"I'm on my way to Rhett." Vince pushed off his chair and halted. "I'll give you an update from my glider."

"Be careful." She wanted to kiss or hug him. Anything, for it might be their last. But not in front of her guest. She would have to take a rain check. He better come back to her.

She directed Joon Soo to divide the crates, some going to Korean ISAN to Russ, and the other to the mountain base. After her special guest left the office, she made a call to Mr. San to fill him in.

Acid bubbled in her throat, the heat burning her cheeks. She clung to the table, its edges digging into her palms as she forced shallow breaths in and out. Her heart raced, pounding against her rib cage. She needed a moment to steady herself before calling Mitch.

As if on cue, her chip rang. She froze. *Please, no more bad news.* Mitch had left a message, and her eyes pooled with happy tears.

Lydia and Zen are awake!

CHAPTER TWENTY-EIGHT—SEPARATE WAYS

AVA

I strutted along the walls holding us prisoners. Brooke and Tamara sat on their cots, staring at the floor, faces pale, shoulders slumped. This facility had drained all the fight out of them.

Tamara ran a hand down her face, keeping her voice low. "Do you think it's possible that Mr. Park was faking the call to Davina?"

"Maybe he's pretending?" Brooke's voice rose with hope. "Ozzie said no one knows it."

Oh, God. A sharp pain in my chest spread like wildfire and my breathing came in short, shallow bursts as I sprinted around the room. I had to do something. Anything was better than sitting and going out of my mind. I marched to the access door and banged my fist against the surface in desperation.

"Hey! Let me out!" I repeated over and over.

Brooke and Tamara joined me. I was determined to get attention from one of the guards, then find Park and order him to terminate his order.

The wall slid open and I came within inches of socking Russ's face. Justine's lips twitched, giving a hint of a smile.

As soon as the door closed, Russ grabbed my shoulders as his green eyes darkened. I thought he was going to scold me.

"Calm down," he said. "I'm getting you three out, along with the Korean rebels. I've already set the mission. It'll be up to you to take down the CODE soldiers in the glider."

"What about Momo, you, and my sister?"

Justine's eyes widened, perhaps surprised I had asked about her.

"Don't worry about us," Russ said. "But—"

"I found Momo, but I didn't turn her in," Justine cut in. "To make a long story short, she uncovered the facility that housed the elders taken from ISAN's secret compound."

Tamara gasped louder than me.

Brooke shook me with excitement. "Damn, the little squirt did it."

Good. Momo was safe for now.

Justine placed a hand to her chest. "I saw Mitch's father with my own eyes. I read his ID."

"I haven't told Mitch, but I will." Russ lowered his voice even more. "I left a message for Councilor Chang to send help to the mountain base. I hope we're not too late. And I've been leaving messages for Rhett, but I don't know if he's gotten any of my warnings."

Mr. Park would likely have sent assassins to implant a gadget to cut off communications. We had arranged with Councilor Chang to pick up survivors at the forest if we were ever attacked, but Rhett would stay behind and fight until everyone was safe.

I had no idea what Russ had planned. It seemed we all had a different agenda. One person needed to take charge, or it would be chaos. The rebels at the mountain base were my people, not his.

"Listen," I whispered. "Russ and Justine, find Momo and ask her how she brought down the two soldiers. When help comes, save the elders. My team and I will head to the mountain. This is it. Stay safe. Do whatever it takes."

CHAPTER TWENTY-NINE–AWAKE

JOSEPHINE CHANG

As soon as Josephine landed at ANS medical facility, she rushed to the lab, her heels clicking echoed down the hallway. She had called Rhett on the way, but she couldn't get through, so she called Mitch and filled him in on the details about the mountain base being found.

She wanted Mitch to stay with Lydia, but Rhett was his half brother and Avary his niece, and he had the right to decide. Besides, she needed all the top agents.

The doors slid open and Josephine entered. Lydia and Zen, sitting on the sofa in white robes, smiled at her. Mitch was next to Lydia, and Cleo beside her father, drinking hot tea. They all looked pale and worn, Lydia and Zen most of all, but that was to be expected.

Josephine couldn't believe her eyes. She had been praying, and finally Lydia had broken through the fever and Zen had awakened.

"Councilor Chang." Lydia pushed off her seat halfway, but Josephine put up a hand as she approached her.

"Don't you dare get up to greet me." She eased onto the sofa and smiled at Zen. "How are you feeling?"

"I feel like an old man." Zen chuckled and patted Cleo's hand. "I was happy to see my daughter's face when I woke up."

"And how about you?" Chang asked Lydia.

AVA

Lydia crossed her legs and sighed. "Much better. I'm so grateful to be alive. Mitch told us what happened to Mr. Novak, Gene, and Ava's mother. And about the CODE girls. It all sounds crazy."

Josephine clasped her hands, her heart pounding. She needed to get things done, but she had to see Lydia and Zen with her own eyes. They were the two people she trusted most aside from Vince, who had been with her since she began the rebel movement.

They were her support, her rock. They gave her the fuel to be strong, to continue to risk her life like she would today. She'd told no one of her plans, but she was going to the mountain base. If she couldn't help Ava, she would save Avary. She had to.

"Our fight isn't over yet," Josephine said. "But we are going to end it."

Mitch took Lydia's hands in his. "Babe, I'm going with Councilor Chang. We have some errands to run." He hiked an eyebrow at Josephine, asking her to play along. "We're going to be gone all day, but I'll be back."

She wasn't sure if Lydia knew the mountain base would soon be attacked, but he had answered her question. Zen and Cleo didn't seem to know, since they didn't say anything.

Lydia grabbed Mitch's hand. "Wherever you're going, let me go with you. I can help."

"I can too." Cleo's eyes gleamed hopeful.

Zen placed a hand on his daughter's arm. "When you are ready. You need more practice."

Cleo nodded and held a smile. She must be happy her father hadn't dismissed her wish to join the rebels, like before. But if she knew Rhett was in danger, she would leave without his permission. Josephine felt she had no right to intervene, so she said nothing.

Mitch kissed Lydia's hand and rose, his tone playful. "Not this

173

time. You need your rest, because when I come back, I'm going to exhaust you."

Lydia's cheeks turned pink, but she pushed to stand by planting her trembling hands on the sofa arm. Tears pooled in her eyes, and her voice cracked.

"Mitch, Councilor Chang—whatever you're doing, I'm with you. Please keep each other safe, and both of you come back. If you don't, then you might as well have left me to die when Novak shot me."

Mitch swallowed and shuddered. Lydia's words gutted Josephine, too. There was no guarantee either of them would live.

Zen and Cleo stood, their expressions grave and worried.

Josephine sauntered toward the door with Mitch. She looked over her shoulder to Zen, Cleo, and Lydia. She memorized their faint smiles and their salutes as she rushed out.

CHAPTER THIRTY-MOUNTAIN BASE

RHETT

Rhett had just finished changing Avary's diaper on the mattress, getting ready to tuck her in for the night, when the door opened and Ozzie entered with a tray and placed it on the table by the medicine cabinet.

"Want some dinner, Papa?" Ozzie said. "I'll watch Avary. Why don't you eat?"

His stomach rumbled. He hadn't realized how hungry he was until aromas of ground meat, beans, and mashed potatoes filled the space. Rhett had been so busy taking care of his daughter and managing peoples' schedules that he hadn't had time to stop by the cafeteria.

"Thanks, Ozzie. What would I do without you?" He took a seat and scooped up the beef with a spoon.

A rebel team had gone scouting recently and had found some silver utensils. They weren't in the best condition, but they were good enough to use, after some cleaning.

Never thought I'd be so excited to have spoons.

While Rhett enjoyed his dinner, Ozzie cooed and rubbed Avary's belly.

"How's everyone doing?" He drank water from a bowl and placed it on the tray with a light thud.

"I checked up on Payton. He's fitting right in. I'm just keeping

175

busy. I have to, or I think I'll go crazy."

He understood Ozzie's concern, but Russ and Justine were there to keep Ava and the girls saf. Hopefully the memo Councilor Chang had sent to Mr. Park would give them the cover they needed.

"I don't know if I can trust Justine," Ozzie said.

He stopped, the spoon going halfway to his mouth. "Ava trusts her, so I will too."

"Your papa is always positive," Ozzie said to Avary, holding her hand.

A beep came from Rhett's chip. He checked through his messages, but came up empty. Strange. That had never happened before.

Something must be wrong with the reception. He had to check soon. But then a text came through from Councilor Chang.

> Your base has been found. Korean ISAN will have soldiers on the perimeter. I'm sending gliders for pickup and will place your people at ANS. Get out NOW. Go to the forest. Stay safe.

What had he just read? Rhett had to read it again. He closed the message and rose. His mind was a jumbled mess, but his body grew deadly calm. No use freaking out and panicking. He was trained to be a leader, trained to face danger and moments like this.

Leave the mountain? This was their home, their safe haven which he had guarded well. How had they been found?

Rhett had to face the facts. He had always known there was a possibility he would have to lead the rebels elsewhere, one day. Novak had been after them, and if not him, he assumed someone might. *Get out now.*

Rhett opened the cabinet above the cot. The diapers tumbled down. He didn't have time to deal with the mess. He grabbed the baby carrier, adjusted the straps around his body, and tucked Avary inside as he told Ozzie about Chang's message.

Ozzie's blue eyes grew wide and he swallowed hard. "Holy mother of all mothers. Are you sure? Did you read the message right? Why go with Mr. San?"

Rhett didn't like the idea either, but there was nowhere else to go that could accommodate all his people. He understood the shock Ozzie must be feeling, and he appreciated him not freaking out.

"I assure you, our people will be safe." Rhett held Avary's hand and the weight of her steadied him for the horror to come. "Anyway, we have no choice." He was about to give Ozzie orders, but the door opened.

Reyna entered. "Something is happening. I'm on aerial patrol and it's beeping, but I don't see anyone on the perimeter. Payton is at the lookout station and he couldn't see anything, either."

His pulse raced. Korean assassins couldn't have come so soon, unless Chang's message had come through late. He told Reyna of Chang's text and shock rendered her speechless.

"Reyna," Rhett said, his heart thundering, "inform our people what's happening and take them to the forest. Ozzie, gather our soldiers and meet at the glider entrances. Bring weapons. Lots of them."

After Ozzie and Reyna left, he opened the medicine cabinet and pushed a hidden red emergency button by the syringes—a button he'd hope he never had to use. A whirling siren blasted through the air. *There: that should speed things up.*

Footsteps thudded in chaos outside the door. He reached

under the cot and grabbed the emergency backpack filled with diapers, formula, bottles, a change of clothes, a blanket, and Ava's father's journal and phone.

Rhett rushed out the door toward the control room, ignoring the frantic footfalls pounding around him, toward the media room where the hidden door led to the tunnel. The long tunnel would take them directly to the forest.

As Avary bounced with the beat of his quick steps, he covered her ears from the shrill of the alarm. He passed the elevator and the garden, then dashed up the stairs. Just as he entered the lookout room, the noise died. *Good.* Reyna had led their friends out.

Payton's eyes grew wide when he saw Rhett, and they got even bigger when his gaze landed on Avary.

"What's going on, Rhett?"

He didn't have time to explain. "First, tell me what's happening."

Payton pointed to the mounted screen. "The infrared motion sensor picked up movement, and the high-tech camera should have shown who or what's out there, even in the darkness. But, nothing."

"Are you sure it's not the wind?"

Payton pointed to the left corner screen. "If it were just the breeze, that whole section of wild grass would sway."

"Turn on the camera light," Rhett said.

"Are you sure?"

He didn't know. On the one hand, they'd already been found, but Councilor Chang's message had been brief. Would he be confirming their whereabouts? Should they wait and do nothing?

A boom resonated from the other side of the peak. The mountain trembled, but not hard enough to cause them to stagger.

If the bombs kept coming, the entire place would blow.

Another blast sounded farther away. Perhaps ISAN wasn't sure of their exact location and was trying to draw out the rebels.

Perhaps Mr. Park didn't plan on destroying them all at once with one explosive. He'd wanted to salvage anyone with powers. This bought Rhett some time. But still, he had to hurry.

He grabbed Payton's wrist. "Listen carefully. I need you to take my daughter and catch up to Reyna. They're already at the underground tunnel. It's located in the media room. The wall cabinet will be open."

"But …"

Rhett unclipped the baby carrier and adjusted it over Payton with Avary still inside. "Everything she needs is in the backpack." He slung the pack's shoulder straps around Payton's arms. "Follow Reyna to the forest. Councilor Chang will be sending gliders there for a pickup."

Payton wrapped his arms around Avary in front of his chest. "What about you? And how did I end up with your daughter again while bombs explode?"

Payton sounded nervous. Being responsible for a child's life was huge.

He recalled Ava handing their daughter to Payton at the ISAN secret base just before the bombs had detonated. He'd protected her before, and could be trusted to do so again.

"I have something to do," Rhett said. "No one will leave this place alive if I don't cause a distraction. Please keep my daughter safe. Do whatever it takes."

Rhett had known fear twice. Once when Ava hadn't made it out of ISAN with him, and today, this very moment, when he had to give up his daughter knowing he might not see her again. But he had no choice. He was doing this for her and all the people who had left the network with him.

Rhett peppered tender kisses on his daughter's forehead as he inhaled the sweet baby powder scent and memorized her beautiful face. Her eyes, so like his own, held his gaze as if she knew. When she began to whimper, his heart splintered.

"I'll be back, Avary, and Mommy will be back home soon." He swallowed hard, trying not to choke up. "I love you very much. Never forget that."

He snapped out of the daze when another boom shook the walls.

"Go," Rhett said, and practically shoved Payton out the door.

He watched Payton enter the media room, then he sprinted to Ozzie at the transporter entrance. Ozzie waited by the first glider with five of their friends. Rhett didn't want anyone else to put their lives on the line, but he couldn't do it alone.

Ozzie handed him a gun and a Taser. "Do you have a plan?"

Rhett shoved his weapon inside his waistband and focused on each person in turn. "I need all of you on foot, with me and Ozzie in the glider. Ozzie will draw the enemy's attention. We need to buy Reyna some time."

Ozzie tapped his chip and the darkness of the night crept in as the grand doorway began to open. He hopped on the first transporter while Rhett and the team slipped out a hidden exit and hiked up a makeshift set of stairs heading up the mountain.

The cool night wind chilled Rhett to the bone. He shivered as he pressed his back to the rocky surface, a Taser in his hand. His foot slipped on the narrow pebbled path, and dirt and rocks fell.

Rhett grabbed a root sticking out from a tree. He tugged at it to make sure it would hold his weight, then used it to pull up and over to a flatter surface. He extended his arm to help the next person and crawled to the nearest boulder to hide as the glider circled where Rhett had been climbing to give them some light and draw attention to ISAN.

Ozzie's voice crackled through Rhett's chip, but only the last sentence was clear. "Did you see me?"

Rhett tried to reply, but it didn't go through. He held up a fist, directing his troop to get ready, then flexed his wrist like he was knocking, and sped ahead. He'd almost reached cover behind a boulder when a flash of red laser light zapped in front of him, barely missing his toes.

He dove over the laser, tucked into a roll, and landed by a cluster of bushes. His team followed him. Rhett peered out. *There.* Five assassins dressed in all-black jumpsuits, figures wearing masks that made them look even more identical, marched toward him.

Rhett led his team to the clusters of thickets. Stomach down on the dirt, he pulled his gun and aimed. Then he hesitated. Taser pellets would bounce off the assassins, bullets most likely the same. They had to have a weak spot.

The assassins spread out, searching for something. A way in to the mountain base? Rhett had to keep them in this area. If the soldiers went farther out, they might see his people exiting the tunnel.

One of the rebels shifted behind him. The sound of rocks falling off the cliff echoed. Rhett bit his bottom lip, his heart pounding.

"Stay down," he barked an order.

Please. Go away. The rebels had no chance of surviving if they got caught.

Rhett aimed for the assassin's chest. It was difficult to see in the darkness, but Ozzie's glider gave him enough light. And with his precision aiming, he wouldn't miss. When he caught a glimpse of the assassin's face, he stalled. He pictured his daughter.

Avary would have become one of those CODE girls if Ava's mother hadn't stolen her from Novak. These girls were someone's daughters, someone's sisters. He couldn't think of that right now. He had people to save.

The soldier halted three yards from the cluster of thickets where Rhett and his crew hid. *What was she doing?* Something arched overhead and thudded next to his feet.

"Run!" Rhett hollered.

While his team dispersed, he somersaulted over the dry grass to avoid Taser pellets and pulled the trigger. His friends didn't call him *Sniper* for no reason. The bullet hit its target in the eye.

The assassin was flung back and collapsed, another bomb rolling out of her hand. Rhett hid next to a boulder just in time, only hearing a hissing sound. It wasn't an explosive, as he'd expected. Perhaps a sleeping gas.

Red Taser lights cut through the darkness, aiming for the rebels crouched behind clusters of trees. Then, whacks and thumps resonated.

The sound of Rhett's gun had alerted the other CODE girls nearby, and so did Ozzie's gliders, hovering.

"Look who I have here," a girl's voice boomed.

Rhett whirled and fired in almost the same instant. The light from Ozzie's glider passed over them, giving Rhett a clear view.

The bullet hit the side of the soldier's neck, blood seeping down her uniform. She should be on her knees screaming from the pain, but she showed no emotion.

She picked up Rhett by his shirt and flung him. He tumbled

downhill until he slammed into a cluster of rocks. Pain rippled through his back, but he pushed off the dirt and ran into the darkness behind a tree.

Rhett tripped over bodies and fell to his knees. He'd stumbled upon his people, who had followed him out of the base.

His team—they were all dead.

Oh, God. No.

One had been shot in the head. Another had a broken back. A third had his heart pulled out. When had this happened? Rhett had lost sight of his unit.

Shock and guilt hit him hard. He shouldn't have asked them to come. He had sent them to their deaths.

He rushed to another boulder, but an assassin sauntered toward him. He stopped and walked backwards, then turned to run the other way, but another soldier approached. CODE girls appeared wherever he turned. He was the prey to the predators.

Being shot by ten Tasers at once would feel like being struck by lightning. But he would not go down easily.

"You're surrounded." Ozzie's voice blasted through a mic, the transporter hovering over them. "Get the hell away from my friend."

Bullets rained from Ozzie, the soldiers dispersing to take cover. Rhett shot at the nearest assassin and then ducked into the bushes. He moved to the next tree and then the next, hiding behind whatever would cover him as he moved as far away as possible.

One Taser nicked his boot. A faint shock went up his leg, but nothing was strong enough to bring him down. He turned his back for a moment and rammed into a tree. No, not a tree. A CODE girl. She didn't even flinch.

Just as Rhett raised his Taser, she punched his chest and

knocked him backward across the darkness. He landed on his back under a faint crescent moon and countless bright spinning dots.

The same soldier grabbed Rhett and tossed him to an assassin, mocking him as Ozzie continued to send down bullets ... bullets that bounced off of them. Five soldiers raced from the shadows, their feet carrying them swiftly as they hoisted ropes around the glider and began to climb.

An assassin knocked Rhett to his knees just as he tried to warn Ozzie he had company. Rhett's shoulders slumped as his chest rose and fell with exhaustion. He had no fight left in him.

"Say goodbye to your friend."

The girl pointed a gun at Rhett's head, but a bright red light shone around her neck. Then her body lit on fire. She didn't scream. She just stood there, burning to her death.

A familiar figure appeared behind the flame, a blazing angel who had rescued him from his sure demise.

Naomi?

What was she doing out here? She was supposed to be ...

Reyna jumped in front of him and thrust her hands forward as streams of blue lights shot out, sizzling. Rivulets of energy circled around them, forming a protective barrier against the bullets that rained down.

Mia stepped up beside Reyna and thrust her arms outward, creating an invisible wave that shook the ground and sent the CODE girls scrambling backwards off the cliff.

"Why did you follow me?" Rhett shouted, anger in his tone.

Mia flexed her fingers. "Why should you have all the fun?"

"Ava will never forgive me if I left you to these machines," Naomi said.

The humor died abruptly as they peered up at Ozzie's glider

spinning out of control, its lights shining all over the place. The five soldiers had reached the top.

A whoosh of air punched Rhett and his friends, forcing the four of them apart as they tumbled on the rocky slope. Mia had blown the assassins over the cliff. He had seen it with his own eyes.

The soldiers must have used some gadget to recover, because they were coming from that direction toward them while more assassins sprinted from the opposite side.

There was no escaping now.

Rhett heaved himself to his feet, wincing at the protests from his aching body. He slapped his chip and sent a message to Councilor Chang. Bullets whizzed, slicing their way into the earth as a blistering whine cut through the air. Ssomething landed just yards away and detonated.

The ground heaved, opening like a gaping mouth and propelling Rhett and his companions into the sinking landscape. Just before they were swallowed up, Ozzie's craft nose-dived in their direction, like an unstoppable missile, with a deafening roar.

CHAPTER THIRTY-ONE—ALONE

MOMO

Momo didn't know how long she had been in that corner of the supply room. The humming and beeping of the machines were her only company. With her knees tucked to her chest, she glanced at the ceiling, tears streaming down her face.

She had been on the run, doing anything she could to avoid thinking about her squad. But here in the quiet, Jo, Coco, Marissa, Debra, Hector, Jessa, Daniel, and Pete were on her mind.

She missed them so much. The tears would not stop no matter how fast she wiped them. ISAN had trained her to have a rock-hard heart, but she didn't belong to that network anymore. She could decide what she wanted to feel, and that was what she did— let the pain finally sink in.

I'm so sorry I failed you. She should have been faster. That second of hesitation when she tried to save Hector had cost her everyone she loved. But she couldn't think of that now. Rhett counted on her. She would not fail him too. She would not fail the one that cared enough to take her and her friends into the rebel family.

Click. A door opened. Momo froze, her heart bouncing inside her ribcage. Two sets of footfalls. CODE soldiers? She had no weapon, but she crouched and readied her hands to shove the gurneys at them.

Footsteps came closer, passing the crates. Closer … closer … almost … one more step, and she would jump out.

"Are you there? It's me, Justine."

Why hadn't she announced herself in the first place? Who was with her? She jolted up. Justine and Russ jumped back, Tasers pointing at her.

"It's just me." Momo raised her hands and offered an innocent smile. She supposed she should have given them a warning too.

"Here." Justine handed her a bundle of cloth.

"Thanks?" She pinched her eyebrows together.

What was she supposed to do with it? Did they plan to take her hostage? If so, she'd hope it didn't include her seeing Mr. Park again. He gave her goose bumps, and goose bumps on top of those goose bumps.

"You must be starving," Justine said. "Sorry. I couldn't bring more."

It must be dinnertime. Momo unwrapped the fabric. Breadsticks and corn on the cob. She loved corn. Her eyes lit up and she bit into the juicy kernels.

She said, through a mouthful, "So, what now?"

Justine and Russ exchanged a glance and smirked. Then he explained. Momo couldn't believe what she was being asked to do, but agreed to do her part.

She couldn't wait to get out of Korea.

CHAPTER THIRTY-TWO—TRAITOR FOUND

AVA

Russ and Justine escorted my team, Hae Jin, Min Hyuk, Sena, and seven CODE soldiers, down the hall. A cool draft greeted us on the glider landing when the door slid open, revealing all the sleek transporters lined up in a row.

Russ had told Park that his ISAN team back home had found Joon Soo, that he had been hiding in the Eastern Sector and was protected at a safe house. Since there was no way to confirm Russ's information, Park allowed his fake mission to go through.

As Russ had predicted, CODE soldiers had to be part of the mission. Russ had entered the fake coordinates, and it was up to me to get to the mountain base.

"Be careful," Russ said, his voice stern. He leaned closer. "I've put weapons and suits inside the back cabinet." Then he retreated to meet everyone's gazes. "I'll see all of you after you've captured Joon Soo. Good luck."

After we went inside the glider, we sat in our assigned seats. The two CODE girls took the front and the rest were situated in the passenger section with us. My skin crawled as the assassins watched every move I made and listened to everything we said.

"You okay?" I placed a hand on Hae Jin's fingers, tapping her Taser. She seemed nervous.

"I think so," she said.

We hadn't gotten a chance to talk. I wanted to reassure her that Russ's plan would be carried out, but I couldn't guarantee there would be no hiccups. She had tried to escape with her team, but had been caught, and here we were, attempting it again.

This time, she wouldn't fail. She had me.

Hae Jin leaned lowered and retied her bootlace. I bent to swipe my ankle, knowing she wanted to talk.

Hae Jin whispered, "Mr. Park ordered me to terminate you on this mission. It's the only reason why he kept me alive. We're good as dead if we return."

"Don't worry. We're not going back. Is there anything else you have to tell me?"

"There's a traitor." Hae Jin sat up when the soldier tapped her shoulder from the seat behind her.

"Who?" I said through a cough.

She stole a quick glance behind us and then turned back to me. I wasn't sure who she was looking at—Min Hyuk or Sena. The boy seemed protective of her, so my bet was on the girl.

I bumped my shoulder against her. "What do you want to do about it?"

She shook her head, which I took to mean that she had no idea. If I'd learned anything from ISAN, it was that anyone could be a double agent—even your best friend. I would keep my eyes on both of them.

When the glider took a turn, the soldier in the driver's seat, the lead, swiped at the hologram monitor. She said something to the girl next to her, her voice growing louder with panic.

"This isn't the way," the lead said. "Something is wrong. I can't control it. It's locked. Call Mr. Park. If you can't reach him, then try Davina."

My cue to get ready. I unhooked the seat belt and jolted up.

The lead turned and glared. "Hey, what are you doing?"

I grabbed Hae Jin out of her seat and tightened my arm around her neck, pressing a gun to her temple with my other hand. "Play along," I said into her ear.

"What are you doing?" Min Hyuk jolted up, a hand to his Taser.

"Don't move" I hissed. "There's a traitor with us. Which one of you is the mole?"

The five CODE girls darted their gaze at each other, confused.

"Brooke, switch places with the driver." I jerked my chin toward the front.

Brooke blinked, hesitant. She arched her eyebrows, as if asking what the hell I was doing. I was going against our plan.

"Go, Brooke, now. Tamara, take the seat next to Brooke. Move it!"

The lead rose and growled, blocking Brooke's way. "Go ahead. Mr. Park told me to kill Hae Jin anyway."

Hae Jin stiffened in my grip. Min Hyuk gawked.

"Did he, now?" Her words gave me an idea. "Who else did he tell you to terminate? I'll do it for you."

The lead's gaze went from Sena to Min Hyuk, and before she opened her mouth to speak, Sena whirled behind him and pointed a firearm at his head. She had a pistol and not a Taser. Park must have given it to her.

My goal had been to flush out the spy, and my scheme had worked.

Hae Jin pointed the Taser at the mole's chest. "Let him go. You told us Jung was the traitor, but we played along. You deceived us, but the truth is out."

"It isn't betrayal if you weren't loyal in the first place," Sena said. The traitor took a fistful of Min Hyuk's hair and yanked him backwards, pressing the gun to his neck. "Turn the glider back to its original location or I'll shoot him." I aimed my Taser at Sena's forehead. "That's not going to happen. When I'm around, I'm in charge, and I've had enough of your shit." I pulled the trigger. The pellet hit smack between her eyes. Blue tendrils engulfed her body as she convulsed and dropped. When a soldier shot her Taser, I shifted to the side and the red laser beam went wide.

Tamara sprinted to the back, and as she removed our suits and a glove out of the cabinet, a soldier tried to punch her. Tamara had managed to put on a glove and pull the trigger. The air punch pushed the assassin backward and she slammed into the teammate behind her.

Brooke grabbed the suits and tossed one to me. I shoved one on like a backpack, yanked a cord from it, and anchored it to the bottom of the chair with a metal hook, as Russ had instructed. My team did the same.

I flipped over a seat and wrung my legs around one girl's neck. She jumped, and I hit my back against the ceiling and collided on a chair. Pain rippled down my spine.

Gripping two armrests to hold steady, I aimed a high kick at her chin. She would have been knocked out cold if she weren't a CODE assassin.

Brooke landed several blows against a soldier's stomach, but the girl just laughed. Hae Jin and Min Hyuk were back-to-back. Tamara used the glove to push back the two assassins, but they kept advancing on her.

"Hold on to something," I shouted.

I leaped over a soldier, my knees bent to absorb the impact, and slammed my palm on a bright red button at the center of the control panel. With a loud clunk, the walls began to descend, whipping up a ferocious gale-force wind.

Russ had informed us that this glider was a new design, and he had given us instructions before we left.

As the transporter plunged, even though the cords kept us safe, I held on to the chair for dear life as all the CODE girls were flung out like trash into the brilliant blue sky.

Extra weight tugged at my feet and I fell halfway out as the transporter righted itself back to its position. I fired at Sena's neck with a Taser, but nothing happened to her. Either my weapon strength was weak, or she must have taken some type of immune serum against the electric shock. With ISAN, anything was possible.

Sena gave a triumphant smirk and pointed a pistol at my cord, her body flapping with the airstream. If that cord broke, I wouldn't be able to hold onto the chair.

"You're the reason this mission failed," Sena yelled over the roaring air. "If I go back, Mr. Park will kill me anyway. And since I'm going to die, why not take you with me?"

Clank! The bullet hit my cord, then I heard a snap. The wind pulled me out of the glider and my stomach dropped. The air stream stole my breath and I couldn't scream as my fingers dug into the leather seat for my dear life.

Rhett. Avary. My friends. Oh, God. Fear seized my thundering heart. I couldn't die like this. I had to get to the mountain base.

Sena scream trailed off into the atmosphere as she freefell. My fingers slipped, and death looked me in the eyes.

And I … I didn't plummet with her. The wind pushed me in all directions, and four arms came into view. Brooke, Tamara, Hae Jin, and Min Hyuk had held on to my suit.

Tears pooled in my eyes, and I wanted to cry.

"Trying to leave without us?" Brooke yelled over the thrashing gale.

"Why do you get all the fun?" Tamara laughed.

"I love you!" I hollered.

After my team hauled me up, I sat on the driver's seat while Brooke slapped the red button. When the glider walls sealed back, I punched in the coordinates and we were on our way to the mountain base.

Hold on, Rhett. Hold on, Avary. I'm coming.

CHAPTER THIRTY-THREE—THE SETUP

MOMO

After Momo filled her stomach with breadsticks and corn on the cob, she entered the lab from her hiding place. The doctors and nurses had come and gone. About half of the elders had been declared dead and they had been sent to the funeral home, but Rhett's father was still alive.

As per Russ's instruction, she climbed inside an empty hub and tapped a button. The top lid sealed shut. No one could see inside, but she could see out.

The door whooshed open. Footsteps approached. Shadows fell over her, and a masked individual pushed her pod. Only the ceiling came to view as the container she hid in sailed across the tile floor, turned the corner, and rode the elevator.

Momo couldn't tell how many floors she went. She only knew it felt like forever.

She shifted and bounced as the pod rolled again, likely over a gravel path. The moon and stars appeared. More footfalls pounded.

A set of dim lights flashed over her hub. It must be a glider. Momo felt a sense of ease when Russ's face came into view.

"Where are you taking them?" Russ's voice sounded muffled.

She couldn't see to whom he was talking.

"A place they can never return from," the voice said.

A few heartbeats later, a fist knocked three times on the hub. Her cue from Russ. It was now or never.

Momo pushed the button. When the top lid opened, she sat up. The wind chilled her bones as she took in the trees, bushes, rocky slopes, and the concrete pathway the CODE girls marched on toward their gliders. They were on the mountain in Seoraksan National Park, at high altitude and near a cliff.

The pods were inside a mega ISAN transporter. Hers was the last in line to be carried in—the only one left by the ramp. Park was nowhere to be seen, but a few assassins were in the glider while the rest were outside.

Russ had said he had no idea how his plan would play out, but she had to get the soldiers' attention.

"Hello!" Momo hopped out onto the concrete platform.

The two soldiers inside the transporter lunged, missed, and grabbed each other instead.

"Get her!"

Momo backed away to the cliff, all the assassins' attention on her, as Justine and Russ darted inside the transporter with all the pods.

Russ planned to steal the glider? How would he get away with \something that huge? She didn't want to think that far. She backed up until her feet couldn't find purchase, the soil sliding off the cliff.

"Trying to catch a ride?" a CODE girl with blood smeared across her cheek said.

She wanted to call for help, but Russ and Justine's cover would be blown. Fine. She could do this. Sacrifice herself so Rhett could have his father back. After all, her squad was all dead. She could join them in the afterlife.

"Stop, or I'll jump." One more step, then Momo would fall to her death. She couldn't even see how far she would drop in the darkness below.

"You're not going to die by falling." The same assassin took out her gun and aimed for Momo's head. "You're going to die at my hands."

Momo wouldn't let her have the satisfaction. She'd rather die on her own terms. She said her goodbyes to the world and pivoted to jump, but then a whistle rang out from behind her. The assassin furrowed her brow.

When the whistle came again, Momo threw a quick glance below, and then gave the soldier a wide grin. She should have known Russ would have backup.

"Not this time, machine." She gave her the middle finger and freefell backwards. Oh, the joy of seeing the shock on the assassin's face.

Momo's stomach plummeted, then her heart slammed against her chest as she bounced on a net. Zeke had caught her—or rather, she'd fallen onto the right spot. The net had metal rods that punctured the rocky surface to hold her weight.

Zeke held onto a rope that anchored on the mountain face just the same. She shifted until she hugged the cool overlay. They stayed there in the darkness, the night hiding them from view.

Dirt sprinkled on her face. The assassins must be pacing on the edge of the cliff, searching for her.

"Are you okay?" he whispered.

"I'm fine now that you're here." She flinched from the sound of bullets.

He put up a hand. "Stay here. I'll go take a look."

She grabbed his wrist. "No. I'll go with you. Russ and Justine might be in trouble."

He waggled his brows. "Then ... hold on tight. It's going to be a fast ride."

She wrapped herself around his back, her knee nudging some of the gadgets hooked around his waist. Then a ropelike material launched from his belt.

Spikes came out of the rope and anchored on the dirt. He pressed something on his chip and she felt a jerk behind her belly button. As she tightened her grip, they soared upward. When they landed on top of the hill, the CODE girls fired their Tasers at Russ and Justine.

Zeke handed Momo a Taser he had pulled out of his back pocket and yanked her under the transporter's rear wheel for cover. More assassins swarmed through the ground opening, onto the concrete path.

"What do we do?" She gasped for air, her pulse racing out of control. There were too many of them.

He gave her a glove hooked to his belt and put his on. He jerked to the side to duck a Taser beam. Momo had seen this weapon on one of the soldiers the day her squad was killed. She knew exactly how to use it.

They dashed to the front wheel and curled their fingers to release blasts of air. The soldiers nearest to them went flying. More assassins attacked with their weapons. Faster and faster, they aimed and released. Then her gadget stopped. She tried again. Nothing.

Did the thing need to be charged?

"I'm out." She sighed.

"Take cover. I'll distract them." He rushed to the back.

At this rate, they might get captured.

Momo threw her glove at the soldier that jumped for her, then ducked a Taser beam and coiled into a ball. She thought she'd escaped, but an assassin pointed a weapon at her head.

This was it. Momo had given it her all. She closed her eyes and thought of her friends as she prayed for a quick death.

She should be shot or dead, but ... *thud, thud, thud.* When she opened her eyes, the assassin was sprawled on the ground. One after the other, bodies collapsed on the concrete around her.

She stood, Zeke beside her, with wide eyes. Russ and Justine stuck their heads out of the transporter. The soldiers lay flat on their backs. Some were running away. There was nowhere to hide. The ground door had sealed.

No way. No way. No way. Momo could cry. She'd thought her squad was dead. How? When?

From the opposite end of the platform, in a line formation, Debra, Jo, Coco, Marissa, Pete, Jessa, Daniel fired their Tasers.

Red laser beams helped them aim, but the pellets that came out of the weapons were neon blue as they darted across space.

In the chaos, Momo lost sight of Zeke, so she ran to the nearest fallen assassin and picked up a capsule that had missed the target. Like the soldiers she had put down at the training room, the veins on their necks protruded and had turned thick and black, wiggling as if worms were buried under their skin.

The capsule was the same as the ones she had stolen from the man she'd thought was Joon Soo. During the fight with the assassins in the training room, she had shoved them in their mouths hoping it would help her. She hadn't known it would work so fast—and thank God it had. She kept the last one inside her pocket for safekeeping.

Momo ran, the light from the Taser beams her only guide, towards her squad. She didn't know what would happen if she got shot by one of the capsules, and she didn't want to find out.

She had made it halfway to her squad when a hand seized her leg. Momo fell flat on her face and the attacker tossed her in the air. Her head smacked the dirt, missing a fist-sized rock by an inch.

"You're dead." The same soldier who had seen Momo dive off the cliff coiled her fingers around her neck.

Momo heard faint voices calling out for her. The team might not find her in time. So close. How ironic to have thought her friends were dead, but she would be the one to die at the end.

Nope.

She wouldn't die today, and she certainly wouldn't die by the hand of the CODE girl.

Momo took out the capsule from her pocket and grabbed the rock by her head with the other hand. Smashing it against the assassin's head with all her strength would do no good. She might as well slap the girl with a feather.

She had to do something drastic. Something that would throw the soldier off. So she slammed the rock into her own head. Warm liquid streamed down her temple. Pain ripped through her skull, but it would be worth it if her plan worked.

The girl blinked, dumbfounded, loosening her grip.

"You don't get to kill me." Momo hit her head again. "I'll kill myself."

"What the hell are you—"

The soldier never finished. As soon as her lips parted, Momo shoved the capsule into her mouth and punched her face so hard, she thought her knuckles had broken. The girl collapsed just as the bright light flashed from the transporter and highlighted them.

Momo stood, her knees wobbly, head pounding.

Zeke and her squad rushed toward her. Jo pulled her into a hug first, and then the rest followed. She felt all their love, and happy tears wet her face.

"Are you okay?" Debra cupped Momo's face and examined her. "That soldier hit your head."

She decided not to explain, or they would be there all night. She nodded instead.

"I thought you were dead." Momo's voice cracked as she looked at every one of her friends.

"We put up a shield in time, but the debris landed on top of us," Jo said. "When we managed to climb out of it after the fire died down, you were gone and we had no reception. After we buried Hector, we walked to the nearest city."

"That took us days." Coco blinked from the brightness from the transporter.

"Hector." Momo lowered her chin.

"You did all you could, kid," Debra said. "Don't be hard on yourself."

Something settled onto her head. When she looked up, Debra said, "It's Hector's cap. He would want you to wear it."

Her lips curled upward in a small smile—but a smile nevertheless. She raised her head high, proud to be wearing Hector's cap and proud to be part of a great squad.

"How did you know where I was?" Momo asked.

"I remember you wanted to go to Korea to help," Marissa said. "So we figured you would find a way to get here because, you know … you always find trouble."

Everyone laughed. It was the truth.

Zeke turned to Jo. "Where and how did you get your hands on those new weapons?"

"I finally was able to get through to Vince." Jo held up her

Taser and opened the component that housed the pellets. "He sent a team to pick us up. They gave us the location and these capsules called CHAVA."

"Thank you, Vince," Momo hollered, then snapped out of the bliss. "Hurry. We need to get to the mountain base."

Zeke scrubbed the back of his head, his eyebrows pinched.

Momo put a hand on his arm, assuming he was worried about a particular rebel. "Don't worry. Tamara is fine. She's with Ava."

As if Russ had heard, he flashed the high beam from the transporter.

"Wait," Zeke said. "You can all ride with me. My glider is faster. I'll tell Russ to take the elders to ANS."

"What about the fallen?" Debra asked. "We can't just leave them."

"They'll be knocked out for a day. Councilor Chang's men are almost here. They're taking the girls."

CHAPTER THIRTY-FOUR–JUST IN TIME

AVA

I landed the glider on the flat surface of the mountain near the transporter entrance. Rhett and his unit might still be inside the base distracting ISAN soldiers.

Instead of entering from the front, I led the team toward the back, way by the waterfall where my people did laundry. I tried calling Rhett, once inside, but there was no answer. I couldn't call anyone from my chip—not even my teammates next to me. Mr. Park definitely had done something to scramble the reception and my map ability.

"This way." I stepped onto a large flat stone that led to the other side of the stream.

The steady murmur of water rushing and gathering into a pool at the bottom drowned out the noises we made. Lit lanterns hung on the bridges, and some rested on the taller boulders. Aside from the dim light coming from the main entrance, these were our only light sources.

Pounding footsteps echoed. I held out a hand to my team and tried again to pull up my map. This time, it worked. Good timing. Park's effort seemed limited.

Brooke crouched, placed her palm on the dirt, and closed her eyes. "There are too many every direction."

"We can hide in the cave," Hae Jin whispered beside me.

I furrowed my brow. "You've never been here. How do you know?"

"I have the same gift as you." She sounded shy as she tucked strands behind her ear. "You've been a role model. I sort of stalk you."

Min Hyuk placed a hand on Hae Jin's back and smiled at me. He was confirming her conviction and wanted me to believe her.

I gave her a curt nod. "Your words mean a lot." I waved a hand toward north. "Lead the way, Hae Jin."

Her eyes widened, as did her smile. We followed her across the bridge, the water muffling our boots thudding on the wood. I thought I heard more footfalls and glanced behind me toward the section we had entered, but saw no one.

We went up the rocky surface and inside the cave, which was not large, but big enough for us to hide in the darkness.

About ten CODE girls rushed across the bridge while the other ten searched by the water.

"I thought I heard something," one of the assassins said.

"No one is here. We should—"

A bullet hit the upper part of the cave entrance and ricocheted into the water. Dirt sprinkled down.

"There!" someone shouted. "In the cave."

Twenty soldiers with guns against five of us armed with Tasers that did nothing to our adversaries was no fair match. I had to buy us time by bargaining, so I told my team to stay.

"I'm coming out," I bellowed, my voice echoing. "Don't shoot." I walked out with my hands up. "I'm Ava. One of the leaders of the rebellion. I'm the one you want. Just take me and leave the rest of my team alone."

Sounds of fabric rustling and weapons clicking resonated as

guns shifted toward me.

A soldier moved closer, but kept her distance. "That's not going to happen. You're surrounded. All of you are coming with me."

I glanced around, checking for hiding places. I could do more damage if I had a pistol, but I only had a Taser—one shoved inside my back waistband. I could hit one of the lanterns with it and start a fire, but water was nearby.

Shadows crept along the wall. Hope bloomed in my chest. Those shadows weren't CODE assassins, or they wouldn't be hiding. Rescue had come.

"Then it's too bad for all of you," I said. "You're surrounded, too. We didn't come alone."

Thank God for Vince and the guards he'd brought with him. They stepped out of the darkness and raised their high-tech weapons. Almost in unison, they clicked off the safeties, and that one little sound drew the attention of every CODE girl.

"Meet my friends." I smirked.

As if my words were a cue, bullets soared across the water, past the laundry on the boulders, and pierced through the CODE soldiers' suits.

I gasped. At first I'd thought Vince was executing these girls, mowing them down without mercy. But a glint of blue in the air clued me into what was happening. Russ had explained about the capsules when we took over the glider.

After the soldiers were down, Vince waved us over. I sprinted ahead of my team, and he handed each of us the same sort of weapon he'd just used.

Shots rang out from the garden entrance. Rhett?

A bomb exploded—not a big one, but enough to put us off

balance. I stumbled and slammed into the rocky wall, Brooke and Tamara beside me. Hae Jin and Min Hyuk pressed against the boulder behind us.

The earth trembling stopped. We had to hurry. There was no telling if ISAN would blow the mountain.

"Have you seen Rhett? Ozzie? Reyna?" I asked Vince.

"No. We're looking for them."

More gunfire erupted.

I led the team up the rocky stairs and past the vegetable section and the citrus trees, weaving around a pile of debris that had fallen from the ceiling. The farther we got from the garden, the louder the gunfire. We halted by the elevator and peered down.

The CODE army below scattered, some hiding in the shadows. And in the center of the firing squad were Mitch, Councilor Chang, and a few guards.

Vince and his team went down the stairs, but I leaped over a metal rail and landed in a crouch behind Mitch. My team landed beside me, one after the other.

"Where's Rhett?" Mitch asked. "Has he contacted you?"

"No. I was going to ask you."

"No one is here. They must be at the forest."

I shook my head, my heart breaking. "Something is wrong. Rhett would have messaged one of us."

Mitch cupped my face, his expression worried, but he said, "We'll find him. He's alive. And Avary is safe."

"They better be." I snarled. "And Ozzie, Reyna, and our friends. Because, I swear, if they're not, I will be the super-soldier ISAN always wanted, and no one will be able to bring me down."

Mitch swallowed hard and his eyes widened with fear. He had overseen parts of my training and retraining, and knew better than anyone the monster I could become.

He pulled a pistol out of his waistband. "Let's go find our family."

"Go ahead." I jerked a chin toward Chang, hiding by the wall with my crew and shooting at the assassins. "I'll be right behind you."

There was somewhere I needed to go first. I sprinted across the other side while dodging bullets. When I arrived at a door, I planted my palm on the scanner to slide it open and waved at the dust clogging the air. Half of our room had been destroyed.

"Rhett?" Even knowing he was likely not there, I had to try. "Rhett?" I pushed through the shattered medicine cabinet and shoved a broken TAB aside. Coughing, I weaved around a cracked table, then to our cot, the only things still intact.

I picked up Avary's stuffed toy and hugged it, inhaling the scent of baby powder. Diapers were scattered on the bed. Rhett had been in a rush. Avary's emergency backpack was not under the cot. *Good.*

If they weren't here, then they had to have escaped to the forest, but ... I dropped the stuffed toy and walked with my heart in my throat to the pile of soil and rocks. A hint of a glider's wings poked through. I backed away in horror and sprinted out the door. Not inside the mountain, but on top.

CHAPTER THIRTY-FIVE–HER TEAM

MOMO

Momo's heart thumped with excitement. She couldn't wait to see everyone at the mountain base. Especially Rhett. She couldn't wait to tell him she'd found his father, and to share how she'd single-handedly knocked out two CODE girls with the capsules she had stolen. But as Zeke's glider circled the peaks, she snapped out of the daydream.

"I just got a call from Councilor Chang," Zeke said from the driver's seat. "Rhett and his crew are under attack. We're to land close to the forest. Everyone, load up your weapons with CHAVA."

She exchanged glances with her squad. They had escaped ISAN, had been separated, and lost cherished friends, but now they were together again. This time, their mission wasn't to destroy. This time, their task was to save lives. Even the CODE assassins.

Zeke parked the transporter at a distance so they wouldn't be spotted. They poured down the ramp, Debra in the lead. Zeke didn't hold a weapon, but instead put on the gloves as he ran.

As their legs propelled them toward the sound of gunfire, they used the grass to their advantage and kept low. People wearing black scattered, and it was difficult to tell who was who. Only the crescent moon and the red laser beams were there to light up the night.

"Take cover!" Jo hollered.

Momo grabbed Coco and Marissa and vaulted under a shield Debra had created. The rest of the team hid under the same umbrella.

Something flew toward their direction, but Zeke triggered his gloves and the blast of air pushed it back. It landed fifty yards away and exploded with a roar. Dirt and grass flew in every direction.

"Move!" Debra shouted.

They trailed her steps, boots shuffling. There … finally. Blue capsules soared out of the weapons, but from whom, Momo couldn't tell.

Debra put a finger to her lips to hush them. Too late. CODE soldiers surrounded them.

Someone jumped on Momo's back and she flattened to the grass. The heavy weight flew off, and Jo hauled her up. Jo shoved Momo next to Coco, lightning from her fingertips zapping at the assassins nearby.

Momo had forgotten she was no longer underground in Seoul. She had a special gift, and now was the time to use it. So she ran as fast as her legs carried her, becoming one with the wind and the earth. As she sprinted, she shot at the assassins' necks.

Momo darted from soldier to soldier as she recalled the day ISAN guards had come and blown up their safehouse. She had thought she'd lost Debra and many of her friends, that day. She thought about how Bobo had died, Coco being stabbed by a CODE girl, and then how Davina had snapped Hector's neck. All these memories fueled her to run faster.

She pitied the CODE girls, but she hated the adults who had created them even more. These girls hadn't asked to be lobotomized and then trained to be killers. And, because of this, she would try to save as many as possible.

A hand gripped her arm, and she halted abruptly. Her shoulders slumped and air puffed out of her mouth. The ground tilted and her legs turned to lead.

"You can stop now." Jo embraced her.

She eased into Jo's arms, but not even a second had passed before something landed beside them with a soft thud, then detonated.

Momo launched in the air and dropped hard, her face rubbing against the itchy grass. She let out a moan as the ringing in her ears began to fade away and consciousness started to return. She tried to push up with trembling arms, but every time Momo tried, she collapsed.

She should have died. So, not a bomb, then, but something chemical. Maybe like the sonic wave that seized their power, this time, in the form of gas.

CHAVA-filled capsules flew past her, blue lights streaking across the night. She caught a glimpse of black suits and Russ and the guards, then Momo's team joined behind them.

Someone grabbed her shirt and yanked her up. "Sleeping on the job. By the way, Mitch's father is safe. And try to keep up."

Momo laughed, but it sounded like a whimper. She loved the newfound friendship with Justine.

"Rhett is going to be so happy when he finds out his father is alive." Momo matched Justine's speedy pace.

"They're so lucky we care." Justine snorted, and then her expression became grave at the sight of the destruction and chaos ahead.

There was one person Momo wanted to find. She was no longer a scared mouse, and she would prove it to Davina.

CHAPTER THIRTY-SIX–UNDERGROUND

RHETT

Rhett groaned and blinked, trying to focus. Where was he? He couldn't see much in the darkness. Only soil above and around him. The high beam from the glider was the only light, and the wings provided pockets of space. Had he crashed?

He tried to push up, his hands on the cold, damp soil, but he couldn't move and pain shot through his muscles. Something pressed on his legs and something warm wet his skin. He touched the side of his waist near the dandelion tattoo and realized that it was blood.

Rhett's heart thundered as he recalled the explosion, being pulled under, then Ozzie's transporter falling on top of them.

His friends. Oh, God his friends. "Ozzie. Reyna. Naomi. Mia."

So cold. Trembling, his teeth rattled. His words wouldn't carry. He didn't have the strength. He spat out grainy sand and blew some out from his nose.

Someone moaned, and the dirt shifted.

"Rhett?" said a soft voice to the left of him.

"Reyna. Are you hurt?" He extended a hand through the damp dirt, but he couldn't touch her.

"I can't move. Dirt is pressing on me. I don't think … I can't breathe."

Reyna's rattling voice told him she felt cold, and Rhett had difficulty taking in air, too.

"Ozzie!" Rhett said. "Naomi. Mia."

"Here." Naomi moaned. "Everything hurts. I think I'm above you, and Mia is beside me. She's breathing, but she's not responding."

"Holy mother of all mothers. I'm here, inside the glider." Ozzie sounded farther away, the light from the transporter blinking.

They must have been underground for some time. Soon that light would die, and soon they would run out of oxygen.

"We're going to get out of here. Help is on the way." Rhett didn't know if his message had gone through to Councilor Chang.

If she had sent her guards, how would they fight off all those assassins? Bullets and Tasers were a joke.

He prayed that Payton had escaped with Avary and they were safe at the selected destination. Oh, Avary … his beautiful daughter. He saw her face, her smile. Inhaled her baby powder scent. He *had* to stay alive for her and for Ava. But it would take a miracle.

The ground above shook, breaking Rhett out of his reverie. Reyna gasped, and dirt fell on Rhett's face. He raised his hand to wipe it off his eyes, but tremendous pain stabbed at him. If he didn't get help soon, he wouldn't die from lack of oxygen. It would be from blood loss.

Sleepy. So sleepy. He shivered as the pain on his side grew stronger. His eyelids felt like bricks. He just wanted to sleep.

"Rhett." Reyna sounded far away. "Are you okay? Rhett!" Her voice boomed this time.

He flashed his eyes open. He must have dozed. The glider creaked and jerked. His stomach dropped as he fell lower, sinking into the dirt up to his chest. Naomi screamed, and so did Reyna.

"Where's Mia?" Rhett said, short of breath. "You've got her, right, Naomi?"

Naomi gasped, panic in her voice. "I've got Mia, but she's … I don't think she's breathing. I'm touching her neck, and there's no pulse. And … it's wet. Oh, God … oh, oh, oh. There's a metal rod stabbed through her neck. What do I do?"

His heart caved in. He didn't know Mia that well, but she had come around. She'd even come on her own to help him. He closed his eyes to say a prayer for her, and to sleep. He just wanted to sleep.

Ozzie cleared his throat. "Just in case we don't make it out, I wanted to say it was an honor to have you all as my friends. Even Mia …" Ozzie gasped sharply, holding in a sob.

"Same here." Reyna sniffed.

The light from the glider flickered a warning. It was on its last leg of power.

"Thank you for welcoming me into your family," Naomi said. "I thought my foster father would kill me, but I'm glad I get to die with my friends."

"I'm still mad at all of you for coming back for me," Rhett said. "And if you die, I will never forgive you. So you better stay alive."

"Funny, isn't it?" Reyna snorted, despite their predicament. "Ozzie, Rhett, and me. The three of us have been a team searching for Ava. I hope she's looking for us now."

She is. Hold on.

If Rhett died here, he would do so in peace. After the escape, he'd found Ava and helped her regain her memories, giving her back the life that belonged to her. And to have been a father to Avary, even for a short time, was a blessing. But he wished for more: to see her take her first steps, hear her call him *dada*, and experience many of her firsts.

He was one of the lucky ones who had family and friends who loved and cared about him. Casualties were inevitable during a war, and to have lived this long was the best gift of all.

His arm with the chip wasn't buried, and he had an idea. The last time he'd attempted to use it, the reception had been blocked, but he had to try. If more bombs went off, they would be buried alive, but regardless, recording his voice would give him some peace.

He didn't care if his friends listened. He pressed a button and spoke.

My dearest Ava ...

Ozzie, Reyna, Naomi, Mia, and I are stuck underground, and we can't call out for help. I know you're looking for us. But just in case I don't make it, I want to tell you how precious you and Avary are to me.

I found love when I first looked at you. And I knew at that moment that I wanted to make you mine. No matter how dire our circumstances were, I was determined for us to be together. Only think of all the happy times we shared, if I'm gone. Because, babe, memories are what keep us alive.

I love you and Avary so much, and I'll love you just the same even when I'm gone. Be the dandelion for our daughter, and always be resilient. Don't look back. Go forward.

I have a place for you and our daughter. Ask Mitch. He'll know where.

I love you endlessly,
Rhett.

Rhett hummed a tune. Their song. The song he sang to Ava at the ISAN compound and when he sang to her on the rooftop of the abandoned building as one last desperate measure for her to remember him.

Put your hand on my beating heart,
as we dance under the stars.
I'll sing you a love song, mending all time's scars.
It was clear and simple you see.
We fell in love with just one glance.
We knew it was special when we took a chance.
A gamble worth taking, true love in the making.
We are forever. You and I.

Rhett had seen Ava across the room at ISAN compound, and the electric charge that ran through him as their eyes locked was stronger than anything he had ever felt before.

She had shot him a coy look and sauntered over with a smirk, and then their friendship had bloomed. Their conversations were filled with jokes and playful banter, a spark of attraction that only grew with every accidental brush of their hands as they trained together. He knew even then that it was only a matter of time before they fell in love.

He could almost feel his girl's arms around him and hear her laughter echoing through the Fun Zone. Her gray eyes sparkled with amusement as snowflakes cascaded around them like confetti. With a smile, she had convinced him to get a dandelion tattoo—a reminder of their first kiss and their resilience in the face of adversity.

"You afraid of needles?" She waggled her eyebrows.

214

"No. I'm not afraid of anything." The playful tone left him, replaced by a somber one. *"Except of losing you."*

"Ava," Rhett said her name like a prayer, for it would be the last time he'd get to say her name out loud.

He had been strong and hopeful until then, but when soft sobs came from Reyna and Naomi, tears streamed down his face as he thought of not just Ava and their daughter, but the friends who would die with him.

The deafening sound of the explosion reverberated, the shock wave rippling through the ground like a heavy punch. The air pressed in around him, becoming even thicker with each shallow breath. His chest heaved as he fought to breathe, his lungs straining against the thick atmosphere.

Any ounce of hope vanished with the light from the glider.

CHAPTER THIRTY-SEVEN—UNTIL THE VERY END

MOMO

Momo crouched behind a cluster of rocks with a rebel unit. The lights from the parked gliders provided some visibility in the surrounding area of the mountain.

"Mitch and Councilor Chang are by the cliff." Justine pointed north, not far from where they hid.

She wasn't the only one with excellent sight ability. Momo blinked to focus on Mitch. No Rhett by his side. He must be with Ava. Or with another team.

"We're moving," Russ said. "Let's go."

The team sprinted in a tight circle, with Debra and Jo in front. They hid behind clusters of rocks and bushes, dodging bullets and Taser pellets, and when they reached Mitch and Councilor Chang, they made a circle around them, shooting at the approaching soldiers.

"Good to see you all," Mitch said, in a hurry.

"Your father is safe at ANS." Russ shot at an assassin near the tree. "But I don't know his condition. Mr. San will update us soon."

On his way to ANS to drop of the survived elders, Russ had informed Mitch about Momo finding his father.

"I owe you both." Mitch ducked low to dodge a Taser beam.

Russ grabbed her and ducked. A passing bullet would have hit

216

Momo's chest, had he not intervened. Then he looked over his shoulder and met Mitch's determined gaze.

"I told you I would help you find him," Russ said, before whirling to face the soldier perched atop the tree. He aimed and fired, hitting her neck. The assassin toppled to the ground like a marionette with cut strings. "And I always keep my word. Till the very end, my friend. Let's bring everyone home."

Russ's words not only inspired Momo, but her teammates, too. She looked at her friends, one after another. Each one tapped the bill of her cap, pushed back her shoulders and held up her chin.

Momo raised an index finger, then another. Her friends knew what she wanted to do, and as her third finger went up, they shouted, "*Renegades forever!*" and ran. But as she took a step, someone knocked off her hat and yanked her into a hard chest as an arm wrapped around her like a rope.

"I've caught you, little mouse," Davina sneered in her ear,

Councilor Chang shot at the CODE girl, but she twisted to dodge the bullet. Mitch knelt and pulled the trigger again and again, and the assassin dodged every single CHAVA capsule.

Russ jabbed the butt of his gun against the back of Davina's head. She should have been knocked out, but she growled and, still holding Momo, tackled him.

The three of them tumbled, mud caking Momo's body. As Davina fell off the cliff, she clawed at soil and pebbles in desperation, but her stomach dropped as she plummeted.

Momo screamed. Her grasping fingers tangled in a cluster of jutting tree roots as Russ did the same above her. Russ fell past her in the same split second, and she snatched at his arm. He stopped with a jerk, feet dangling.

Oh, God. Please let the root hold our weight. But when she peered down, her eyes grew in horror. Davina had seized Russ's ankle.

"Momo, I've got you. Russ, climb up." Mitch latched on to her wrist, holding on to something above him she couldn't see.

She swallowed hard. Mitch didn't know about Davina, hidden in the darkness below him.

"Little mouse, I guess we're all going to die together after all."

Even with her strength, Momo couldn't hold the weight of two larger people, with gravity against her.

"Russ, grab anything." Mitch's words were strained.

Momo screamed when the root she held pulled out from the cliff and settled lower, dislodging a rain of soil.

Davina wiggled with great heaving tugs. She was trying to bring everyone down with her.

"Stop!" Momo yelled at Russ, who was trying to loosen her hold on him.

"Let me go." Russ's voice was low and raw. "If you fall, Mitch will, too. Lydia is waiting for him."

"What about you?" She teared up, her voice cracking. Her trembling arm strained, and any second her shoulder might pop out of its socket.

"I don't have anyone," he said.

She knew he wasn't trying to sound pathetic. He meant to say he wouldn't be leaving someone who loved him behind, but it didn't matter. Neither would she.

Momo groaned, her face burning in heat and the pressure. "You have friends waiting on you to come back. Please, don't let go."

"Russ, grab something." Mitch sounded desperate. "I swear that if you let go, I'll never forgive you."

Davina gave up pulling on the human chain and began

climbing up Russ's leg, a wild gleam in her eye as she glared at Momo. CHAVA capsules flew toward Davina from Mitch's gun, but she shifted, dodging them effortlessly.

"Mitch," Russ bellowed, "tell Ava I gave it my all. Tell her to be happy. Tell her I love her. Thanks for the good times, buddy. I promised 'until the very end.' This is the end, my friend."

Russ braced his feet against the cliff and twisted, and Momo … her fingers were free, and Russ became smaller and then lost in the darkness with Davina.

"No!" Momo screamed until her voice broke, her heart crushed.

It happened so fast, she couldn't believe it. This was a nightmare she would wake up from. But she didn't wake up. She only saw the darkness and her empty hand.

She barely heard Mitch calling out for his friend, and didn't know how she'd gotten back up onto solid ground. She only recalled Mitch pulling her up, her back pressed on dirt and dried grass, the moon her view as she gasped.

She wanted to cry. She wanted to scream. But she could do neither. ISAN had trained her well on how to push away the horror and the pain. It didn't seem real. She had to get up. Get back to the battle.

She rolled over, her knees digging into the earth as she looked for Mitch and assessed her surroundings.

Mitch dropped to his knees, looking out into the darkness as if he thought Russ would climb back up. One last fake-out.

He didn't seem to care about possible assassins sneaking up on him, so she kept an eye out. She didn't know how long he would just stare into the blackness, but any longer and she would intervene.

Momo put a hand on his shoulder, the only comfort she could offer. She didn't have the heart to tell him his buddy would never return. She looked down at her fingers, felt the absence of Russ's hand, and thought of all the rebels who had each died too soon. She made a silent promise that their deaths would not be in vain.

Momo flinched when Mitch shoved fingers through his hair and made a pained noise, the sound of coming to terms with Russ's death. Her resolve broke when he pounded his fists against the earth repeatedly as he let out a gut-wrenching holler, and she unleashed the tears she had been holding for far too long.

Mitch raised his head and blinked, snapping back, determination in his scrunched features.

"Rhett," was all he said and ran.

CHAPTER THIRTY-EIGHT—THE BATTLE

AVA

I climbed to the top of the highest boulder away from the battlefield and closed my eyes, the wind tousling my hair. A warm, tingling sensation coursed through my veins as I pulled up my map. Hae Jin stood beside me and did the same, Min Hyuk encouraging her.

I concentrated on the bright red dots against the cobalt-blue hologram chart, but that only confused me, since the fallen CODE girls were everywhere and I couldn't pinpoint Rhett among them. I groaned, my frustration building. But I still searched, tugging and yanking at my power, scrutinizing for dots that stood out. That felt right.

My heart is my map, and it will lead to you. My priority was to find Rhett, Avary, and whoever was with him. Everyone else could handle the remaining CODE soldiers with CHAVA.

"Maybe he's not here," Tamara said.

"But Rhett and Ozzie would be the last to leave." Brooke rubbed her face, sighing with worry. "What if they're hurt, or what if they're—"

"Underground." Hae Jin grabbed my shoulders, forcing me to meet her gaze. Excitement danced in her dark eyes. "Ava, they're underground," she said louder. "Over there." She pointed away from the battlefield. "I see four red dots."

"You can track people below land surface?" I parted my lips, jealous but impressed.

The parked gliders around the mountain gave us some lighting, but we would be heading toward the back in the darkness. I turned on my chip to use it as a flashlight, and my team did the same.

I leaped and sprinted across the field. Lights from our chips were beacons in the night. The closer the destination, the harder my heart pounded. And no matter how fast I ran, it still wasn't enough.

The ground had parted. A bomb had caused it, but a glider had sealed the hole up and pushed down into the earth. Might have been the same transporter wing I had seen pierced through our room. It didn't look good, but Hae Jin had said she had seen four dots. And I held on to hope.

Hae Jin halted beside me and panted, her eyes widening, concern marring her features. "There's only three now."

Not the words I wanted to hear. We had to hurry. But we also had to be careful. We might bury them deeper with the wrong move. Worse, we might kill them.

Min Hyuk pointed outward, the light from his chip lighting his face. "We could try to dig, but that would take forever."

"I can lift the glider."

I knew that voice. I swung around to see Justine. She braced her shoulder under one of the wheels and waited for my answer. Mitch and Councilor Chang had come, too. The rest of the unit was likely holding off the CODE soldiers. But the way Mitch avoided my eyes, something was wrong. Lydia? I would ask him later.

"My men are on their way to help," Councilor Chang said.

"They're coming on foot as we speak. We can't land a transporter here. And, Ava, I've just been informed that Payton has your daughter and they're both safe."

I closed my eyes as I released a long sigh of relief and returned to my duty.

Brooke placed her palm down. "I'll part the land so it will be easier for Justine."

We had no time to waste in discussion. I gave Justine the order. We backed away as the ground trembled and cracked. Spider lines traveled around the glider, rippling out from where Brooke had knelt.

Justine inhaled a deep breath and lifted with her whole body: legs, back, and arms. Her face turned red and sweat beaded her forehead. Brooke, Tamara, Hae Jin, and Min Hyuk helped her lift while Mitch, Councilor Chang and I peered down, ready to jump in.

The transporter jerked forward and sprang from the ground with a sickening lurch, ripping up grass and soil before clattering to a stop. Justine fell to her knees, breathless and dizzy from the effort.

One wing was still partially buried in the earth, but where the front windshield had been, there was now only a jagged opening. Ozzie groaned in the driver's seat, his eyes opening and closing.

Brooke rushed to him.

Ozzie held up a hand and then dropped it. His lips parted, trying to talk as Brooke and Councilor Chang attended to him.

Mitch and Tamara followed me as we scrambled down the steep bank and into the deep crater. Rhett lay motionless on the broken wing, the dandelion tattoo visible through rips in his crimson-soaked shirt.

Naomi and Reyna were both unconscious beside him, their clothes caked in mud and blood. My heart raced and I felt an urge to scream, but instead remained calm.

Mitch's eyes, full of fear and panic, darted all over Rhett. A curtain fell over his expression as he wiped his brother's face and placed two fingers on his neck.

"He's breathing." Mitch eased his stiff posture. "That's a good sign."

Mitch waved at Chang's men. One grabbed the upper part of his body, the second held the middle, and the third the lower part, cautious about any broken bones, and supporting his spine.

"Rhett. I'm here." I caressed his face and kissed his forehead. "You're safe now. Can you hear me?"

"Ava," he murmured, his voice hoarse and hardly audible. "Avary."

"She's fine. Don't talk. Rest. I love you."

I wanted to go with him, but I went back down and attended to Naomi. Thank goodness she had a pulse. Two of Chang's men hauled her up while Tamara checked on Reyna. Was there anyone else?

Hae Jin had seen four red dots, then three. If Ozzie, Rhett, and Naomi were alive, then …

My heart stuttered, and I knew before Tamara shouted Reyna was dead. But I refused to believe her. It couldn't be true. I pushed through the soil again, ignoring the cold, and looked at my first friend at ISAN.

No, no, no. Oh, please God, no. I sat down in the mud, hugged her lifeless body, and sobbed. My tears fell on her forehead, leaving pale spots in the grime. I dusted the sand off her face and her hair.

I gently placed my palm over her eyes to close them and kissed her cheek.

"I'm so sorry, my friend. I will win this battle for you. I swear I will."

Brooke stood on the edge, peering down at me. She crossed her arms and clutched at her sides, as if to hold herself together. "Ava, Ozzie said Mia is down there. Find her. Hurry."

Mitch, Tamara, and a few of Chang's guards searched. I used my arms like a rake and plowed through the soil, even though I knew she had no chance of surviving. *Only three red dots.*

Hae Jin was beside me, her eyes closed in concentration. "There." She pointed toward the other side of the wing.

I dug and dug. My team did the same. An arm stuck out. I swallowed hard, and with my friends' help, we pulled. Mia's beautiful face emerged from the buried dirt, a small metal rod piercing through her neck, her shirt soaked in blood. Soft whimpers escaped me and I held her in my arms and wept.

"Thank you, Mia," I whispered, and kissed her cheek, grains of sandy dirt clinging to my lips. "I know you're in a better place, but you will be missed."

Ozzie had told Brooke that five had gone under, but only three came out. But Hae Jin had seen four red dots because Mia was already dead.

This was war, and there were casualties. That was what we'd learned in ISAN. But every person at the mountain base was a friend, no matter how long I had known them.

We were a family, all with a similar goal. We only wanted to live. The CODE girls had been no different before ISAN had stolen their ability to think for themselves. It was time to end this, and I had a plan.

While Chang's men took care of the wounded and the dead, I ran back to that damn battlefield with purpose, my squad falling in line beside me. Momo came sprinting from a distance, almost a blur with her powerful speed. She skidded to a stop and nearly collided with me.

"Russ ... Russ ..." Panting, she couldn't speak. Tears streamed down her face, and she hyperventilated. "Russ. Cliff. Gone. I tried. Davina. I'm so sorry."

I understood her broken words, and a powerful shudder racked down my back. Something in me broke. Russ had fallen off the cliff? I would ask a team to search for him. He could still be alive. He'd better be!

My heart couldn't take any more sorrow. More people would die if we didn't win. This war would determine what the future held for ISAN, the rebels, and the world.

I pushed away the agony of loss and my worries over Rhett and Russ. As I ran, I barked orders. When I climbed to the top of the slope, Jo and her crew and Vince and his men rushed toward us. Vince's men, with backpacks full of CHAVA capsules, passed out supplies.

The CODE soldiers' weapons pointed at us from a distance, and a cohort turned and headed our way. They were too far, and their bullets would not reach us, so we had seconds to spare.

I peered downward, watching them dash uphill towards us with purpose and determination. This had to be the spot: close enough to do damage and yet far from danger. I'd told my team my plan, and it had better work.

"They're fast," Momo said. "They'll reach us soon."

Her voice was calm and without fear, as she'd been trained. And she trusted me the way my rebel family did, all of them lined up on either side of me. Even Councilor Chang and Mitch. They reloaded their weapons and waited for my order.

"I believe this is yours." Hae Jin, standing on my other side, reached around and gave Momo something metal and round. "One of our assassins told me she took this from your pocket when Davina kidnapped you. Sorry about the chocolate bar. The girl ate it."

"My penny." Momo offered a small smile. "Thanks. It'll bring us good luck. I wished I had it when I was with ... Russ."

Russ is alive. He has to be.

I guessed the coin meant something to her, but I had no time to ask. The CODE soldiers had come.

"When I count to three, fire and do not stop until I say." I hollered an order, then turned to Hae Jin beside me. "Pull up your map and find all the CODE girls."

She nodded and raised her arms halfway, like me.

"One ..." Inhales of breath reached my ears. "Two ..." Weapons fell into position in steady hands. "Three. Fire!"

Neon blue streamed through the air all at once, one after the other, illuminating the night. According to my map, I directed the capsules to the red dots and Hae Jin did the same.

This was my plan. It would ensure that no one escaped and would keep the rebel unit safe. No more deaths.

Thud. Thud. Thud. CODE soldiers collapsed. No matter if they leaped or shifted to dodge the capsules, they had no chance. But there were so many of them. Mr. Park must have sent half his army.

As I continued to direct the capsules, I thought of Reyna, Mia, Russ, and so many more who had sacrificed their lives so that these children would have a better future. These children who knew no better were attacking the very people trying to save them.

Sweat dampened my skin. My arms strained and energy flowed out of me. I was so tired of running and hiding from ISAN. So tired of watching people die. So tired of fighting. I'd had *enough*.

As I pushed harder and yanked on my power, the reloading of my team's weapons filled my ears. Faster and faster, I sent those capsules to their targets. Bright waves of lightning-like lights sizzled through and around my and Hae Jin's bodies, crackling. Her eyes illuminated, and I wondered if mine did the same.

We glowed brighter, like a thunderstorm ready to strike. Our tendrils intertwined, our powers connected and became stronger and more potent. It seemed my plan was smooth sailing, but then bombs and bullets came toward us from the CODE soldiers. I'd thought this might be the end for us. I was about to break away and tell everyone to run for cover, but then …

"Incoming," Vince hollered. "Ava, do something!"

"Do not leave your post!" Josephine shouted. "Trust the mission."

She meant, trust me.

So many lives to consider. So many who believed and relied on me. I couldn't let them down. I pushed through my nearly drained energy and extended my arm toward my team. The hissing tendrils stretched and arched to create a dome-like shield around them.

The first bomb that struck us melted on contact. The bullets did the same, but each time they hit the barrier it felt like a hammer to my bones. Dividing my power to do two things took too much effort.

My body shook and I bit my lip through the horrendous pain. Every inch of me felt like I had been stabbed with a knife, my chest blazing with unbearable heat. I felt as though I might burst into a ball of flame.

Hae Jin's chest rose and fell quickly. "Ava, I can't … I can't …"

Her head had to be pounding like mine. But we couldn't stop. No CODE soldier could escape. I had to save them all.

Min Hyuk, firing his Taser next to Hae Jin, stole a glance at her, but closed his eyes from the brightness we emanated.

"You can do it. Keep going," he said.

"Hold on, Hae Jin, hold on." Blood rushed to my ears in a wave of throbs. Never had I tested my limits this much. So exhausted. I wanted to collapse, but I couldn't. I would not, until the very end. "You're doing great. Almost … almost … almost …"

Hae Jin collapsed into Min Hyuk's arms. The lightning-like tendrils vanished. Icy chills replaced the scorching heat from my body. I shivered, my teeth rattling. So cold.

The last red dot jerked and fell, and I dropped to my knees and sobbed. I thought of Rhett, Avary, Russ, Reyna, Mia, and my mom. My mother would have been proud. She was the reason these children had been saved and would get to live. She was the unsung hero.

As cheers filled my ears, Brooke and Tamara gathered me in their arms. I leaned into them, my sisters, and they leaned into me. The three of us wept.

"We did it," I said. "We did it."

Brooke started. Her head popped up from my shoulder. I heard the grass shuffle and an intake of breath at the same time that she did.

"Watch out, Ava!" Mitch hollered.

My instinct kicked in and I raised my hand to stop a bullet in midair, inches from my head. Either I had missed this girl, or she had pretended to be hit. I'd bet on the latter.

I jolted to my feet while the bullet still in midair rose with me, controlled by my hand. The assassin sprinted. I could have released the hold on the bullet or turned it back on her, but instead I jerked a chin to Tamara and Brooke, who aimed their CHAVA-loaded guns at the escapee and fired.

CHAPTER THIRTY-NINE—ANS FACILITY

AVA

The CODE soldiers hadn't blown up the mountain, but the damage had destroyed our home. But we were safe, and that was all that mattered. Thankfully, ANS generously agreed to house all the rebels in one of their facilities.

I walked down the glider ramp, taking in the view of transporters parked side by side on the polished floor. When I halted in front of Mr. San and Payton, my team did the same.

Payton had Avary in a baby carrier, and a backpack hung on one of his shoulders.

I bowed to Mr. San and then shifted my attention to my daughter. I kissed her forehead again and again, taking in her fresh scent. I'd missed her so much.

"Thank you, Payton, for taking good care of her."

He unbuckled the clip and shifted the carrier onto me. After I closed the straps, I wrapped my daughter in my arms and held onto the moment.

Payton caressed Avary's hair, looking at her with adoration. "I've already fed her and changed her diaper. Rhett's in the medical room. The doctor operated on him and took out the bullet. He's going to be fine."

I'd already heard Rhett's update, but I thanked him anyway.

San had sent his people to bring every CODE girl back to the medical base. He ensured they would be well cared for. Some were too young to live on their own, but a handful could get jobs and live a normal life, under guidance.

"Thank you for welcoming my people into your home," I said. "I don't know what we would have done without you."

San grinned meekly and glanced at my team behind me. "This is what ANS is all about. For our children and our future. Please don't hesitate to ask my assistants or myself if you need anything. Payton can guide you to the medical station."

My team and I were escorted, while Momo's squad followed someone else to get settled with food and water. Mitch and Councilor Chang told me they had something important to take care of and would meet me in the medical center.

The door slid open to a spacious room, and soft hums from the machines greeted me first. With the weight of Avary in the carrier, I entered, but stayed close to the door, my team beside me.

Looking exhausted and worried, Ozzie, wearing a white robe, was seated on a chair. He smiled big when he saw us, then blinked and dabbed at his eyes. I had never seen him cry before. He must have been thinking of Mia and Reyna, and at the same time was relieved to see us alive.

"I fractured my arm, but Dr. Machine fixed me up," he said. "I'm not breakable. You can come closer."

Brooke ran to him first, then we all hugged him. We greeted Naomi, who sat up in her hub in a white robe. I helped her out, and she settled on a chair next to Ozzie. She looked tired, but she'd recovered well.

Closest to the wall, Rhett lay inside a medical hub, sleeping, with a tube up his nose. When we surrounded him, I wiggled my finger to Momo and gave her space so she could stand next to me.

Blue and green laser beams moved horizontally across his body, and the monitor to his heart beeped in a steady rhythm.

"So this is Rhett," Min Hyuk said. "I've wanted to meet him. Ava is Hae Jin's idol, but Rhett is mine."

"He's going to be fine. Right, Ava?" Momo flipped a penny. "I'm giving Rhett good luck, but I'm also praying for him."

I scuffed her hair. "That's what I've been told."

"He's our hero." Payton sounded proud, weaving around Naomi to me. "He trusted me enough to hand over Avary, and he stayed behind so we could escape. But Ozzie and Naomi are heroes, too." His tone turned somber. "And Reyna and Mia."

Silence filled the space.

"That's Sniper for you," Ozzie said, bringing life back to the room. "He's always thinking about others before himself. When he found out about the mountain base, he led our first escape from ISAN. He and Ava were the last to leave, except ..."

Ozzie's blue eyes met mine, and he didn't need to say anything more. Those days were long gone, and I never wanted to revisit the separation again. We had a child now, and a clear set of priorities.

"How about we go to the meeting room?" Justine cocked a thumb toward the door. "Maybe Ava wants some space?"

Tamara and Justine draped their arms around Naomi and helped her up. Brooke and Payton did the same to Ozzie. And they all walked out of the room together behind Momo.

Quiet. Just the sound of three beating hearts.

I turned to my side so our daughter had a clear view of Rhett. "Look, it's your papa. He was hurt, but he's better and resting."

I swiped at the panel on the glass atop his hub and the top released with a hiss. Rhett looked so peaceful and beautiful. I ran a light touch across his thick eyebrows and over his cheekbones, then kissed his lips.

Avary fussed and made a soft sound. Payton had said she'd already had her milk and her diaper had been changed. I lifted the carrier and sniffed her bottom. Baby powder. No stinker.

"Do you want to hug Papa?"

I took her out of the carrier and lay her in the crook of Rhett's neck and shoulder. Her small fingers brushed down my arm and accidentally pressed my chip. I had been so occupied during the battle, I didn't realize I had a voice message.

The letter began with "Dearest Ava." Tears streamed down my face, the pain in my heart still raw as I listened.

> *Ozzie, Reyna, Naomi, Mia, and I are stuck underground, and we can't call out for help … I want to tell you how precious you and Avary are to me.*
>
> *I found love when I first looked at you … because, babe, memories are what keeps us alive.*
>
> *I love you and Avary so much … I have a place for you and our daughter. Ask Mitch. He'll know where.*
>
> *I love you endlessly,*
>
> *Rhett.*

"I love you endlessly too." I kissed his forehead and pulled back, but he gripped my arm.

Rhett's eyes were closed, but a slight grin played on his lips. "Why not kiss a little lower? I see you finally got my message. Geez, it took you long enough. What's a guy to do to get his girl's attention? Get buried?"

He squinted and then finally opened his eyes. My gaze met his.

Relief. Grief. Terror. All emotions flooded out of me.

I wrapped my arms around him and sobbed. Rhett cupped my face and kissed my lips, short and sweet, again and again. Then he twisted his neck just enough to kiss Avary's cheek.

"You're safe, as I knew you would be," he said. "Payton took good care of you." He pushed a button on the side of the hub to sit up. "You're here. We're here together. We're never parting again."

I wiped my tears and laced my fingers through his hair. "It's time we both retire. So, tell me about this home you've been hiding from me."

Rhett chuckled and shifted Avary on top of his chest. She had fallen asleep.

"I've been fixing it up in secret." He stroked her back. "You're going to love it. I'll show you when I can get out of here. And …"

His features grew strained, water pooling in his eyes. He glanced toward the hubs. "Ozzie. Naomi. Reyna. Mia. Where are they?"

"Ozzie and Naomi are fine. But …" A lump formed in my throat.

He scrunched in his shoulders and furrowed his brow. His eyes widened like he remembered something. "No, no, no. Reyna and Mia. They didn't …"

I wiped his tears as they fell, then I embraced him. "It's not your fault. You don't get to choose who lives or dies."

I gave him the words he used to say to me, but he only sobbed harder. He hadn't known Mia well, but Reyna had been like a sister to him.

Rhett pulled me back. "Did you recover their bodies?"

I nodded, my voice softer. "They're going to be cremated." The word was so hard to say. "We'll throw a proper funeral. And there is one more person …" I blew out a breath to stop the tears, but it didn't help. "Russ …" I shook my head as I wept.

Vince had informed me before I got here that they had found Russ's body. I knew he'd fallen off the cliff when he'd sacrificed himself to save Mitch and Momo, but I asked not to be told of his condition. I couldn't bear to hear it.

"I'm so sorry." He pulled me into him.

He knew how much Russ had meant to me. Aside from Brooke and Tamara, Russ had been my rock and my savior. And he had helped us escape from ISAN.

"He'll always be in your heart," he said. "He'll always be remembered."

The door slid open. Councilor Chang, Mitch, Lydia, Zen, and Cleo walked in. Mitch dashed across the tile floor and grabbed Rhett in his arms. Then everyone followed suit.

"You scared the life out of me." Mitch lightly socked his brother's arm. "Don't ever do it again."

"He won't." I winked at Rhett.

"I'm so sorry about Reyna and Mia," Cleo said, then smiled at Avary, still on Rhett's chest sleeping. "She's beautiful."

"May I?" Zen asked.

Rhett handed him our daughter and Zen held her with ease.

"Wait, I get to hold her first." Mitch took her from Zen, but his arms around her stiffened when she opened her eyes. Then his muscles eased. "I'm your uncle. I can't wait to show you how to use a weapon, just like I taught your mother."

Lydia let out the cutest snort, her dimple indenting.

"But, unlike me, she won't be training to be an assassin," I said.

"Oh, hell no." Rhett frowned. "She's going to have rules. Lots of rules. Especially when she's at a dating age."

"I'm right there with you." Mitch narrowed his eyes. "I'm going to be staring down at a boy right next to you, Pops."

"Boys ..." Chang shook her head. "She'll have you two wrapped around her finger. You'll do anything she wants."

Laughter rang in the room.

"I want your opinion," Chang said, her gaze set on me. "I need to send teams to Singapore, China, Japan, Africa, India, and Europe. I'm considering asking Hae Jin, Min Hyuk, Naomi, Jo, Debra, and Momo to lead a team. What do you think?"

Josephine was indirectly asking me if I would head the missions, but we had already talked about this. There was only one answer.

"I think that's a great idea. Hae Jin has the mapping ability, and everyone you mentioned has great leadership skills. If Momo agrees, then her squad will likely volunteer. What about Justine and Payton?"

Councilor Chang smiled. "Thank you. I believe my decision has been made. As for Justine, I asked her to take Russ's position, and asked Payton to assist her. They will reorganize ISAN to ANS and take down the international sectors with help from the teams I'm organizing."

"Good." I offered a curt nod.

She placed an arm around Lydia. "Do you want to tell them the good news, or shall I?"

Lydia dipped her head sheepishly, then looked at Mitch with Avary in his arms. "I've been asked to take over Verlot's spot. If all goes well, I'll be officially announced as a Remnant Councils member. I'll be trained by the best." She smiled at Chang.

"I'm so proud of you." Mitch hugged Lydia. "I'll be your

personal bodyguard."

Lydia snorted. "You can oversee the guards who will be assigned to me. And I'm not joking. I'm appointing you, if you'll take it."

Mitch beamed a smile, his eyes glinting with joy. "It will be my honor, Councilor Lydia Lee." He rocked Avary from side to side. "Did you hear that, niece? I'm going to be a captain."

Chang cleared her throat. "There's one more thing I'd like to discuss with Rhett and Ava, if you can all excuse us."

Mitch met Chang's gaze and nodded, then handed Avary back to me. What was up with these two?

Everyone went out the door, but Mitch walked back in with a striking older man who was the same height as he. Mitch had to hold on to his arm, supporting him under the elbow.

The man dragged his feet, looking fragile, like he had been through the wringer. He had black-and-white hair and was old enough to be Mitch's …

"Dad?" Rhett's voice cracked, and his eyes rounded. He tried to get up, but the machine beeped in warning.

Rhett and his father were similar in the eyes, with thick eyebrows and perfect noses. With Mitch, Rhett, and their father in the same room, the resemblance between them was unfathomable. Rhett's father embraced him and sobbed.

Chang and I wiped away tears. I mouthed *Thank you* to her.

"Dad. Where have you been?" Rhett asked.

Rhett's father told him how he thought it was a great idea for his sons to be part of a network that would change the world. Being a council guard to Verlot, he had been able to get them in without a background check.

On the day of the meeting, the parents had been kidnapped

and taken to a facility where ISAN tested the new serum on them. They'd created countless orphans, allowing the network to have easier access to their kids.

"Mitch and I tried to find you," Rhett said. "We never stopped looking."

His father placed a hand on his shoulder. "I know. My sons were always with me." He met Mitch's gaze and grinned. "I suppose we got lucky when we were sent to Korea. I was told that a little girl named Momo found me."

"She did?" Rhett chuckled. "She's all over the place."

Rhett's father said, "After all the CODE soldiers were taken to ANS, us old folks were safe inside the hubs when Russ and Justine bombed Korean ISAN."

My throat burned, and I bit back the tears. I didn't have the heart to tell him our friend had passed away.

Rhett shook his head and cleared his throat. "Dad, Randy, meet my girl Ava and our daughter Avary."

Randy's eyes widened, as if seeing me for the first time. "It's so nice to meet you." He hugged me and kissed Avary's head. "She's got your eyes, Rhett. No, my eyes." He cackled with so much joy that the lines on his forehead deepened. "I have a granddaughter." His voice got louder. "I had lost hope I would get out alive, but so much has happened. It's all wonderful."

His happiness and laughter filled the room as we all shared a chuckle.

Randy furrowed his eyebrows, confused. "Where do we live?"

Mitch and Rhett looked at each other, grinning. They had something up their sleeves.

"Dad, do you remember our cabin?" Mitch placed an arm around his father's shoulders.

"I do. The cabins were so cheap, I bought three of them. Two for each of my sons, and one for me. I doubt anyone wants to live in the mountains. It seems this generation is all about technology. Why do you ask?"

Rhett's smile grew bigger. "It was supposed to be a surprise for Ava, but I can't hold it in anymore. We're going to live there as soon as I get out of here. And Mitch and I would like to propose something for one of the cabins."

I couldn't wait to see it. We had left ISAN, and we would start a new life ... the life Rhett and I had dreamed about since the day we'd fallen in love.

Sometimes wishes do come true when you blow on a dandelion.

CHAPTER FORTY-FUNERAL

AVA

Rhett and I sauntered out of our glider, our friends following us in a grim procession. The only black outfit I'd had was the ISAN uniform, so we had all taken a miserable shopping trip for funeral clothing.

The scuffling of our shoes echoed in the long tiled hallway. At the end, double glass doors slid open and the scent of flowers permeated the air.

A chill spread over my back and pulled my shoulders tight. The white walls were lined with short, narrow shelves from floor to ceiling. Each shelf contained a ceramic box of someone's ashes. In the center of the room, flower wreaths on wire stands clustered next to a metal table.

On the table were three framed photos—Reyna, Mia, and Russ—and in front of each photo sat a box holding their cremated remains. All thanks to Councilor Chang, who had arranged and funded this funeral.

A lump formed in my throat, and I swallowed hard. I placed a hand to my chest as a breath shuddered out of me and my knees threatened to give out. I had already grieved in private, but these large framed pictures of my friends next to rosewood boxes that held nothing but ashes shattered my soul.

When Chang had asked what kind of flowers should be on the

wreaths, I'd only requested lavender for Russ. He'd loved that scent, and it would always remind me of him.

"It smells like Russ's office." Brooke smoothed a finger over the tiny purple blossoms.

None of us had been to a funeral before. I only knew that a minister or a priest presided over a solemn ceremony in some sort of sacred space, but the team had decided to hold a private gathering.

Justine stepped closer to Brooke, her gaze trained on Russ's photo. He was dressed in a classic black suit and vest, with a polished white dress shirt underneath. His face shone with a kind smile, revealing a perfect set of teeth, and his dazzling emerald eyes sparkled like sunlight reflecting off a precious stone.

"Whenever I would storm into his office ..." Justine's voice cracked. "Russ used to tell me to take a deep breath. He said lavender relieved stress, anxiety, and agitation. I told him it didn't work on me, and he agreed." She snorted. "I gave you such a hard time, Boss, but you were still so nice to me. I wish you were here so I could apologize and hug—"

Her head lowered, she sobbed.

The tears I'd tried to keep at bay streamed down my face, and I squeezed Rhett's hand.

Mitch cleared his throat. "Hey, buddy. I just want to thank you for finding my father. We both knew it would take a miracle, but somehow you, Momo, and ..." He glanced at Justine as she wiped away tears, and he smiled at her. "You three did it. But do you know how mad I am at you right now?" His hand trembled as he placed a fist by Russ's photo. "Why did you ... you shouldn't have ..." He lightly banged his forehead on the table. "You let go so Momo and I could live. You sacrificed yourself so—"

Mitch released a stuttering breath and pressed his eyes shut. He had never displayed such raw emotion in public before, but we weren't just anyone. We were his trusted friends and family. And, out of ISAN, we were allowed to be human again.

Lydia pulled him into her arms and he wept harder, pressing his head to her shoulder.

"He let go." Mitch gulped air between halting words. "I couldn't help him. I should've …"

Lydia stroked his back. "You held on until the very end. You need to forgive yourself."

While Brooke crouched in front of Mia's photo, whispering her farewell, I stood with Rhett and Ozzie by Reyna's urn. Instead of a professional portrait like the one Russ had, hers was an informal one—mouth curved in a sly grin, eyes twinkling with mischief.

Reyna wore a flannel shirt and jeans, with one hand resting on the Taser tucked into her waistband. Her thick curls were pulled back into multiple braids that framed her face.

Rhett got down on his knees and took a deep breath, staring at her photograph. "Thank you for coming back for me, or I would have been good as dead." He rubbed his thigh and bit his bottom lip. "Thank you for putting up with all my shit, especially during the times when Ava and I were apart. Because of you, I made it through another day. I'm sorry I couldn't save you, little sis." He pressed his forehead to the floor and sobbed. "I'm going to miss you so much, Reyna." He curled his fingers into fists. "Why did it have to be you?"

I lowered myself between Ozzie and Rhett and wrapped my arms around them.

"We were a good team," Ozzie said, tilting his head on my

shoulder. "It's not going to be the same without her." Ozzie sniffed, wiping at his reddened eyes.

"No, it's not," Rhett said. "But she'll live on in our hearts.

Brooke leaned into Ozzie, then Justine to Brooke, while Mitch and Lydia kneeled on the other side of Rhett. The seven of us stayed like that in the quiet with our heads down, but I peered up to Russ's photo. I was the only one who hadn't said a word.

As if Russ was standing before me, I spoke in my mind.

I didn't want to say I told you so, but … I told you so.

Russ would say: *But I did what I had to do, and so did you.*

True. We're both crazy.

In my mind, Russ snorted. *You said it, not me.*

I laughed. *Thank you, for everything.*

Russ came closer and placed a palm on my cheek. *I'm very proud of you. Because of you, the CODE children have a chance and the rebel teams worldwide will move forward to bring down the rest of ISAN. Please, be happy and live. You deserve the best.*

I leaned into his hand and closed my eyes. He brushed a thumb over my wet face. I'd sworn I wouldn't shed any more tears, but saying goodbye broke my resolve.

I love you, my friend. And if you see my mom, please give her my love.

Russ kissed my forehead. *I love you, Ava. I always will.*

CHAPTER FORTY-ONE – SISTER

JOSEPHINE CHANG

Josephine sat at her dining table in her penthouse, hot steam wafting out of her mug. As she drank her favorite tea she swiped at the hologram file on her sister, who didn't know she existed.

She took another sip, savoring the taste of honey. Ginseng, not so much, but it was good for her health. At least, that was what her mother had always said. Josephine wished her mother was still alive to witness her two daughters, born of different fathers, finally meeting for the first time.

Josephine took a sip, the gorgeous view of the city lights through the window keeping her company. When the bell chimed, her heart thundered.

A voice said, "You have a visitor. Vince is at the front."

Josephine went to the kitchen to pour him tea, placed the mug on the dining table, and by the time she opened the door, he was standing in front of her with his arms behind him.

"Good afternoon, beautiful." His gaze raked her from head to toe, then he arched his eyebrows. "I love you in jeans. You look so playful."

He had overseen transferring all the CODE girls to ANS, and she hadn't seen him until now. She couldn't stop daydreaming about him, and she just needed to … What was she waiting for? Josephine grabbed his strong shoulders and gave him a kiss he would keep thinking about long after she let go.

"Wow." He blew out a breath. "I should be regularly absent for days and come back, if this is the greeting I'll get." He kissed her cheek and handed her two dozen roses.

She pressed her nose to the petals and inhaled. "That kiss was for helping me with the funeral details. And, *two* bouquets? I must have done something right. Come in."

"I missed you, that's all. And I have two hands."

Josephine took the roses to the kitchen and placed them inside a glass vase she had recently bought. Perhaps she should have purchased two. When she ambled toward the family room, he sighed after drinking tea.

"Ginseng with honey." He raised his cup. "My favorite, now."

She snorted as she slipped into the chair across from him.

"Are you nervous?" he asked. "Excited? Going out of your mind from anticipation?"

She let out a belly laugh as her mug thudded on the table. "All of the above. I can't believe today has come. I told security to let your men in. No need to call for me."

"Good. You know your package ... I mean ... your sister is fortunate you found out in time, and it's a miracle she survived." His chip buzzed. When he looked at the message, his eyes grew wider. "They're coming up."

Josephine walked toward the door, rubbing her hands. She had been calm and composed, but her chest tightened and her stomach twisted in nerve-racking knots.

"Don't worry." He gathered her in his arms. "She's going to love you."

She nodded, then cracked the door open. Ten of Vince's guards had escorted her sister. She gave Vince an *are-you-serious* look.

He shrugged, grinning. "Just keeping her safe, boss. If she means the world to you, then she means the world to me." He leaned closer to her. "Good luck, and tell me how it goes when I see you tonight.

"I can't wait," he said, and directed the guards to the elevator.

How had she gotten so lucky, finding a man who adored her? When she settled down, she would try this thing called 'a relationship.'

"Councilor Chang?" the visitor gasped. "I didn't know I was going to your home. I didn't bring anything with me."

Always bring a gift when going to a person's home for the first time. It seemed their mother had ingrained those words in her sister, too.

Josephine didn't mean to stare. She already knew what her sister looked like, but it was so strange to finally meet her, and she wanted to hug her. She'd never been the affectionate type, though that had been changing lately. Vince had softened her.

"Please come in and have a seat." Josephine cringed at how cheerful she sounded. She didn't need to try so hard. "Would you like some ginseng and honey tea?"

"It's my favorite, but no thank you." Her sister eased onto the sofa and glanced out the window, then back to her.

Josephine picked up the data chip from the dining table and sat across from her sister. "How are you feeling?"

"Much better." She folded her arms across her stomach. "I want to thank you for everything you've done for me." Her eyes pooled with tears. "I don't even know how I'm still alive."

Josephine smiled. "Helping others is my job."

It was the truth, but she would have gone to hell and back for her.

Her sister rubbed her arms. "I don't mean to sound rude, but why did you want to see me?"

She handed her the chip from across the tea table.

Her sister scanned it against her chip reader. As she read the file, Josephine studied the woman's features. Dark hair. Pale complexion. Sharp nose. Full mouth. But the shape of their eyes was different, and unlike Josephine, who'd had a white father, she had changed her last name to her mother's maiden name when her father had left them.

Her sister crinkled the corners of her eyes and her pitch rose higher. "My mother had a second child and she never told me? I suppose that when she left, there was no obligation to tell us. She moved to the Western Sector and I never saw her again. I never told my daughter. But why are you showing me this? I'm grateful, but I'm confused."

"What happened to your parents?" Josephine asked. "I'll explain why I'm asking, after."

Her sister regarded her for a moment, as if contemplating whether to share her family secrets, but then gave in. Josephine was one of the Remnant Councilors, after all—someone she should trust.

Her sister took a deep breath and clasped her hands. "It all makes sense, now. I was only ten. My parents got into a big fight." She leaned back and sighed. "My mom walked out and she never came back. My father must have found out she was pregnant with another man's child. She must have felt so guilty that she ... why didn't she reach out to me? I was her daughter."

"I'm sorry. Ou ... your mother had a good reason." She'd almost said *our*. That would have been awkward.

"This is crazy. I have a sister out there somewhere." She shook

248

her head and laughed, but not with humor. "No, I've been through a lot worse. You wouldn't believe a fraction of what I've been through. Anyway, why did you want to see me, again?"

Josephine rubbed her palms on her thighs, heat rising to her neck. Her heart pounded, and she didn't understand the nervousness. She could hear Vince giving her the courage. *She's going to love you.*

Josephine cleared her throat. "I was wondering if you would like to meet your sister?"

She placed the data chip on the table and pinched her brows together. "Yes, but I wouldn't know where to start."

Josephine shuddered and beamed a smile. That joy traveled down to her heart so fast, she thought she would burst from happiness. After the meteor devastation, many married couples hadn't had children, and if they had, it was usually just one. So, to have a sister, even a half—she considered herself one of the lucky ones.

Josephine grabbed her sister's hand and told her everything.
***

Before heading out to meet Vince for dinner, Josephine took a detour to ANS. Mr. San escorted her to Verlot's cell and turned on the speakers for both ways. Then he stepped to the side, out of sight from the prisoner.

Verlot sat on his cot and held a hamburger. The wrapper crinkled as he peeled away a layer over the buns. He opened his mouth to take a bite, but paused.

He smirked. "Hello, beautiful. What brings you to my humble home?"

"I have some news for you," she said, her voice cool but with a hint of mischief.

He took a bite, his eyes gleaming. "And what might that be?"

She leaned closer, her nose almost touching the glass barrier. "I want to thank you for your donation."

His fake grin fell as he placed the burger on the bed. "What do you mean?"

"Due to your generosity, we have taken down all the CODE girls in the US. We are going to educate them and give them their lives back. The teams I've dispersed recently will bring down all the international ISAN."

"That's interesting, but you're lying." He rose and took a step.

She crossed her arms, her lips curving upward. "Oh, I forgot to mention that you're dead to the world. We even had a funeral. It was sad and beautiful. The citizens adore you for donating all your 4Qs to research."

He clenched his jaw and approached closer, his voice louder. "What do you mean?"

She snarled. "You keep asking me the same question, but you know what I mean. How do you like having your rights taken away? Now you know how it felt for all those girls who had been turned to assassins without their consent."

"Chang." He growled, his fingers curving into tight balls.

"By the way." Her lips tugged at the corners. "This is the last time you'll see me. Have a wonderful life in the hell I've created for you. Goodbye, Verlot."

"Chang!" He grabbed his burger off the cot and mashed it against the barrier. The sauce smeared on the glass, but the bun and the meat dropped with a splat.

She didn't flinch as he dropped to his knees. He picked up the broken pieces and shoved them in his mouth.

Her heart softened for a heartbeat.

No, she would not feel sorry for him—she had no empathy for the man who had ruined many lives. She'd sealed up that Verlot wall, never to think about him again.

"My burger! Look what you did!"

Josephine slapped the button so she could no longer hear his crazy voice, and walked away.

CHAPTER FORTY-TWO—CABIN HOME

AVA

R hett tucked our daughter inside the carrier and grabbed Avary's backpack. He took a silk fabric square out of his pocket and tied a blindfold around my eyes.

"I already know we're going to our cabin home." I placed a hand on the passenger's seat in the glider to steady my stance. "Is this necessary?"

"It's supposed to be a surprise. Just humor me." He took my hand, guiding me down the ramp.

The soft breeze kissed my face, and I bathed in the warmth of the sun. We had spent three nights at the ANS facility, and I was so glad to be out of there.

Hae Jin, Min Hyuk, Jo, Debra, Naomi, and Momo and her squad had said their goodbyes and headed off to their destinations. They were to report to Councilor Chang, who would oversee their missions, but I worried about them and planned to ask for reports.

My feet slid over pebbles, then flattened on the dirt-packed ground.

"Almost there," Rhett said. "Keep in mind that I didn't have much time to furnish our home, so you can rearrange or buy more things."

Light beamed in my eyes when he took off the blindfold. I blinked and adjusted my vision as the scent of pine filled my nostrils and mountain peaks surrounded us in the distance.

It was not the old run-down cottage I had imagined, but a modern one, with tinted windows that took up the front wall.

"Wow," I said. "I didn't think it was this big."

He raised an eyebrow. "Do I do anything small?"

He had a point.

I passed a cluster of pine trees looming over us that hid the cabin well, even from being spotted from above.

Bushes with pretty flowers adorned either side of the structure and dandelions grew near the cobblestone walkway. I smiled, thinking of my mother.

A noise came from the direction of our glider by the back of the cabin. Rhett grabbed my shoulders and faced me back towards the house. *Suspicious.* He didn't want me to see something. What other surprises did he have in store?

He jerked his chin to a metal panel by the door. "It's all set. Stand in front of it."

I shifted. The blue laser scanned my face, then my eyes. The double doors clicked and swung open automatically.

"Surprise!" voices boomed.

I jerked, startled, then turned to Rhett with my jaw dropping. He had his palms over Avary's ears.

He kissed my forehead. "Welcome to our home, babe."

Ozzie, Brooke, Zeke, Tamara, Justine, Payton, Cleo, Zen, Lydia, and Mitch had scattered in the large living area. And, sitting on the sofa, Randy grinned. He was seeing a therapist, advised by Councilor Chang. Speaking of which, I would have expected her and Vince to have been invited. Perhaps they would come later.

"We wanted to throw you a surprise party," Mitch said, his arm around Lydia's waist.

I needed to get used to addressing her as Councilor Lee.

Zeke gave me a salute and kissed the back of Tamara's hand, which he held. I was glad those two had resolved their differences.

After the hugs, we gathered at the kitchen and the family room. Brooke, Tamara, Zeke, and Ozzie came with me on a tour hosted by none other than my man.

"I feel like I've gone back in time." I climbed the wooden stairs, Brooke beside me. "Does your cabin look like mine?"

Rhett had informed me that Randy lived with Mitch and Lydia, and the empty one would go to our friends. That house was going to be loud, and so much fun, but I had to admit I would enjoy our quiet space with just the three of us.

"Ditto," Brooke said, and pushed open a door to the master bedroom.

"The best part is: we're just a house away," Zeke said.

The wooden floor creaked under my feet as I walked in and examined the grandness of the space. A king-size bed was set in the middle, the headboard against the wall. I walked past a sofa in front of a fireplace and went into a bathroom with marble flooring.

Two sinks. Two showers. One large standalone tub. The bathroom was as big as the walk-in closet. I touched the hanging clothes, silk and cotton pants soft between my fingers. Shirts, skirts, sweaters, jackets, pants, and dresses—when had he had time to shop online?

"Wait until you see Avary's room." Tamara tugged me down the hallway.

My daughter's room was decorated in delicate pink and white. Above her crib was a musical mobile with hanging dandelions, matching the mural of a field of dandelions that filled a side of the wall. Some leaves floated in the air, catching the sun's rays and glowing in golden hues. Across in the middle of the field were the words: *Be resilient.*

I choked up, and tears welled in my eyes. Rhett leaned against the doorframe with his arms crossed, wearing a smirk. It was the exact way he'd looked the day I'd fallen for him in ISAN.

I teared up even more when he placed a necklace around my neck, the one he had gifted me, and the one I had told him to hold onto until I returned. He had put so much effort into our home.

Yes, he'd done it alone, but he'd wanted to surprise me. And, frankly, I'd rather have him do the decorating. I wasn't good in that department. He was the romantic type, and a planner.

I hugged him, our precious daughter sandwiched between us in the carrier. "I love everything. I love our home. And I love you." I kissed him on the lips and licked his ear. "I'll finish thanking you when we're alone."

"I'll be waiting." His tone dipped playfully as one of his hands brushed my butt. "There are more surprises yet to come. Let's go to the garden."

Tamara, Zeke, Brooke, and Ozzie shrugged when I looked at them. I hoped one of them would accidentally spill the beans in their excitement. My friends went to the kitchen, and only Rhett, Avary, and I went outside through the sliding glass door.

The backyard was just as big as the house, surrounded by a fence to keep the wild animals out, unlike my apartment in the city, where Mother had gardened on the balcony.

"Did you plant those?" I pointed at a large plot of vegetables toward the back of the fences.

Carrots, tomatoes, squash, and cabbages lined up vertically, separated by a wooden panel. Behind the section of garden were stone benches under the trees.

"Yes and no." He checked a message that popped up for his eyes only and kissed my forehead. "I'm wanted in the kitchen, and it looks like Councilor Chang and Vince have arrived. She wants to talk to you."

I kissed Avary's cheek and strolled toward the benches.

I expected Chang to come out from the house, but she came through the gate. Her gait toward me was poised and confident. I admired that woman.

She'd put her life on the line and fought for her people, the children, and our future. I didn't know anyone braver than her, besides my mom.

Chang smiled, standing before me. "Good afternoon, Ava. There's something important I want to discuss with you."

I put up a hand. "I'm sorry, but we've already discussed this. I have a child. And—"

"That's not it. And I don't know where to begin."

I had never seen her flustered before. Something must be terribly wrong, or ...

"What is it?" I said. "You can trust me."

"I'm going inside, but I want you to wait here. I would like for you to talk to my sister."

"Your sister?" My voice rose. Where were my manners? "Of course. I'm just shocked, that's all. I'm excited to meet her."

"Half sister, but why do people make such a point of saying half? It sounds silly." She snorted. "I'll go get her."

I supposed she was right. Justine was my sister, regardless of our different mothers.

I sat down on the hard bench and admired the vast land filled with green grass. A soft breeze caressed my hair and I took a deep breath. There was nothing like the smell of spring mountain air.

I'd thought there would be more cabins nearby, but there weren't, besides the three Randy owned. I preferred it that way, anyway—no one but our family and friends.

Soft footfalls brought my attention toward the gate. And then I saw a ghost, because it had to be. My mother was dead.

I rubbed my eyes and blinked as I rose. The spirit was running, or rather limping, toward me and calling my name. Impossible, and yet …

"Mom?" A lump stuck in my throat. My heart pounding, I ran. She'd better be real, otherwise I was losing my damn mind.

"Ava!"

I knew that voice. That voice had scolded me so many times. That voice had said *I love you* every day. That voice had told me to be resilient and never give up.

My mother had sacrificed her life to save me from her husband. She would have done anything for me.

Rhett had told me there were more surprises. Had he known she was alive?

"Mom! Mom! Mom!" My legs wobbled, wanting to give out from the shock.

We slowed and I   stopped when we were six feet apart, between the garden and the trees. Happy tears poured down our faces.

"How?" I couldn't wipe my tears fast enough with a trembling hand. "How?" I said it louder.

I collapsed on the grass and Mom rushed the final steps and embraced me. She pulled back to touch my face, as if she needed to know I was real, and then hugged me again.

"I have missed you so much!" she cried out.

Her voice was smoother than it had been at the ISAN secret

base, steadier and more fluent. She was alive, and that was all that mattered.

We wept in each other's arms as time seemed to slow.

I had pushed away the pain of losing her and kept busy, the battle occupying the forefront of my thoughts. But now, even seeing her physical form, I still cried for the loss of her. And then happy tears gushed, to have her back.

A miracle, indeed.

I had a feeling Councilor Chang had a hand in saving my mother's life. Her sister's life, I realized. *Holy cow, Councilor Chang is my aunt!*

I couldn't wait to tell my friends.

CHAPTER FORTY-THREE—A MIRACLE

AVA

Mom, Councilor Chang, and I sat on the bench under the trees. No, not Councilor Chang: Aunt Josephine. Would I ever get used to it?

"So, can one of you explain how this all happened?" I couldn't stop smiling.

Mom explained how her parents had separated. My aunt had found out she had a sister just before her mom had passed away, which happened before I joined the rebel team.

"I wanted more information on your family, Ava," my aunt said. "When I looked into your mom's profile, our mother's name showed up. I tried to find her, but—"

"Novak had kidnapped my mom," my mother said, and she pushed back strands of hair that had fallen on her face from the breeze. "He did many terrible things."

Even to his own wife and children before we were born. I thought about my father's journal, tucked inside Avary's emergency backpack. I had to put it somewhere safe. I never wanted to lose it. It was research. Science. A part of me, my past. Something to learn from, and to never let happen again.

Josephine had told Mr. San to give Mom a dosage of CHAVA, and parts of the brain tissue that Novak's inhuman experimentation had damaged had been healed. She hadn't known if it would work,

259

but she had thought that if the serum mended the CODE girls, it might help Mom, too. It was the reason why my mother seemed whole again.

"I can't believe it." I shook my head, still in disbelief. "And I can't get over the fact that you're my aunt. All this time, and we never knew. Good thing we were nice to each other."

She placed her cheek next to mine. "I've always seen the resemblance."

"Beautiful." Mom's eyes sparkled in the sunlight poking between the leaves.

We shared a laugh.

"Now that you've been released," I said to Mom, "would you like to live with me?"

Mom took my hands. "Thank you, sweetheart, but I'm going to stay with my sister. You, Rhett, and Avary need space. And, before you ask, he found out about me this morning, and so did everyone else. I wanted to tell you in person."

"I'm glad we had this moment together, but do they know Councilor Chang is your sister?"

My aunt shook her head. "You can announce that surprise during dinner." She winked at me. "They can't know all the secrets before you. You've got to have at least one."

I adored her so much. "Speaking of secrets and surprises, are there more? You're not going to tell me that Novak or Gene survived, right?"

"No, oh hell no." She furrowed her brow, cringing. "Mr. San had planned to blow up the ISAN secret base and had one of his spies place a net contraption under the structure by the glider landing below—mainly for his guards, just in case they fell through the cracks. But I had convinced him to give us time to get your team out, first. And I had another reason. I found out that your mom had been kidnapped by her husband, and where she was located. She survived because she fell into the net. We have to thank Mr. San for that."

Aunt Josephine smiled at Mom, waiting. I supposed she felt like it wasn't her story to tell.

Mom cleared her throat. "I climbed out of the net and crawled away as the structure began to collapse. The debris hit me a couple of times, but I managed to get into a pod. As the pod traveled through an escape tunnel, I fell unconscious."

My aunt held up her hand. "And … I had each pod tagged. Only one made it out intact, and I prayed that it was my sister and not Novak."

"When I woke up," Mom added, "I'd arrived in the East Sector at ISAN, and I met Russ. He took me to ANS."

"I told Russ not to tell anyone," Aunt Josephine said. "He didn't know she was your mother. I had to keep my sister safe. If word got out she was alive, there was no telling what ISAN would do."

I felt grateful, but … *Oh, Russ.* My heart squeezed, and the tears pooled. I swallowed hard and kept them at bay. I thought about telling Mom that Russ had died, but I decided to do it later, when we were alone.

"Anyway …" Aunt Josephine stood and stretched her arms to the clear blue sky. "I'm starving. Let's go eat."

I hooked one arm with Mom and the other with my aunt. We walked together side by side and entered through the glass door.

The aroma of rich spices from homemade cooked food filled the cabin. Platters of roasted chicken, mashed potatoes, beans, and assorted vegetables of squash and carrots from the garden were set out on the dining table. Even the wine glasses were filled. Everything looked delicious.

Mother grabbed Avary from Rhett and sat next to my aunt and Vince. My friends pulled their chairs close. I weaved around the table and settled between Mom and Rhett.

"Raise your cups." Aunt Josephine lifted a wine glass. "I would like to make a toast for your dedication and your sacrifice, and for the heroes who lost their lives. They will never be forgotten. We wouldn't have been able to save thousands of children, had it not been for all of you."

To Russ, Reyna, Mia, and all the fallen rebel soldiers.

Glasses clinked, and I took a drink. The liquid felt cool on my throat. I needed something to settle my heart and the rushing of adrenaline which still raced through me. I still couldn't believe Mom had survived the blast even as I looked at her, smiling at Avary in her arms.

"This is by far the best meal I've ever had," Brooke said through a mouthful of chicken.

"What do you mean?" Ozzie's cup stopped before it touched his lips. "You don't like my cooking? We were limited at the mountain base, but—"

"I like your meals." Justine smiled and scooped up some carrots. "I like your baked potatoes the best."

Ozzie rolled back his shoulders. "Thank you, Justine."

"I like your cooking, too," Zeke said.

"No comment," Payton murmured.

Chuckles rang in the air.

Mitch's spoon clanked as he scooped up squash. "Do you remember when Ava fell out the window with Thomax Thorpe?"

"Ava!" Mom gasped, and then her attention went back to

Avary as she fed her with a bottle.

"I thought she was good as dead." Tamara frowned.

"I'd like to hear more," Aunt Josephine said after she took a sip of her wine.

"Ohhh …" Brooke's fork clanked on her dish. "Remember when Ava took her top off during training and brought Mitch to his knees?"

"I was so proud of her." Lydia giggled.

"Clever." Vince forked a piece of chicken and took a bite.

Mitch raised a hand and an eyebrow. "What can I say? She learned from the best." He winked at Lydia.

Zen glanced down the table. "Well, let's not pick on just Ava. I've got lots to tell about Rhett."

"I have some stories, too." Cleo snickered.

"I can't wait to hear," Randy said.

Rhett stopped chewing a piece of chicken. "Just you wait." He waved a hand, snorting. "I've got tons on all of you."

Rhett held my hand underneath the table and squeezed once before letting go. We continued to share stories, and laughter filled the room. This was the moment I had been waiting for. My friends and family, gathered at the same table and sharing a meal outside of ISAN. But we were missing a few friends.

I inhaled a deep breath, keeping the tears at bay as I smiled at the empty seats reserved for Reyna, Mia, and Russ, and observed a moment of silence. Then I shared stories about them.

Memories will keep them alive forever.

CHAPTER FORTY-FOUR—WHATEVER IT TAKES

AVA

Sunlight bathed my skin as dusk neared. The hues of violet and magenta made the summer sky even more breathtaking.

Rhett held my hand and we strolled across the prairie behind our cabin without our daughter. He wanted us to be alone, so Mom and my aunt took Avary. Whatever he had planned must be special, because we typically never left our daughter behind.

"Where are we going?" I asked. "How far is it?"

Rhett chuckled. "We've only been walking for five minutes." His tone became serious. "Are you okay? Do you need to rest?"

I rubbed at the little bump on my tummy. At four months pregnant, I was already showing. No one could tell, thanks to the long dress I wore, but my family and friends knew about the pregnancy.

"I'm fine, Rhett. I just want to know."

Avary had been born from an incubator hub, so I hadn't known what to expect. I didn't have morning sickness, and the first trimester had been a joy—an amazing experience, and everything I'd hoped it would be.

Rhett halted. He pulled out a long piece of material from his pocket and dangled it in front of me, smirking.

I frowned. "You've got to be kidding. I *am* a map."

"But, where we're going, there are no people. Humor me,

264

babe." He winked. "You're going to love what I'm about to show you."

I let out a breath as I showed him my back and closed my eyes. After he tightened the cloth, he guided me down the hill slope, and then we slowed to a stop.

"Take off the blindfold," he said.

The soft breeze pushed back my hair, and when I got a clear view, my jaw dropped. I stood in a vast field of dandelions that stretched for miles.

"How did you know of this place?"

He occasionally flew around the perimeter with Ozzie to check for intruders. We were out in the middle of nowhere, so there was no reason for anyone to come in this direction, but we still had to be careful.

Justine, who had taken over Russ's position, had informed us that ISAN knew of Avary. And though she had conquered the US, Hae Jin and Momo's team were still working on bringing down the international network.

I lowered my gaze when he didn't answer. Down on one knee, he held a small black box. In perfect timing, the setting sun refracted in the diamond ring. I sucked in a breath and my view became blurry from my forming tears.

We had talked about making it official online and throwing a small banquet with our family and friends, but I never imagined he would propose to me. It wouldn't have mattered if he hadn't. I didn't need the romance. His love had been enough.

Rhett swallowed, though not an inkling of his nervousness came through his tone. "I love you, Ava. I've loved you from the moment I laid eyes on you, and I never wanted to let you go. Will you be mine forever?"

I pressed my hands to my face as tears streamed down my cheeks. "Yes, I will be yours forever."

"She said yes!" he hollered.

He kissed my lips and twirled me around.

"Look who's joining us." Rhett tilted his head behind me.

Brooke, Ozzie, Justine, Payton, Mom, Aunt Josephine, Vince, and Avary in Randy's arms, ran down the slope. Rhett had timed everything perfectly. I held up my hand to show off my ring, and then we all hugged.

"Mama," Avary said with open arms.

Ever since she began to walk, she didn't like being held.

I took her from her grandfather and set her down. After I plucked a dandelion, I took a deep breath and blew. She gave the cutest peal of laughter as the seeds floated in the air.

"Be strong," I said. "Be resilient like your father, grandmother, grandfather, great-aunt Josephine, and all your aunties and uncles."

She had many role models and people who loved and cared about her. She and her yet-to-be-born brother were the luckiest children.

"And, just like your mother," my mom said, placing her hand on my shoulders, "she's the most resilient of us all."

I disagreed with her, but smiled as I plucked a flower and placed it in front of my daughter.

Her cheeks puffed out as if she understood what to do. And maybe she did. She was special, no doubt, but I didn't know if she would have her own unique power. Time would tell.

"Make a wish," I said. "Sometimes wishes come true when you blow on a dandelion."

Avary puffed out air, but her spit-filled breath passed over the leaves and missed the target. Flustered, she twisted at the waist with her arms crossed.

We snickered. She was too adorable, even when she threw a tantrum.

"It's okay." Rhett held a white puffball in front of her. "I'll help you."

Avary squinted, pointed to the field, and ran off in that lurching toddler way.

"She's going to be a handful." Her grandfather grinned.

"Maybe she's had enough of us." Vince chuckled.

"Holy mother of all mothers," Ozzie murmured.

"Where is she going?" Aunt Josephine giggled.

"Aww. She's just like Ava," my mother said.

"Wait for me." Justine ran after her.

"I'm coming." Payton sprinted.

"Let's run." Brooke followed.

Everyone chased her except Rhett and me. She ran fast—faster than a one-year-old should.

Dandelion seeds fluttered in the air like first snowflakes falling. And so did the flowers Avary touched as she sprinted. She became lost in a blanket of dandelions.

Impossible. She couldn't have plucked them fast enough. My eyes must be playing tricks on me. I blinked to clear my vision.

Rhett's mouth opened. "Babe, are you seeing what I'm seeing?"

If he saw the same thing, then … I gasped, my hand to my mouth. As Ozzie would say, *Holy mother of all mothers.*

Rhett ran a hand down his face and blew sharp, quick breaths. "When did she … I better get her."

I knew our daughter was special, but I would never have guessed she would be able to manipulate objects by touch, at her age. She was more powerful than I had imagined.

Avary's laughter resonated, and fluffy white dandelions fluttered in every direction. Some circled in a wind tunnel, while others flew up to the sky. Such a breathtaking moment.

I rubbed at my little bump. My son, named after Russ, would soon be born, and I wondered if he would have a unique power, too. If so, double trouble. All the more reason to stay at our hidden cabin to keep our children safe from ISAN.

Rhett and I would protect them. *Whatever it takes.*

I'd better go after Avary before she did something else, like touch the trees and make all their leaves fall off.

I ran toward Avary.

I ran with my family and friends.

I ran to live.

ABOUT THE AUTHOR

Mary Ting is an international bestselling, award-winning author. Her books span a wide range of genres, and her storytelling talents have earned a devoted legion of fans, as well as garnered critical praise.

Becoming an author happened by chance. It was a way to grieve the death of her beloved grandmother, and inspired by a dream she had in high school. After realizing she wanted to become a full-time author, Mary retired from teaching after twenty years. She also had the privilege of touring with the Magic Johnson Foundation to promote literacy and her children's chapter book: *No Bullies Allowed.*

www.ISAN.Agency
www.AuthorMaryTing.com